TAMPA BAY NOIR

TAMPA BAY NOIR

EDITED BY COLETTE BANCROFT

BROOKLYN, NEW YORK

This collection consists of works of fiction. All names, characters, places, and incidents are the product of the authors' imaginations. Any resemblance to real events or persons, living or dead, is entirely coincidental.

Published by Akashic Books
©2020 Akashic Books

Series concept by Tim McLoughlin and Johnny Temple
Tampa Bay map by Sohrab Habibion

ISBN: 978-1-61775-810-2
Library of Congress Control Number: 2019943606

Akashic Books
Brooklyn, New York
Twitter: @AkashicBooks
Facebook: AkashicBooks
E-mail: info@akashicbooks.com
Website: www.akashicbooks.com

In memory of John Bancroft, my partner in crime

ALSO IN THE AKASHIC NOIR SERIES

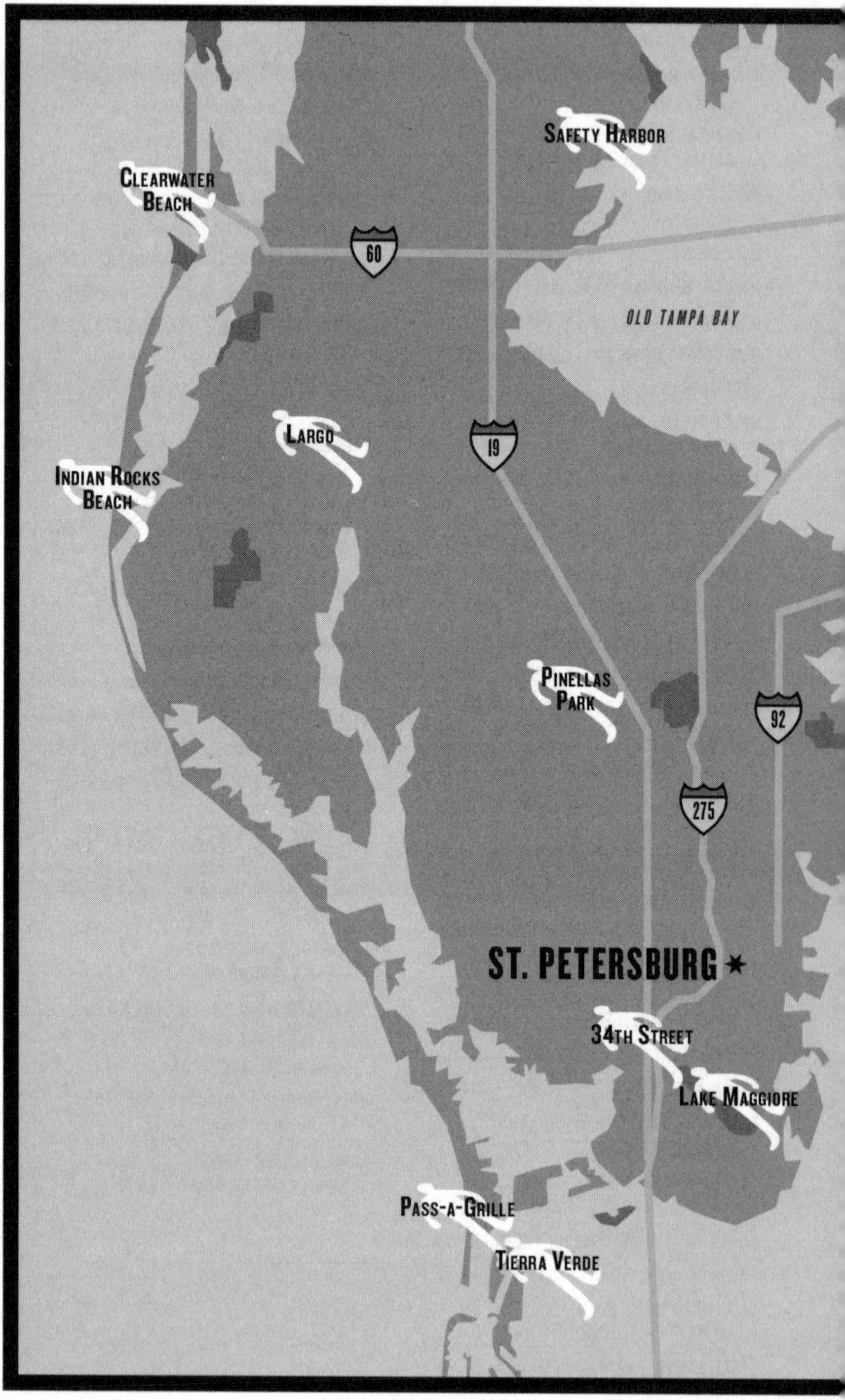

Safety Harbor
Clearwater Beach
60
Old Tampa Bay
Largo
19
Indian Rocks Beach
Pinellas Park
92
275
St. Petersburg
34th Street
Lake Maggiore
Pass-a-Grille
Tierra Verde

★ **TAMPA**

Westshore

Hyde Park

Palma Ceia
Davis Islands

Rattlesnake
HILLSBOROUGH BAY

Gibsonton

TAMPA BAY

41

75

TABLE OF CONTENTS

INTRODUCTION
SHADY STUFF IN THE SUNSHINE

Ask most people what the Tampa Bay area is famous for, and they might mention sparkling beaches and sleek urban centers and contented retirees strolling the golf courses year-round. But it's always had a dark side. Just look at its signature event: a giant pirate parade.

Not only does Gasparilla honor the buccaneer traditions of theft, debauchery, and violence; its namesake pirate captain, José Gaspar, is a fake who probably never existed. And if there's any variety of crime baked into Florida's history, it's fraud. From the indigenous residents who supposedly conned Spanish explorers seeking the Fountain of Youth through the rolling cycles of real estate scams that have shaped the Sunshine State for the last century or so, the place is a grifter's native habitat.

For a large chunk of the twentieth century, Tampa had a reputation as a Mafia town. Santo Trafficante Jr. and his family ran assorted extralegal operations in west Florida and, for a while—until Fidel Castro threw them out—in Havana. Mob killings were standard newspaper fodder in the 1950s and '60s, and oddly went unsolved even when they happened in public.

In the twenty-first century, the "Florida Man" meme has found its ground zero around Tampa Bay, a metro area of about three million people that includes Tampa, St. Petersburg, and several other cities and towns. A website dedicated to it calls Florida Man "the worst superhero ever," but Florida Man stories are real. A guy impersonating a cop pulling over a real cop? A naked man caught on video stealing hot dogs from a concession stand? A small-town mayor who is charged with drug dealing and medical fraud—and shoots at the SWAT guys when they come to arrest him? All real, all arrested around Tampa Bay—in the span of a few months.

With that kind of real crime, it can be tough to make anything up. But the fifteen writers who contributed to *Tampa Bay Noir* (myself included) found inspiration in its darker corners. Florida is the kind of place where almost everybody is from someplace else, where people come to make themselves over. Sometimes they make themselves into victims—or very bad people.

In the stories in Part I: Suburb Sinister, the authors take us into some of the elegant Tampa Bay neighborhoods where the hibiscus bloom and the mockingbirds sing and, occasionally, blood flows. In "The Guardian," Michael Connelly brings his iconic LAPD detective Harry Bosch to town to help a former lover, and Bosch finds he still plays an unexpected role in her life. Lori Roy's "Chum in the Water" pits a real estate flipper against a rumored mob guy on Tierra Verde. A woman buys a house on posh Davis Islands and finds it has an eerie connection to a man from her past in Karen Brown's "I Get the Same Old Feeling." In Tim Dorsey's "Triggerfish Lane," a nice Midwestern family relocates to sunny Palma Ceia only to find Florida-history enthusiast and occasional killer Serge Storms living across the street.

The beaches of Tampa Bay and the Gulf of Mexico are world-famous. In Part II: Blood in the Water, writers take their characters to the yacht clubs, waterfront restaurants, and island neighborhoods for some bad times. In Lisa Unger's

"Only You," a rich girl and a bartender's son who were once in love reunite on Clearwater Beach years later, now that he's a millionaire. Sterling Watson sends an ordinary guy to the Hurricane's rooftop bar in Pass-a-Grille for a sunset drink and a serving of "Extraordinary Things." In Luis Castillo's "Local Waters," a surfing high school teacher in Indian Rocks Beach has a run-in with a student and finds out more than he wants to know about himself.

Cons and fraudsters work their marks in Part III: Grifters' Paradise. Ace Atkins writes about a middle-aged woman (another migrant from the Midwest) who thinks she's found the man of her dreams at a Westshore hotel in "Tall, Dark, and Handsome." Sarah Gerard sends a journalist living in a seedy 34th Street motel in St. Petersburg on the trail of a sketchy Internet evangelist in "The Midnight Preacher." In "Jackknife" by Danny López, an ex-cop pursues the stripper who dumped him to Gibsonton, the town known for its population of circus sideshow performers—in the middle of a hurricane.

Part IV: Family Secrets explores some of the area's darkest neighborhoods. Ladee Hubbard's "It's Not Locked Because It Don't Lock" reunites two high school friends in Lake Maggiore, and one of them knows what the other did to his relative. In Gale Massey's "Marked," a teenage girl struggles to deal with her parents' sudden death and finds comfort on a gun range in Pinellas Park. The young narrator of Yuly Restrepo Garcés's "Pablo Escobar," newly arrived in Largo from Colombia, encounters the image of the Virgin Mary on the windows of an office building and a happy American family that might not be. A divorced father takes his son on a resort vacation in Safety Harbor, which might belie its name, in Eliot Schrefer's "Wings Beating." And in my story, "The Bite," a girl growing up in the neighborhood of Rattlesnake learns that even a dead snake can bite.

Add it all up and it's not a Tampa Bay postcard. But these noir stories will draw you in with the shady stuff people get up to in the sunshine.

Colette Bancroft
St. Petersburg, Florida
June 2020

PART I

SUBURB SINISTER

THE GUARDIAN

BY Michael Connelly

Hyde Park

I t had been almost twenty-five years. Years that had taken a toll on Bosch, both inside and out. He was hesitant and drove by the house twice, working a wide loop around it by taking Swann to Bayshore to Howard and then back to Swann. He knew he was invited. His presence was, in fact, requested. But he had never been in such a position; revealing himself to an old lover after so long. And she revealing herself to him.

But that wasn't what this was about. They lived different lives now. And her request was not based on their past as lovers but on his past as a detective. Her call had gone to the detective bureau of the Hollywood Division of the Los Angeles Police Department. It had been years since he had worked there but that was the number she had on an old business card he had given her on the first day they had met. The person at that number and Bosch's old desk knew of Bosch and knew how to get in touch. And Bosch got the message: "Something has happened. I need a detective. I need you."

Bosch would not have traveled from Los Angeles to Tampa on such a mysterious message from Jasmine Corian. He called and in the conversation the mystery deepened. So did the hook she had planted in him so long ago. A damaged woman and a damaged man longing for a connection. He had come to Florida on an investigation and had met her by happenstance.

She was an artist and at first he was as equally enamored of her paintings as he was of her. Back then, she lived in the guest quarters above a garage behind a stately old house at the corner of Swann and Willow. They spent a weekend in her rooms, Bosch studying her work in the adjoining studio while she slept and he roamed about, firmly set on Pacific Standard Time. He then had to go back to his work and his home. He came back to Florida several more times and she came to LA once. She loved the light but didn't like the city. The geographic distance ultimately put distance into their relationship. It was Jasmine who ended it, telling Bosch to stop coming unless it was to stay.

Now she needed him.

After his second loop he finally turned at Swann and stopped in front of the house. The neighborhood was called Hyde Park, close to downtown and one of the oldest in the city. The houses were built at a time when there was no air-conditioning. Large covered porches fronted most of them while up above there were screened porches for sleeping on warm summer nights. Her house was clad in yellow brick with large windows behind the full-length porch. She had told him she now owned the house. The garage apartment was still her studio.

Years earlier, when Bosch had first learned how to use the Internet to search for people, he had put her name into Google. Their relationship was long over but he thought about her often. He plugged in her name and found that she had become a successful artist both critically and commercially and her work was sold in galleries across the country, including New York, and she had her own gallery on MacDill Avenue in Tampa.

She had painted him once. He didn't sit for it. It was a

surprise he found on an easel in the studio. It was a dark, brooding painting, abstract and exacting about his character at the same time. She had depicted his eyes as piercing and haunting.

She had never sold the painting, nor had she given it to him. And now it was gone, stolen from a wall from inside her home. She had tried to explain to Bosch on the phone that the painting was vital to her, that she could not complete another painting until she had it back and knew it was safe.

Bosch parked at the curb in front and looked into the house through the windows. He could see an empty wall and could make out the nail and hook from which the stolen painting had hung.

He got out of the car and looked down the street, through a tunnel created by the canopy of the hundred-year-old live oak trees that lined the sidewalks. Down at the end he saw sparkling sunshine on the surface of the bay.

She answered the door before he could press the button below the brass *No Solicitors* sign and they engaged in an awkward hug. She was wearing a long white tunic over pale-green slacks. Like Bosch's, her hair was gray with dark streaks through it. She kept it long and braided in a tail.

"Harry, I'm so glad you came," she said.

"Not a problem," he said. "It's good to see you, Jasmine."

She told him to come in. The entry area split a wide space with living room and grand fireplace to the left and a formal dining area to the right. Directly in front of Bosch was a curving staircase to the second floor.

"I know," Jasmine said. "It's a long way from when I lived in the back."

Bosch nodded. "Congratulations. You deserve it."

"I'm not so sure," she said. "In the art world, it sometimes seems to be more about luck than craft or anything else."

"Don't kid yourself. From way back your paintings had a power. They held people. They held *me*." He glanced at the blank wall where the missing painting had hung. She followed his gaze.

"It was the first thing I put up when I bought the house thirteen years ago."

Bosch nodded and turned his eyes to the fireplace. Another painting with her distinctive style hung above it. He could tell that paintings on other walls in his view were not her work. That would have been too narcissistic. He looked back at the painting over the fireplace. It was of a man with a face turned away from the painter. He had a sharp jaw and an almost cruel look, as if he was almost intentionally holding something back from the painter.

"My father," Jasmine said. "I worked on that one for twenty years before finishing."

Bosch's memory was fuzzy but he remembered her telling him something about her fraught relationship with her father. He had died just before Bosch had met her. "So," he said, "why did they only take the one painting?" He pointed to the blank wall, and then to the painting of her father. "Isn't that one just as valuable?"

"A painting is valued at what it sells for," Jasmine said. "I never attempted to sell either painting. They were not for sale. *The Guardian* was one of my oldest pieces."

"How much are we talking about here?"

"My more recent pieces sell in the twenty to thirty thousand range. My commission fee is twenty-five. My agent told me in the past that *The Guardian* could sell for as high as fifty but I said no. I did not want to part with it."

Bosch glanced at her for a moment, then nodded and

looked away. He didn't know she called the painting *The Guardian*. "What did the Tampa police say?"

"That they're investigating," she said. "Detective Stone said they're watching the art markets to see if someone tries to sell it."

"That's a long shot. Whoever stole it will know not to do that. Who else wanted the painting besides your agent?" Bosch knew that someone coming in and taking one of the paintings and not the other put this on a different path. He didn't think it was a crime motivated by money.

"I can't think of anyone," Jasmine said. "Very few people have seen it. I don't entertain very often. I keep to myself. I didn't realize it was gone until someone came to the front door and when I turned I saw it was gone."

"You're saying you don't know exactly when it was taken?"

"Right. I knew it was there and then it was just gone, you know? I don't use the living room that often. I'm in the studio in the back and I use the kitchen here and then the upstairs. My bedroom."

Bosch gestured to the grand staircase. "When you go up-stairs to your bedroom, don't you glance in here? Just to check things out?"

"I don't use those stairs," she said. "There is a set of back stairs off the kitchen. All of these old houses in the neighbor-hood have back stairs for the help."

"Got it. What did Detective Stone say about when the burglary happened?"

"Nothing. They can't pinpoint it either."

"No sign of break-in?"

"Not that the police found. They think it's my fault."

"How so?"

"I go back and forth between the house and the studio.

Sometimes several times a day. I don't lock the back door every time. Sometimes I just don't because I think I'll be right back and then I get caught up in the studio. I sometimes work into the night. Anyway, the police said this may have been how the painting was taken. It was opportunistic. Somebody came off Swann, went through the gate into the yard, and found the back door unlocked. They went in and grabbed the painting."

"You don't keep the gate locked?"

"It's locked from the outside but you can reach over and release the lock."

Bosch took in the information but found himself disagreeing with the conclusions of the local police. The painting seemed targeted, not something that was grabbed in a random burglary of opportunity. "Nothing else was taken?" he asked.

"No. I mean, nothing that I've noticed missing."

"Where do you leave your car keys and your purse on a regular day of work?"

"Well, the keys are in the purse and sometimes I leave it upstairs, sometimes in the kitchen. It all depends."

"Do you take it with you to the studio?"

"No, almost never. I don't need it. I don't even take my cell phone to the studio."

"And it wasn't taken or touched."

"No, only the painting."

Bosch thought about that for a moment.

"Do you want to sit down, Harry?" Jasmine asked. "Or . . ."

"I want to see the backyard," he said. "And the studio."

Jasmine led the way. They walked down a hallway and through a kitchen to a back door. Outside, there was a stone path across a lush green lawn to a wooden staircase leading to the studio over the garage. Bosch paused and took in the yard. It was perfectly manicured and protected by a six-foot wall that ran the length of the property and connected to the walls of the garage. Bosch remembered that the garage was accessed by the alley behind it.

He stepped over to a wooden gate set in the wall. It had a flip latch located about six inches from the top on the inside of the door. Anybody who stood at least five and a half feet could easily reach over, flip the latch, and allow themselves entry. Besides that, the wall itself would be easy enough to scale. The security measures protecting the backyard were deterrents to entry, not denials.

"Let's go up," he said.

Once again Jasmine led the way. Bosch took the steps to the studio slowly, his knees extra sore from being cramped in the airline seat for the five-hour flight.

The place where Jasmine painted was much as Bosch remembered it. An apartment living room converted into an artist's studio. With a workbench—Jasmine stretched her own canvas—and paint and brush station on the right, and her easel and painting area at the far end of the room where there were windows that allowed the morning light to hit the surface she was painting. There was a work underway on the easel. It was in the sketch stage and was clearly going to be a portrait of a child—a girl with dark circles under her eyes. Bosch recognized Jasmine as a child.

"Do you remember being here?" Jasmine asked.

"Of course," Bosch said. "I remember everything."

He looked at her and waited. This was the place where she created, where she felt safest. If she wanted to reveal something, it would be now. She looked at her work in progress for a moment and then back to him.

"You asked about the money—what the painting was

worth," she said. "It's not about the money. It's not even about the intruder. That piece . . . that painting is when everything changed for me. I found my art. I found the confidence in what I was doing with my life. It's a portrait of you but it's also of me. Coming out of darkness. I don't know if that makes sense to you but it—"

"It does," Bosch said. "I understand."

"Then you see. I have to find it. I have to get it back. I'm not sure the local police understand that. That's why I called you." She was silhouetted by the light coming through the windows.

"I'll do my best," he said.

"I believe you." She came to him and put her arms around him and leaned her head against his chest. "You must be tired," she said. "You took a red-eye. I have a room set up for you if you want to rest."

"I just need some coffee and I'll be fine," he said. "I want to call Detective Stone and just tell him I'll be poking around on this. I also thought maybe I should stay at a hotel or something. I don't want to im—"

"Don't be silly. I have a big house and you can have half of the top floor. You won't be bothered . . . unless you want to be." She landed the last line with a tilted smile Bosch remembered very well.

Back inside the main house, Jasmine made coffee while Bosch walked back to the living room, where he studied the wall on which the missing painting had hung. Up close he saw the smudges of fingerprint powder on the plaster. It was good to know the locals had tried but he also knew that a painting could be removed from a wall without having to touch the wall. He expected that the forensic effort had been for naught.

He turned away and looked out the large plate-glass window to the street. Anybody driving by could have seen the painting and become enthralled by it. Narrowing that down to a suspect list would be impossible. He called to Jasmine, who was still in the kitchen.

"Were there any cameras?"

"What?"

"Cameras. Here or at homes on the street. Did the police check?"

"They checked. Detective Stone said it was a bust. Cream and sugar?"

"Black is fine."

She entered the room carrying a mug of steaming coffee. "I should've remembered. No cream, no sugar," she said. "Let it cool."

She carefully handed him the mug. He was tempted to take a gulp and get the caffeine working inside him, but he followed her directions and stood there awkwardly holding the mug. It said *Girl Power* on the side.

He turned and looked out the window again, his gaze carrying to the house across the street. It was another large craftsman-style house with a full porch. But he could tell it was empty. No curtains on any window. And empty rooms beyond the glass. There was a real estate sign on the lawn that said, *FOR SALE*.

"When did they move out?" he asked.

"A couple weeks ago," Jasmine said.

"Did you know them?"

"Not that well. I keep to myself mostly. I know Pat and George next door. We have a drink at Christmas every year— we alternate porches. I have the odd years, they the even. But that's about it."

"Do Pat and George have a spare key to your house?"

"No."

"Does anybody?"

"Just my manager."

"I think I should talk to your manager. Where is he?"

"It's a she. Monica Tate. She works out of the gallery on MacDill."

Bosch took his first sip of coffee. It was good and fully charged and he thought he could feel the spark hitting his bloodstream, going to work. "This is good," he said. "Will Monica be there today?"

"Yes. The gallery hours are eleven to three but she goes in earlier to handle the business end of it."

"You don't like the business end of it?"

"No, I don't."

Bosch took another hit of coffee. "I should go over there then," he said. "Can I take this or do you have a to-go cup?"

"I have cups," she said.

Bosch followed her into the kitchen and poured his coffee into a foam cup she got out of the pantry. "How long have you known Monica?" he asked.

"About fifteen years. She changed everything for me. Got my work in front of the right people, opened the gallery. This house, everything I have really, I owe it to her."

Bosch knew that many successful artists had trouble accepting accolades and money. Many didn't care about it and others craved it. He put Jasmine in the former category. When he thought about their past times together, he knew that all she wanted to do was be in a room by herself and paint.

"Don't sell yourself short," he said. "I'm sure Monica is good at what she does, but it starts with the art and that's all you."

"That's nice of you to say."

"What is Monica's cut?"

"Do you really need to know that?"

"I need to know everything. Then I can tell what's important."

"She takes out the gallery expenses, all the shipping, and 25 percent for herself. It's standard."

"Do you know if Detective Stone spoke to Monica?"

"Yes, he had to speak to her so they could value the loss. The higher the loss, the higher the level of the crime, I guess."

"Yeah, that's how it works. What was the value?"

"Eighty thousand. But I have to tell you, I've never sold a painting for that much. Not even close. Monica said it was worth that because it was a seminal work and part of the artist's personal collection."

"Was it insured for that much?"

"I have a general policy on all my work. I won't get that much unless I want to hire a lawyer. The insurance company is trying to say that because it was on a wall in my house, it doesn't count under the policy for the studio. It's part of the homeowner's insurance and included in home furnishings. There's a maximum payout of twenty-five thousand."

"That's crazy."

"Tell it to *them*. I'm not going to fight it. I don't care about the money. I just want my painting back. I haven't been able to work since it was taken."

Bosch nodded. He knew she wanted more assurance than *I'll do my best*. She wanted a promise that he would find the painting and bring it back. But he never made promises like that. When he worked homicides in Los Angeles, he made too many promises like that, telling grieving parents he would find the killers who took their sons or daughters. He never made good on some of them and the promises kept him awake at night.

"Okay," he said, "I'm going over there to see Monica. Do me a favor: don't tell her I'm coming."

"I won't. But if you think she may be involved in this, you are wrong. Monica would not betray me like that."

"It's good that you have somebody like that. But I don't think anything about anybody right now."

Bosch took Swann to MacDill and turned south toward the air force base the street was named for. He knew from prior visits that Tampa didn't rely solely on tourism like most of the cities that crowded Florida's coastline or sat in the middle of the state where only an iconic mouse could draw people on humid summer days. Tampa was unique. It was a peninsula that had water views and beauty from almost all angles—he had been reminded of this as he drove along Bayshore while getting up the courage to knock on Jasmine's door. It was also a military town. MacDill AFB was the location of CENTCOM, from which the country's most recent wars were directed. The base took up the entire southern tip of the peninsula and it was not unusual to see fighter jets and huge Stratotanker refueling planes on maneuvers in the sky over Tampa Bay.

But long before MacDill Avenue reached the end of the peninsula, it moved through a small art district where there were a handful of galleries and frame shops. On his way, Bosch called the number Jasmine had given him for Detective Stone at the Tampa Police Department.

"Burglary, Stone. How can I help you?"

"Detective, my name is Harry Bosch. I got your number from Jasmine Corian. I'm a friend of—"

"Excuse me, who gave you this number?"

"Jasmine Corian."

"And she is . . . ?"

"The artist whose painting was stolen off the wall of her living room. I thought it was your—"

"Yes, yes, sorry—a lot going on here. I know who Jasmine Corian is. What can I do for you, Mr. Bush?"

"It's Bosch. As I was saying, I'm a friend of hers and I'm retired LAPD and she asked me to come out and take a look at things regarding the theft."

There was a long silence before Stone finally responded. "LAPD—what are we talking about here? Lake Alice Police Department?"

"No, Los Angeles."

"Really. *The* LAPD. I'm honored."

Bosch could hear the sarcasm clearly.

"How long have you been retired?"

"A few years."

"And what did you do for LAPD?"

"I worked homicides for about thirty years."

"Good for you, but this is not a homicide."

"I know that, Detective. Ms. Corian and I have an acquaintance going back twenty-five years or so. She asked me to come out and take a look at this."

"A *look*—what does that mean?"

"It means I am going to look into the theft of her painting. I just thought you should know and I wanted to see if you want to get together to discuss the investigation."

"Why would I want to do that?"

"Look, I know what it's like. Crime victims going to private investigators and all of that. You don't want the headache and I promise you I won't be a headache. If you don't want to talk to me, that's fine. But I'm here and I'm working it. And if I find anything that you don't have or know, then you will be the first person I call."

"Mr. Bush, you already are a headache to me. This is a police matter and it's under investigation. I respect that you were a police detective—at least you say you were—but stay away from this or you could get yourself into trouble."

Now Bosch paused while he composed an answer. "What does that mean? Are you threatening me?"

"No, I am telling you that if you interfere with a police investigation, there are consequences. Now, I'm in the middle of things here. I have multiple cases and I need to go."

Stone disconnected. Bosch held his phone to his ear for a few seconds before dropping it into the cup holder in the center console.

A few minutes later he pulled into a space in front of a gallery called Jazz, which was how Jasmine signed her work. It was just opening for the day. And as he stepped to the glass door, a woman appeared on the other side and unlocked it. She looked at him for a moment through the glass as though she knew him. She pulled the door open.

"You're him," she said.

"Excuse me?"

"You're him. The one in the painting. I recognize you. Jasmine said you were real but she never told me about you."

"Can I come in?"

"Of course."

She stepped back and he stepped in. It was not a large gallery. A square with a display wall running down the center. It allowed for four walls holding two paintings each. At the back was a desk in front of a doorway that led to what Bosch assumed was a storage and packaging area.

The paintings on display looked to be part of a linked series of studies of a woman. It took Bosch a moment before he realized they were self-portraits. Though each was unique in terms of pose and color—ranging from shades of black, gray, and red—the eyes in each painting were unmistakably Jasmine's.

"Are you Monica Tate?" he asked.

"Yes. We haven't met though. I would remember."

"Harry Bosch. I'm here about the painting. The one that was stolen."

"She told you."

"Yes, she asked me to look for it. I'm a detective."

"You mean like a private eye?"

"Yes. Who do you think would have wanted to steal it?"

Tate shook her head like it was stupid question. "Anybody who knows her work," she said.

"But why *that* painting?" Bosch asked. "It's never been for sale. How would people know about it?"

"It's been in a few catalogs. Jasmine wasn't happy about it, but I convinced her. The painting is powerful. I put it on the cover of one catalog. It drew people in. They would find out they couldn't have it, but then they would pick something else. It's also been on the website. It's a sales tool. It has that rare thing. People who know true art want it."

"Any customers who wouldn't take no for an answer?"

"You mean who would then steal it? No, none. That's insulting. I don't deal with people like that."

"Good to hear. Where is your key to Jasmine's home?"

"Are you suggesting that I took the painting?"

"No. I just want to confirm that you still have the key. If you don't, then we may have a clue to what happened. Because there was no sign of forced entry. Whoever took the painting either walked in through an unlocked door or had a key to unlock it."

Tate turned with a huff and walked to the desk at the back of the gallery. She took a set of keys sitting on top of it and used one to unlock a drawer in the desk. She then opened the drawer, reached in, and held up a key.

"Happy?" she asked.

Bosch stepped over to the desk. "You keep it in the desk rather than on your own key chain," he said.

"Yes, it's not my key. I have it in case there's an emergency or she locks herself out. I don't carry it with me everywhere I go."

"Have you ever used it? In a case of emergency or if Jasmine locked herself out?"

"No, never."

"And you can't think of anyone you've dealt with who might take it upon themselves to steal that painting after you told them it was not for sale?"

"No, no one."

"Is there anyone who has bought more than one of her paintings? Anyone obsessive about her or her work?"

"I don't know about obsessive, but it's not unusual in the art world for collectors to have multiples of the artists they love. Sometimes it's investment and sometimes it's purely love of the art."

"Who does Jasmine have that's like that?"

"I would have to look through the books. I've been selling her paintings for fifteen years. There have been many people who have come back for more. One man on Davis Island has four or five paintings."

She pointed past Bosch to the center wall. He turned and looked at a painting that depicted the artist sitting huddled over, cradling her face in her hands, one eye peeking between two splayed fingers. It was painted in black and gray gradations. It was haunting, as were all of the self-portraits.

"He just bought that one, in fact," Tate said.

"Did he ever ask about *The Guardian?*"

"I'm sure he did but I don't remember."

"What's his name?"

"I'm not going to give you his name. Not unless Jasmine tells me to."

"She will. Thank you for your time." Bosch headed toward the door.

In the living room at the house on Willow, Bosch reported to Jasmine that he had alienated both the detective assigned to the painting theft and her gallery manager. He also told her he wanted the name of the collector who had purchased multiple paintings by her.

"Can you call Monica?" he asked. "She said she'd give the name to you. He lives on Davis Island, wherever that is."

"That would be Paul Danziger," she said. "I don't need to call her. I know him."

"Where is Davis Island?"

"It's right across the bay. You take the bridge by the hospital. It's actually called Davis Islands—it's three islands connected by small bridges."

"You have his address?"

"Yes, but he didn't steal the painting."

"How do you know? I need to—"

"I know he didn't. I know Paul very well. He didn't take the painting."

Bosch studied her. There was something else there. "How well do you know him?" he asked.

"We had a relationship. It ended five or six years ago."

Bosch waited. Silence was often the best way to tease out information.

"Even though the relationship is over, he still buys my paintings to support me," she finally said. "He would not steal from me."

"Okay. Who ended the relationship?"

"I did."

"Why?"

"That has nothing to do with this. It's private and painful and you don't need to know."

"Okay, then did you ever discuss the painting with him?" He pointed toward the empty wall.

"We might have," Jasmine said. "I don't remember."

"Sure you do," Bosch prompted.

"He liked the painting. But he liked all of my paintings and has bought several. For himself and as gifts to others."

"Did he know who was in the painting? Did you tell him about me?"

"I don't remember."

"I think you do."

"Okay, yes, I probably told him the story, okay? I told him who it was a portrait of."

Bosch stepped away and moved to the front window. He saw a white van pull into the driveway of the house across the street. On its side panel was a sign that identified it as part of a fleet from a commercial cleaning service. Two men in white overalls got out and started unloading equipment and supplies from the back of the van. Then a Range Rover SUV pulled in behind the van. A man got out of the car, acknowledged the other two, and walked to the front door. A key lockbox was attached to the knob on the front door. He started working the combination.

"Is that your old neighbor?" Bosch asked.

"No, that's the realtor," Jasmine said. "Charlie. I used him when I bought this place."

Charlie opened the door with a key from the lockbox and went inside.

"Pat next door told me that they left the place a complete mess," Jasmine said. "Food rotted in the refrigerator when they turned off the power. Holes punched in the walls. Toilets clogged, the whole nine yards."

"Why would they do that if they're trying to sell the place?" Bosch asked.

"They're not. The bank is. It's a foreclosure."

"What happened?"

"I don't know. It was a husband and wife, no kids. He had some sort of business that went under. Remember when the stock market dropped a thousand points on Christmas Eve? He had just made some kind of move with their investments and lost everything. His wife left him, he stopped paying the mortgage, the bank took the house."

Bosch thought about that as he watched one of the cleaners carry a water vacuum into the house. He saw the realtor's full name on the *For Sale* sign. *Charlie Hounchell.*

"Did Paul Danziger stay here at night?" he asked. "Or did you go to Davis Islands?"

"Harry, please. It's none of your business."

"Just tell me his address and I'll stop asking questions."

"You can't go over there. If we falsely accuse him of this, he'll be very hurt."

"And what, stop buying your paintings? Look, if I have to call a friend and run his name through the police computer to get his address, it will leave a flag on his record. Would you rather me do that?" It was a lie but Bosch doubted she would know it.

"Fine," Jasmine said. "He lives on Ladoga. I'll have to look up his exact address because I don't remember it."

"Fine. Look it up. Then I want you to call Monica and tell her to pack up the painting she has at the gallery for Danziger. Tell her to call him and say it will be delivered today."

"She won't want to do that. It will break up the series she has on display. It may hurt her ability to sell through. She says that when people see that one painting is sold, it makes them feel better about buying their own."

"Don't worry. I'll take care of that. Just tell Monica to get it ready and I'll deliver it. I'm going to sleep for an hour and then I'll be by to pick it up. Can you show me to the guest room?"

Bosch drove over the curving bridge off Bayshore that took him past Tampa General and onto Davis Islands. He was following directions on his cell phone app. They took him down Davis Boulevard and then over another bridge, this one spanning a canal that apparently separated two of the Davis Islands. After the bridge there was a hard right onto Ladoga. Paul Danziger lived at 520 Ladoga. Bosch pulled into the driveway of a *Gone with the Wind*–style mansion that was fronted by six two-story pillars.

He arrived at a cobblestone parking circle in front of the door. He studied the facade of the house for a few moments before getting out.

He removed the painting from the backseat and lugged it toward the door. Its wooden crating—designed to keep the painting safe in transit—easily outweighed the painting twenty-five to one. Bosch was huffing when he got it to the door.

Danziger answered himself. A man nearing seventy with a completely shaved head to hide his baldness in plain sight. He looked surprised to see Bosch. "You're not the usual guy," he said.

"I'm filling in," Bosch replied. "A favor to Monica."

"Do you need help with that?"

"I can manage, thanks."

"This way. Watch the walls."

Danziger led Bosch into the house and to the left. They walked down a short hallway and through a living room where there were large paintings over a fireplace and a couch by the opposite wall. They did not appear to be from the brush of Jasmine Corian. It indicated to Bosch that Danziger might be a collector of many artists.

They went through a set of double French doors into what looked like a second living room, this one smaller but with a large fireplace with a seating arrangement in front of it. There was a desk table and chair at the far end of the room next to a window that looked out across the bay. Bosch could see cars moving on Bayshore Boulevard far on the other side.

Standing next to the table was an artist's three-legged easel with nothing on it. Bosch put the heavy painting crate down on a rug but kept one hand on it to make sure the thin wooden package didn't fall over. He pulled the screwdriver Monica had given him out of his pocket. He had to loosen two screws in the top wooden panel of the crate and then the painting could be carefully lifted up and out. He looked around as he worked the screwdriver. There were three paintings of the same size and equally spaced on the wall above the couch. All three were signed *Jazz* and seemed to be part of a study of a young man in a white shirt and tie. On the wall over the fireplace was a larger canvas that was a painting of Danziger that made him look strong and upright, peering off into the distance at something meaningful. The wall to Bosch's left was covered by what looked like velvet floor-to-ceiling curtains.

"Looks like you're out of wall space for this one," he said.

"Just put it on the easel," Danziger said. "When I'm ready I'll find a place for it."

Bosch moved to the second screw. He waited a beat before speaking again. "You used to go out with Jasmine, didn't you?"

Danziger turned from looking at the painting of himself to stare at Bosch. "Why do you ask that?"

"I don't mean to be rude. I saw the painting of you there and that made me remember you two had a relationship."

"It's none of your business."

"You're right. I'm sorry."

"Who are you exactly?"

"A friend of Jasmine's. That's all."

"Have we met? You look familiar."

"That's unlikely. I'm from Los Angeles."

"Then you should mind your own business."

"You're right. I definitely should."

Bosch felt the wooden plank release and he lifted it out by the two screws. He then reached into the crate and brought the bubble-wrapped painting up and out through the narrow opening. Leaning the package against his legs, he used a folding knife from his pocket to cut the tape that secured the wrapping and carefully unfolded it. Holding the painting between his palms in the way he had seen Monica handle it, he walked to the easel and placed the painting on display. From the canvas, Jasmine's eye looked between her fingers at him.

Bosch stepped back and studied the work for a moment. "Twenty-two thousand bucks," he said. "That's a lot for something you just hang on the wall."

"It's an investment," Danziger said. "Her work has appreciated markedly over time."

"I heard her old stuff is really valuable. Wish I had invested way back when." Bosch moved back to the crate and started gathering up the bubble wrap. "You want to keep the crate?" he asked. "In case you can't find space for it and you just want to store your investment?"

"I told you, I'll find a space for it," Danziger responded. "A painting should be seen and appreciated, not put in a closet."

"I totally agree. But if you think that, why do you have the curtain closed?"

"What are you talking about?"

"The curtain."

Bosch dropped the bubble wrap to the floor and walked over to the velvet curtain. He reached behind the left edge and found the draw line. He started opening the curtain.

"Leave that alone!" Danziger cried.

"I studied your house before I came in. This room has no window on the front wall. I look familiar to you because . . ."

The curtain opened, revealing the missing painting hung on a windowless wall. *The Guardian.* Bosch stared for a moment at his own image of twenty-five years before.

"I don't know what you think you're doing," Danziger said. "But I want you to get—"

"A man covets what he can't have," Bosch cut him off. "You couldn't have Jasmine so you bought her paintings. She'd sell you anything but the one on her own wall. So you coveted it and you took it."

Bosch reached up and took the painting off the wall. He judged that it was roughly the same size as the painting he had delivered. He took it to the crate and folded the bubble wrap around it before slipping it securely inside. Danziger just watched.

"What are you going to do?" he finally asked.

"I'm going to take it back to Jasmine," Bosch said. "After that, she's the one you should ask."

Bosch screwed the top plank back into place. "I'm not a cop," he said. "If I was, you'd be in cuffs."

"Please, tell Jasmine, we can work something out," Danziger said, a whine in his voice now. "The police don't have to be involved."

Bosch lifted the crate, ready to go. "Like I said, I just came for the painting. You can talk to her about the rest."

Bosch put the crate into the backseat of the rental and drove away. In a few minutes he was on Bayshore. The sun was going down and the sky was orange and blue over the bay. He turned onto Willow and drove under the thick arms of the oak trees.

A few minutes later Bosch helped Jasmine hang her painting back on the wall.

"Thank you, Harry," she said.

"You're welcome, Jasmine," he said.

CHUM IN THE WATER

by Lori Roy

Tierra Verde

D ale pushes open the door to Smugglers and straight-away sees a new girl working behind the bar. As he walks inside Tierra Verde's only real tavern, a place where a man can still smoke a cigar, the late-day sun follows him into the dark room and throws a glare. He leans to get a better look. The girl pushes off the bar when the sunlight falls across her, turns toward Dale, and smiles. He drops the door and as it falls closed, snapping off the stream of light and hot August air that followed him inside, she comes into focus. White teeth shining against bright-red lips. Pale-blue eyes that linger on him. Pulling a bar towel from her back pocket, the girl laughs at something, tips her face, arches her back, and blots her neck and chest. Dale drops into a chair at his usual table, or rather the sight of that girl knocks him from his feet, because, damn it all, walking in on something that inviting is almost painful. And then he sees Chum.

Sitting on his stool at the end of the bar, Chum is the one making the girl laugh. He's telling her how he got his nick-name some sixty years ago. He's going on about sharks hav-ing a taste for him and ancient burial grounds just down the way that protected him. Protected this island from hurricanes too. Look it up, he's telling her. Dale wants to turn and leave, but that would make Chum suspicious, and he'd come after Dale for sure. Or he could stay and hope the old man forgets he's here, a possibility given the distraction behind the bar. Quietly, Dale scoots his chair until he's out of Chum's sight line.

The past year has been tough for Dale—lost his business, wife left him, got himself deep in debt to Chum, and he's never felt so damn old—but he has good reason to believe things will start looking up in the next few weeks, and maybe the new girl is another sign of better days ahead. With a girl like that, Dale damn sure wouldn't feel old anymore. Just the thought of what her hair would smell like when fanned across his pillow starts him feeling happy about the days ahead. Yes, he'll stay and hope Chum forgets he's here.

Most nights, Chum's gone home by the time Dale gets to the bar, at least that's how Dale's tried to work it since he borrowed $150,000 from the old man.

Chum—real name Santo—is the last living Giordano brother. He's no more than five foot four, wears black-rimmed glasses, is mostly bald, and has a round, doughy nose. There were four brothers at one time, and before that, two generations of Giordanos ran Tampa's organized crime. One brother died in a plane crash over the gulf, another was shot in his Tampa driveway, and the third is rumored to be stashed in the fifty-gallon drum that sits outside Smugglers. And it's rumored that Chum put him there.

The Giordano family's days of running bolita and rum over in Tampa, and more recently drugs and women, are long over. Chum likes to say his people were cigar makers and that he's retired, but he also likes to talk about all the shit he's seen and how these Tierra Verde types in their cargo shorts and fishing shirts can't begin to imagine. Mostly Dale has always figured Chum for a nobody who made a living by trading off his family's history. Hell, Dale hadn't even believed the rumors about the drum outside Smugglers or that Chum was loaning money for a living, at least not until he needed to borrow some for himself.

Dale never figured on being one of the guys who borrowed from Chum. But he also never imagined that one season of bad storms would stall the housing market and he'd get stuck upside down in so many condos. But those things did happen and when he needed money quick, borrowing from Chum meant no paperwork and no credit check. Dale's wife didn't even need to know. He sure never thought he'd end up having to sell his home of twenty years to pay Chum back, but in two weeks, that's what's happening. Two more weeks of keeping clear of the old man and then the sale will close. He'll pay Chum back and Dale's life can begin again. Maybe it'll begin again with this new girl.

Even though from his table Dale can't see Chum, he can still hear him.

"Was bit five times by the age of fifteen," he is saying. His voice rattles in his throat, some say from having had a telephone cord wrapped around his neck, back when people still had telephone cords. "Right there in the channel running alongside Egmont Key. Most shark-infested water on the whole coast. I was like chum in the water."

Dale stares hard at the Rays game playing on the big screen, so he doesn't smile or laugh at hearing this story yet again. He isn't as good at pretending as the other guys. He has pride, is the way he figures it. That's been the hardest part of borrowing Chum's money—having to tuck away the very thing that makes Dale a man.

"What's her name?" Dale asks when Donna, the bar's

owner, slides a highball in front of him, the glass leaving a slippery trail on the table.

"Elise," she says. The tendons under her wrinkled skin run like slender cables from her wrist to her elbow. Since her husband died last year, she's been running the place alone and the strain is showing. "Elise from Birmingham. Doing my bookkeeping too."

"Do any on the side?" Dale asks, taking a sip of whiskey and giving the new girl a nod to let her know she did good with his drink. "Bookkeeping, I mean. You know I'm needing someone part-time."

"Couldn't say. Worth asking, I guess."

"Single?"

"Far as I know," Donna says, and as she turns to walk away, she knocks one bony hip against his table. "But you ain't. And don't you forget it."

Late in the fourth inning, though Chum still hasn't left, Dale finishes his drink and when the new girl glances his way, he gives his empty glass a shake. Smiling with those bright-red lips, she nod and pulls the Woodford from the top shelf. He hasn't even talked to the girl yet, but he already knows she's something special. It isn't just the lips shining like they're wet or the bright eyes or the tiny waist that gives way to a full chest and round hips, it's that she's kind. She's really laughing at the stories the guys are telling. Not just pretending for tips. That's what makes her different from every other girl who's passed through here.

As the girl, Elise, walks from behind the bar, Dale gets a good look at the rest of her. She wears tan shorts that hit midthigh and a white V-neck. Her skin, pale, almost pink, would be smooth to the touch, he's sure of it. When she reaches his table, she rests a hand on his shoulder and stretches across him to set down the glass. Her chest brushes against his head. He closes his eyes and inhales. For the first time since he stopped being able to service his loans and his wife left him for borrowing from Chum, that thing that makes Dale a man, that searing thing that makes him want to attack the world for his share of it, is racing through his veins again.

"I don't believe a word of it," the girl calls out to Chum. She smells of lavender-scented lotion and Dale imagines her rubbing it on her arms and legs. "Sharks don't have a taste for one man over another." She squeezes Dale's shoulder. "You believe that?" she says to him.

"Tell her it's true, Dale."

Dale looks to the bar at the sound of Chum saying his name, and the image of bare legs, one stretched out next to the other, disappears, and so does the girl as she picks up his empty and walks away.

"Sure is true," Dale says, taking a long swallow that nearly chokes him. "He's even got scars to prove it."

"You know that spot I'm talking about, Dale?" Chum says, slapping a bill on the bar and walking toward Dale's table. "You been to that channel? Been there at dusk, Dale? Damn good fishing."

This is what Chum does when he's honing in on a man— keeps repeating his name. Dale saw him do it to a dentist who lived on the island and who borrowed a quarter million to buy out his partner.

"Yep, that's me," Chum says, adjusting his thick glasses before resting both hands on Dale's table. "Just an old man who likes to help out his friends on occasion. You think my friends appreciate an old man's help, Dale?"

Taking another long swallow, Dale nods. "Course they do. I do too."

Chum's sour smell drowns the smell of sweet lotion rubbed on bare legs.

"I'm all set to close on the house," Dale says, clearing his throat of the whiskey burn. "Did I tell you? Two weeks. I'll have all your money wired the second the papers are signed."

"I gave you cash in hand," Chum says. "And that's how I want it repaid. Cashier's check will do." He leans closer, his hot breath making Dale turn away. "Don't usually see you in here, do I?" He pauses as Dale slowly shakes his head. "Myself, I promised Mrs. Giordano, God rest, I'd always get myself home in time for supper." Another pause. "What about you? How late does your missus let you stay out?"

"She's out of town," Dale says, and takes another long drink because Chum wanting to know what time he's leaving is not good. "Besides, got a nice-looking distraction here tonight. Hell, might stay until close. But don't you worry, two weeks and we'll be even."

Chum slaps the table and pushes away, hobbling toward the door on mismatched legs.

"Just an old man," he says, "with old stories."

Ever since Dale listed the house for sale, which was his only hope of paying Chum back, a part of Dale has been wishing Chum would drop dead before the house closed. Surely the debt would disappear if Chum disappeared. Dale knows people. He could ask around, find a few guys who might take on the job. This is what meeting a girl like Elise will do for a man. She's making Dale believe he can have the thing he's been wishing for, making him realize he deserves it.

Pulling on the wooden door, Dale stumbles onto the boardwalk outside Smugglers. He draws in a deep breath. Island air. It's salty and heavy, tinted with the smell of fish, too thick to go down easy. Behind him, the bar's lights switch off. At some point during the evening it rained, but not enough to break the heat. The lights in the parking lot throw a glare on the damp concrete that stretches out below him. It shimmers like black ice.

Leaning heavy on the railing so he won't fall, Dale pulls out his phone. The lights on it blur as he squints and holds it close. He sets an alarm for nine a.m. tomorrow morning, doing it now so he doesn't forget. Elise is coming to the house at ten a.m. sharp. That's what she said. Sharp. And she also said she was happy to help Dale with his bookkeeping and that she needs every extra penny she can get. Maybe, if the business bounces back, he can bring her on regular.

Every guy in the bar tonight saw Dale getting what they couldn't. Elise. They're all worn out, old guys, looking in from the outside, but Dale proved that even at fifty, he's still on the inside. He's still in decent shape, even has all his hair. And his bank account will bounce back. He's nothing like all the others. Every one of them will want to hear the details of what happens between Dale and the girl tomorrow, but he won't tell. She's beautiful, sure. That's all the other guys noticed. The lips and legs. The curves that spilled across the bar every time she reached out over it. But he saw her real beauty. She's worth more than one night. She's young and new and a fresh start on a tired life.

The pain in his upper arm is the first thing Dale feels. He swats at it and then he's stumbling off to the side, struggling to keep his balance. Someone has grabbed him and he's falling. But then someone grabs the other arm and he's straight again and they're dragging him toward the side of Smugglers where the lights from the parking lot don't reach. His toes bounce over the curb and then over the rough ground.

There are two of them. They pull Dale by the arms, shove him so he'll keep moving forward, don't say who they are or what they want. They don't have to. When they're beyond the glow of the streetlights, they drop him. He hits the ground and they start kicking him. He curls up on himself, pulling his knees to his chest and wrapping his hands over his head. And then they're gone. By the time he can stand, pressing one hand to his ribs and touching the other to his top lip, he knows this was Chum's reminder that he doesn't give a shit about stagnant real estate or foundation problems in one of Dale's flips or a barrel-tile roof for his own house that cost him forty-five thousand dollars or a seawall he had to replace along eighty feet of frontage. Two weeks means two weeks, and Dale's house better damn well close. Standing in a patch of St. Augustine left to grow too long and waiting for the ground to settle underfoot, Dale wonders if those two guys might be the right kind of guys, if they might be the kind Dale could hire to make sure Chum disappears along with Dale's debt.

Elise shows up at Dale's house right on time. She's dressed in blue jeans and a loose-fitting polo, both meant to disguise her body, likely because she thinks she'll be meeting Dale's wife. Dale didn't tell her that Patty left months ago when he finally confessed he had borrowed $150,000 from Santo "Chum" Giordano. Patty, like Dale, knew the name. She knew about the dentist too. According to her friends, the wife still lives in the house but her husband, the dentist, disappeared when he couldn't pay Chum back.

"Beautiful place," Elise says. The arched entry shades her from the morning sun, but even the short walk up the ten stairs that lead to the front door has caused sweat to break out across her upper lip. She rests a hand on the stucco siding. "Never been inside a house like this."

"Me neither," Dale says, moving aside to invite her in. "Until I bought one."

Before closing the door, Dale steps outside and looks down onto the street. A dark-blue sedan sits in front of the house two doors down. It's rusted around its front wheel basin, has the large, squared-off body of an older model, and has been parked there since Dale woke this morning. People on his street don't drive cars like that, but men who work for Chum do.

"This is just beautiful," Elise says, peering up at the ceiling that lifts two stories overhead, and then she notices Dale's face. "Good lord, what happened to you?"

"I'll give you a tour later," he says, ignoring her question and waving her off like it's nothing, though breathing still hurts and he's been wondering all morning if he should go to the emergency room. Patty would probably come back if she knew he was in the emergency room, yet she'd also want to know how he ended up there.

In his office, he pulls out the leather chair from under his mahogany desk, and with a sweeping gesture, he helps Elise to sit. She slides in front of him and he can't help but lay a hand on her waist.

"All this from flipping houses and condos?" she asks, glancing back at him with raised brows.

"Among other things," he says, winking so she'll think there's more to the story. Once she sees Dale's books, she'll know he's broke, and he wants her to think he has other deals going.

When she begins tapping on the keyboard, Dale leans close as best he can with the pain shooting through his right side. She smells of that lotion again. He tries to breathe it in deep.

"You don't look so good," Elise says, glancing up at Dale. Her hair brushes the side of his face. "You should go lie down. I'm fine here. I'll let you know if I'm missing anything, and I can let myself out."

Dale nods because he's having trouble taking a full breath and a little rest will do him good.

"And I see here you're only reconciled through February," Elise says, continuing to tap on the keyboard as she talks. "Is that right?"

Dale shrugs. He used to have an accountant, back when he could afford one, who took care of everything.

"Just download your bank statements before I come back next time," Elise says as he starts up the stairs to the bedroom that's mostly empty because Patty keeps coming by and taking things when he isn't home. "Don't you worry. I'll get you all straightened out."

By the time Dale wakes again, he's sweated through his T-shirt and the sheet is damp where his head is resting. Without moving, because he's stiffened up while he slept and maybe all the sweating is a sign of infection or a fever, he reaches for his pillow. Not finding it, he sits up. Both pillows are gone, as well as the blue comforter Patty bought for them last Christmas. On Patty's side of the bed, where her head used to rest, is one of her notes. She leaves them when she comes and goes with more of their belongings. This time, she's taken the pillows right from under his head and the comforter from on top of him. She's even taken the top sheet. He picks up the note and unfolds it. *This is the last time. I won't be back.*

Downstairs, the house is somehow quieter than before, because Patty is finally gone for good. His office chair is pushed up tight under his desk, the keyboard is centered, and the lights are off. Walking across his office, he flips open the slats on the plantation shutters and looks down on the street. The squared-off car is still parked two doors down. Pulling back, he closes the slats because even the filtered light is hurting his eyes, which is probably a sign of a concussion, and the spot between his eyes is pounding and he's still worried about the ache in his side. Not only is Patty gone for good, but it's as if Elise was never here, which makes the quiet in the house heavier. And then he gets a whiff of her lavender-scented lotion and smiles.

At his desk, he signs into his bank account, the sound of his fingers on the keyboard echoing in the mostly empty house, and downloads the monthly statements Elise asked for. When he goes to the bar tonight, long after six so he doesn't happen upon Chum again, he'll be able to tell her she can come back anytime, tomorrow even, because he's done what she asked. Just thinking about seeing her makes him feel better.

While he's still able to smell Elise and feel her hair on the side of his face, Dale walks outside and down the stairs to his driveway. He'd never be able to do something like this if he was still with Patty, but Elise is different. A good woman will have this effect on a man. He's always known that, and he can't fault himself for making a mistake with Patty. Squinting and wishing he'd grabbed his sunglasses, he looks for any sign of neighbors. Overhead, the fronds of a coconut palm rattle with the breeze, but the street is otherwise quiet. Most of his neighbors have homes up north. When summer rolls around, they install their hurricane shutters, make sure their flood insurance is up-to-date, and flee the Florida heat and humidity.

Both guys startle when Dale knocks on the car window.

They'd been asleep, which Dale is certain would upset Chum if he knew about it. That could be leverage if Dale ends up needing it. He's already good at this, already thinking like he needs to. Even with all this pain fogging his head, he's thinking clear, thinking a few steps ahead. This is the Dale he used to be.

"The hell you doing?" the driver says. He has black hair, slicked back so it shimmers. His smooth skin shines and a tan sleeveless shirt shows off slender arms and a sunken chest.

"You fellows work for money, yes?" Dale says, leaning against the doorframe in a casual sort of way and because it's easier to breathe.

The men look at each other. The one in the passenger seat is broad through the chest and shoulders and wears a baseball cap over a head of stringy blond hair. He lets out a laugh and nods. Dale has asked a stupid question.

"Chum's an old man too, ain't he?" Dale says.

The driver dips his chin and looks out at Dale over the top of a pair of dark sunglasses. "Suppose he is."

"And you know I'm selling my place," Dale says. "That place right over there."

The driver hangs one arm out of the car and looks toward Dale's house.

"Well, here's the deal. You two see to it that Chum doesn't live past closing day," Dale says, not able to stop himself from swallowing midsentence and giving away how nervous he's feeling, "and there's fifty thousand dollars in it for you."

Dale's new place is a two-bedroom on a slab with a flat roof and cinder-block walls. The marble windowsills are etched with water stains, and while the walls have been freshly painted in a pale gray, the air vents in the ceiling are trimmed with black mold. "The place'll do well in a storm," the leasing agent told him, "but if the flood insurance goes up, you should expect your rent to go up too." Sitting at the small table off the kitchen, Dale flips open the lid on the rubbery eggs and cold sausage Elise brought him when she came by to set up his computer and finish the last of the accounting. Taking one bite and then pushing the food aside, he stares out at the browning backyard and the lone cabbage palm. No reclaimed water here. No green lawns trimmed weekly by a lawn service. No towering royal palms. No saltwater pools.

"Chum come into the bar last night?" Dale shouts over one shoulder so Elise will hear him in the back room.

Yesterday morning, his house closed as scheduled, and when he walked out of the title office, he texted Chum to say the funds would hit the bank no later than noon today and that Dale would hand Chum a cashier's check at the bar when it opened at three. He stared hard at his phone while he waited for an answer. He never got one, and Dale has been hoping ever since that no text means the guys finally made good on their deal and that Chum Giordano is dead.

"Yes," she calls back, "I saw him. Pretty sure I did."

"What do you mean, you're pretty sure?" he shouts, swinging around and almost tipping his chair. "Either you saw him or you didn't!"

When Elise doesn't answer, Dale leans forward, rests his elbows on his knees, and hides his face in his hands. Fifty years old and he's going to have nothing. Chum is alive and Dale's going to have to give him damn near every last cent he has. The roofer took what was owed him right off the top. Another chunk went to pay off the equity line and the seawall company. And once he pays off Chum, he'll be wiped out. Hell, he isn't even sure how he'll make rent next month. At the sound of footsteps, he turns.

"Yes, he was there," Elise says. "I remember because he told me you were having a rough go of it." She presses up close behind Dale and works her hands and fingers along his neck muscles. "Said you're a good guy too. That true?"

Dale closes his eyes. Her hands slip down his chest as she presses closer. He glances at the clock. He's got plenty of time to get to the bank and then over to Smugglers, where he'll meet Chum. From his old house, he could walk to Smugglers, but it'll probably take him twenty minutes from here.

"Yes, that's true," Dale says. "I'm a good guy. The best."

Elise must know he's broke since he's living in this shithole, and yet she doesn't seem bothered by it. Dale leans his head back, resting it against her as she runs her fingers down one arm and takes his hand. She tugs so he'll stand and then leads him to his bedroom.

Dale can still smell Elise on him as he stands at the counter and waits for the teller to pull up his account. His skin is damp from the late-day heat and the cold air blowing down from overhead makes him shiver, or maybe it's the memory of Elise. As he waits for the teller to hand over the cashier's check that will wipe him out, he closes his eyes, letting himself slip back to that first moment of seeing her and touching her.

"There's a problem with your account, sir," the woman sitting behind the computer says. Her short brown hair is cut at a sharp angle that makes her look older than she is. She taps the screen.

"How so?" Dale says, leaning to get a look.

"You don't have the funds."

"They were supposed to clear by noon."

"Yes," she says. "A deposit cleared late this morning."

"So what's the problem?"

"And a withdrawal was made at . . ." She pauses, tucks her angled hair behind one ear. "Twelve twenty-three. Yes, twelve twenty-three this afternoon."

Outside the bank, Dale drops against the stucco siding. The ground underfoot tilts. He braces himself with one hand to the building. "Did you ever use a public computer to access your bank account?" the teller had asked him. A man joined them, asked if Dale needed to take a seat. "Who might have access to your accounts?" the man asked. No one, Dale kept telling them as the room began to spin. And then the man, the branch manager, had asked . . . "Who else might have access to your home computer?"

Three calls to Elise's cell phone roll directly to voice mail. Inside his car, he tries to take slow, steady breaths so he might remember where she lives. Or if she ever told him. After she climbed out of his bed, she said she was headed to work. From the bank parking lot, within walking distance to the house he owned until about thirty-six hours ago, he can look across the street and see Smugglers. Leaving his car at the bank so Chum won't see it parked outside the bar, Dale runs across four lanes of beach traffic, up onto the boardwalk, and yanks open the door to Smugglers.

"Good lord." It's Donna. She's standing behind the bar, a paring knife in hand and an orange on the counter. "What's got you in such a hurry?"

"Elise," Dale says, scanning the room for Chum or his men. "Where is she?"

"Darned if I know. Supposed to be here to open things up. Thought I'd found some decent help, but . . ."

"Her address," Dale says, swinging around at the sound of a car's gears popping into park. "I got to know where she lives."

The door opens and sunlight spills into the bar. Dale squints, and while he can't make out the figure standing in the threshold, he can see the hand that waves him outside. His shoulders drop and he walks head-on into the stream of light falling across him. He'd left her in his office when he went upstairs to sleep. "When you get a chance, just download those couple of other bank statements," she'd said. "I'll take care of everything else." And while he slept, she'd put something on his computer to capture his password. That's what the bank manager said as he helped Dale to a seat and handed him a glass of water. It had to be Elise. It really was so easy.

At first Dale can't be sure it's Chum standing outside the bar, but as his eyes adjust, the old man turns from a fuzzy outline into a solid figure. He's leaning there against the barrel that hasn't moved in twenty years.

"It's all gone, Chum," Dale says. "That girl, the new girl, Elise, she took it all."

The air blowing across his face is what wakes Dale. At first he thinks it's the overhead fan in his bedroom and that Elise is lying next to him, naked, her slender legs tangled in his. But there's a noise too and he's bouncing. He's on a boat. Warm saltwater sprays across his face, warm like bathwater. And the boat is slowing down.

The sun is low in the sky now. He must have been out a long time because it's nearly dusk. His head is pounding and muffled voices come from nearby. He closes his eyes when everything comes back to him. The computer Elise used, the log-in information she stole, the money that's gone. Hell, he'd even told her when the money was supposed to clear the bank, and while that was happening, she'd been leading him to his bedroom. Elise in bed with him. That meant someone else had to have been using the stolen log-in to clear out the account. His eyes fly open and he struggles to push himself up, not because he's strapped down in any way, but because he's dizzy and the motion of the boat is making his stomach swirl.

"She didn't do it alone," Dale says, but no one hears. Again, louder this time: "She didn't do it alone. Donna. It had to be Donna."

It's the one with stringy hair. He tells Dale to shut the hell up and turns back to his work. He's throwing something overboard. It splashes and then he throws something else. Dale has done enough fishing to recognize the smell. The guy is throwing buckets of fish guts into the water. He's chumming.

"Did you hear?" Dale says. "The two of them, together. They stole everything."

Someone cuts the motor but the boat continues to roll with the waves. Dale wraps one hand around the side that's still aching.

"That's a damn fool way to try to save your hide," Chum says, stepping up to Dale and blocking the last bit of sun bouncing off the boat's white deck. "I was betting you'd blame your wife."

Dale shakes his head. "No," he says, his chin puckering. Sweet Patty with the silky brown hair that fell past her shoulders and the hands that were always soft and warm. Patty who cooked yellow cornbread just the way he liked and was always there when he stumbled home from Smugglers. It had been her idea for Dale to sell the house to pay Chum back. She took what was in their savings and left the house to Dale and now she's never coming back.

"She'd never hurt me like that," Dale says, his voice breaking before he can say anything else.

Stretching out a hand, Chum helps Dale to his feet, but instead of letting go, Chum keeps hold of that hand and nudges the guy with the sunken chest.

"I'm telling you," Dale says, "it was both of them. Donna, she told me the girl did bookkeeping. She knew I needed someone. Jesus, they played me. And Donna knew about my house being sold. She did it. Had to have. Both of them played me."

The sunken-chest guy takes Dale's wrist from Chum. He pulls so Dale's arm is good and straight, and with a small knife and one smooth motion, he cuts Dale from wrist to elbow. Crying out, Dale tries to pull away, but the man holds tight. As if afraid his shoes will get stained, Chum steps back. Blood begins to drip onto the boat's white deck.

"Not too deep," Chum says, steadying himself with a hand to the railing. "Don't want him bleeding out first."

The same man grabs Dale's other arm, cuts it in the same way, and then folds Dale's arms to stem the bleeding.

"Legs too?" the man asks.

Chum nods, and as the man squats down, Dale stumbles backward but something stops him. It's the stringy-haired guy. He wraps his arms around Dale's chest and yells at him to stop moving.

"Go easier if you stay still," the sunken-chest man says, and one at a time, he slices the inside of each of Dale's thighs.

"We're good to go!" Chum hollers, and sticks a cigar in his mouth.

Dale is kicking and punching as they lift him. They swing him twice and let go. Chum is laughing. That's the last thing Dale hears when he hits the water. Coughing and choking, he pops back to the surface. Before he sees them, he feels them.

First it's a bump to his leg, a glancing blow that could have been an undercurrent. But then he feels another. And then another. Like chum in the water.

I GET THE SAME OLD FEELING

BY KAREN BROWN

Davis Islands

They moved into the house in September. The last time they'd been there, following behind a real estate agent's clicking heels, the rooms had seemed open and friendly. Now the walls were marked by tree shadows, an uneasy flickering of light off the canal. Eva told her husband it wasn't the same and he said it was too late, and gave her that look: part caution, part dismay. Didn't he always want to please her, and was she never happy? Eva crossed the terrazzo floor and opened the doors to the patio and let the breeze move through the rooms. Small insects came in, bobbing off the kitchen counter, hovering slow and dazed like bits of dark ash.

Her husband left for work, agreeing to drop the children at their new school. It was better if she didn't take them at first—her littlest would cling to her and make a scene at the drop-off line. The doorbell signaled a delivery or another neighbor stopping to introduce herself bearing a willow basket of muffins or a box of locally confected toffee. They all said the same thing: "You didn't tear it down!" Eva wasn't sure whether they were pleased or disgruntled—the exclamation kept vague, waiting for her response. "Not yet," she might say. Or, "Never!"

She opened the door to a man she knew she should remember. He stood on the front walkway bewildered, blinking, his hands stuffed into his pants pockets.

"Eva Langford?" he said.

Eva laughed, and his expression dulled. "Dr. Harcourt?"

Her old college professor. He was gray now, his same eyes peeking out of an aged face, the same clothing—jeans, corduroy jacket, Converse sneakers. He took a step back, as if finding her there was a trick of some sort. "What are you doing here?" he said.

They went back and forth this way, an awkward reunion. She explained they'd moved in last week, that her husband's company had reassigned him to Tampa.

"Of all places," she said. "It's Eva Kinsey now."

"This was my mother's house," Jim Harcourt said.

And Eva remembered a day she spent with him—sex at his condo and then the drive around town in his Alfa Romeo with the top down, drinking beer, winding through a suburban neighborhood—had it been this very Davis Islands neighborhood?

They'd driven curving roads under oaks and magnolias, seed pods fluttering into her hair, into her lap, and he'd pointed out houses of horrors.

A low-slung ranch, its lawn a swath of dead grass: "This is where my friend was run over and killed by his brother. High on cocaine. Family station wagon."

A Spanish Mediterranean with green-striped awnings like a candy shop: "Allan Tinker, decapitated in a waterskiing accident."

A two-story contemporary, its stucco crumbling: "There's a plexiglass floor upstairs above the pool. One or two ODs at parties. Heard they took the bodies somewhere it would look like suicide. One of them even survived."

A 1960s mid-century modern, all windows and architecturally sharp landscaping: "Speaking of suicide. Woman was found by the neighbor boy in the kitchen. Former beauty queen. Tampa's *Valley of the Dolls*."

Dr. Harcourt had grinned, pointed his long finger, his hair blown back by the wind. Eva had only half believed him. "Not really," she said, enjoying the bubble of fear. "You're making this up."

He had Barry White's *Can't Get Enough* playing. The car's leather seats were soft and sun-warmed. He'd given her a Valium earlier and she still felt the effects, the wind cottony in her mouth, her arms and legs leaden.

Like the insects bobbing now, just out of her line of sight.

"Jesus, how long has it been?" he said. He brushed an old man's hand through his hair.

Eva said it was fifteen years at least. She'd been a freshman then. "I have two children now."

At the time they'd known each other, Dr. Harcourt had children, a wife. Once, driving in the Alfa Romeo, he'd told her to duck, and she'd slid down in the narrow bucket seat and curled herself up below the glove box. "Look at you," he'd said, surprised, her tiny body the provider of feats for him.

Eva sensed he'd come now to the door for her. Even though he claimed this was his mother's house, she still doubted him after all these years.

"Did you want to see the house? I'm still unpacking."

He put both of his hands up. "I wondered if the place was sold," he said. "I couldn't impose."

But she insisted. "Did you grow up here?"

Dr. Harcourt stepped uneasily over the threshold. Eva led the way into the living room, but when she looked back he was still there in the entry. "I lived here for a little while," he called to her. Slowly, he came forward and stood across from her. "This is—" He took in the boxes stacked against the wall, the shining floors, the new sofa still wrapped in its plastic.

Eva told him the former owner had taken up all the carpets and polished the terrazzo.

"They reconfigured it some," he said, cautiously. "There used to be a wall there."

Eva asked him if he wanted to look around. She remembered how it had ended with him—how cold and unthinking she'd been. She felt sorry for him now, and she reached out a hand to clasp his arm. But Dr. Harcourt's shoulders tightened in his corduroy coat, and he told her it was nice to see her, welcome back, but he had to go.

That evening her boys had baseball practice. Eva took a photo of them in their too-large caps, the gloves grotesque claws at the ends of their small arms. She was going to unpack some more, she told her husband, set up the house. She watched them drive off, and then she went for a walk. Dr. Harcourt had told her the neighborhood was designed by a man named D.P. Davis in the 1920s as an exclusive resort with hotels and a golf course and luxury Mediterranean Revival–style residences. The islands were man-made, built on top of swamp and mudflats at the mouth of the Hillsborough River. The old stucco houses had been replaced here and there with mid-century ranches, but those were now being threatened by mansions—two- and three-story places, with three-car garages and paved driveways. Eva's house was one of the remaining 1950s ranches—one that at the time of its construction would have signaled affluence, with its geometric iron gate, a courtyard, and walls of glass. Large birds of paradise filled the front beds, and banyan trees grew along the side of the house. "A tropical paradise," the agent had said. "Room for a pool."

The night was balmy, as if they might get a bit of fall

weather—although she told her husband not to expect it. She'd only gone to college in Tampa for a year. Of her time here, she claimed dim memories. "My clothes stuck to my skin," she said. "It always smelled of magnolia and river muck." She never graduated. Her parents had made her come home, and she had no choice. She had no way to support herself in Tampa and wasn't in the best shape at the time to find work.

Later, in bed, she told her husband funny stories about the neighbors that visited while she'd been unpacking. She didn't tell him about Dr. Harcourt.

"Why did they all assume we planned to tear down the house?" she said.

Her husband, turned away from her in bed, was half-asleep, a signal for her to stop talking. He grunted. "It's just what everyone is doing," he said. "Tell them we like the house's style."

Eva got up from bed and went down the hallway. She stood in the place where Dr. Harcourt had stood that morning. Beyond the sliding glass doors, the sprinklers hissed. The canal seemed oily and dark. Dr. Harcourt had told her about a husband who'd accidentally killed his wife in an argument. He'd stood her in a galvanized bucket and poured in concrete and dumped her in the bay. He'd been caught, somehow. He'd served his time and gotten out of prison and spent his last years working as a salesman in the mall, selling men's suits.

Maybe this had been a house on Dr. Harcourt's tour and that was why everyone thought they'd tear it down. She returned to bed, but could not sleep for the bright slice of moonlight that cut the room in half, like a torn photograph.

Eva wanted the story of the house. She'd seen Dr. Harcourt's haunted expression, his jittery movements when he stepped through the doorway onto the cool terrazzo. The way he fled—that was the only way to describe his leaving. If the house had ghosts she wanted to be prepared for them. If they were angry or distraught, if their lives had been cut short, if they'd been the victims of their own or others' violence—surely these things would alter the atmosphere of the rooms.

She located his e-mail address at the college and sent him a note.

Two days later, Eva swatted at the small flies she'd let in. She followed through the motions of unpacking that her husband expected—stacking plates on cupboard shelves she'd wiped clean of dust, the bits of spices spilled from their jars, a piece of macaroni, dried and yellow like an old toenail. On one shelf, she'd encountered a small piece of broken glass, and it had imbedded itself in the pad of her middle finger and she could not remove it. Each time she touched anything, the glass announced itself there below the surface. That afternoon, for no reason at all, she felt trapped, held by the house, terror making her heart race. If only she knew what had sent Dr. Harcourt to her door, she might face it down. Maybe it was only a fleeting, sorrowful memory of a lost parent.

She didn't want her husband to know about her past. That time in her life, the brief year of college—she'd kept that private all this time. She could not confess details that would surely alter his perception of her. The revelation might even cause a breach in their marriage. Too much time had passed, and she could not adequately account for her silence, her secrecy.

That had been one of the vows he'd written when they married: *We will keep nothing from each other, no secrets between us, something, something.* She could not remember it all now.

Time diffused some things. And others it highlighted, a spotlight cast about a dark room full of shelves disappearing into the rafters of an impossibly high ceiling, the memories stacked on the shelves in labeled boxes like a museum warehouse. She imagined her husband's face crumpling with disappointment, but she could not predict what he might do or say after.

Later that morning, Dr. Harcourt returned. She found him at her door in his signature clothing—the jeans, the Converse, the corduroy jacket.

"Let's start over," he said. "I was incredibly rude running off the other day."

Eva set down a basket of her sons' dirty clothes. She said she understood. "It's hard to go back to places from the past."

Dr. Harcourt agreed, eagerly, his eyes brightening. "Some of it's a blur, and then the rest is so real and vivid. For instance, I remember *you* so well."

Eva crossed her arms over her chest. She wore her pajamas—a T-shirt and a pair of loose cotton pants. "And this house?" she said. "Is this part of the vivid past?"

She saw his smile falter, but his eyes stayed on hers. "The house."

It was as if he did not want to look past her into its depths.

"Let's go for coffee," he said. "And then I promise you a tour. How's that?"

When she was a college student it had been the Alfa Romeo he used to lure her in. She'd seen him getting into it one muggy afternoon as she crossed the faculty lot and called out to him asking for a ride. It had been a joke, but she knew now he'd seen her real desire to leave campus and its pressure of school and roommates behind, and he'd played along. Now, it was the house. As much as she tried to pretend the story of the house didn't matter, somehow he knew it did.

His car, parked at the curb, was a silver Prius. She got in and tucked her skirt under her legs.

"This takes me back," he said, turning the key in the ignition. She half expected the old R&B songs, but the radio was silent.

They didn't drive far—just along one of the curving roads to the small shopping plaza. Eva and her husband had taken the boys to the nearby Mexican restaurant. The coffee bar had chairs set up outside, but Dr. Harcourt held the glass door for her, and she slipped into the dim interior.

"Coffee or beer?" he said, pulling out a chair for her.

Along the wall were bottles of wine, taps for beer behind a counter. "Beer, for old time's sake," she said.

Dr. Harcourt ordered two pilsners. It was ten a.m. Eva imagined her boys at their school tables, their pencils shaping letters on worksheets. Her husband downtown presiding over a meeting. She should have asked Dr. Harcourt about his wife and children, but she didn't want to know. She drank the beer and said, "So?"

Dr. Harcourt took a long sip, set his glass on the tabletop. "Patience," he said.

"Patient Griselda," she said. They'd read Boccaccio's awful story in his class.

Griselda's husband saves her from poverty by marriage. He believes all women to be faithless and wicked and he tests her by taking her children away and claiming they are dead. He banishes her to her father's small impoverished hut under the pretense of marrying another woman. Dr. Harcourt had been obsessed with the story. They'd even read Perrault's fairy tale written about her. At the time, Eva had not cared about the story's intent as a guide for young women and wives. She had not ever thought she'd be a wife, a mother.

She pressed her finger against the tabletop and felt the sting of the glass beneath the skin. The beer made her woozy.

"Do you think I'm not a faithful wife?"

"You are who you always were," he said, cryptically.

A bell on the door rang and Eva glanced up. She didn't know any of the neighbors yet—barely remembered their welcoming faces at her door—but this woman might have been one of them, the way she eyed Eva with a faint smile. Eva understood it mattered who she was seen with now.

Dr. Harcourt slipped from his chair and returned with two new glasses of beer. Eva tried to protest but he set the tall glass beside her, and she found herself finishing her first, reaching for the second. He leaned back in his chair and crossed his ankles.

"The house," he said. "And my mother."

He told her his mother was no Griselda. She was everything the husband in the tale feared—faithless and conniving. He ran his hand over his cheek as he talked, as if trying to rub off a smear of lipstick. She was a bank teller, or a receptionist, or a ladies clothing store clerk, he couldn't remember which. "A lowly sort, when my father met her," he said. "It was 1958."

His father was bewitched by her and married her, believing that her gratitude for the marriage and everything it would bring her—the sprawling ranch house, the yacht club, the garden club—would be a guarantee of her love.

"But is it ever?" Dr. Harcourt said. He sat forward suddenly in his chair, and Eva, startled, leaned away. She remembered the way he would lecture, pacing the room, his Converse sneakers squeaking on the wood floors.

"For some women it might be," Eva said.

He smiled and took a sip of his beer. "She met someone else and had an affair. My father heard rumors and hired a private detective who took photos of her at a motel with the man. Then he confronted her. I was ten or so. My brother was twelve."

His father spoke to his lawyer about divorce, and his mother knew it was coming: the loss of everything she loved—the clothes, the jewelry. "According to our father, she never worried about losing us," Dr. Harcourt said. "She worried about her Cadillac."

Eva felt her apprehension beneath the effects of the beer. She wondered if she should offer some sympathetic comment, but she could not speak, waiting for the end of the story.

"Not many people acknowledge the other side of this grim tale," Dr. Harcourt said.

"*Her* side," Eva said, her voice an underwater sound. The barista steamed milk and roasted beans. Customers came in, and maybe they were Eva's neighbors, or not.

"What she endured from him—this pillar of society, this much-loved man. Those nights he berated her, accused her of things she had yet to do, ripped her clothing from the closet and drove it in the car to Goodwill. Deprived her access to the bank account so we had no money for food. These things happened—I remember them happening. And still, she stayed."

"Like Griselda?" Eva said, confused.

"I'm not sure what the breaking point was," he responded, drumming his fingers on the table.

"Maybe the man she met was kind. Maybe she wanted a bit of happiness for herself."

Dr. Harcourt drank his beer in one long swallow. Eva saw his throat move. His hands cradled the empty glass. "She hired some thug to kill him. He came into the house and waited for my father to return from work one evening and he bludgeoned him to death."

Eva felt the cold of the glass move through her arm, down the length of her torso. "Is this all true, Dr. Harcourt?"

"It's a notorious local story," he said. "And please, call me James."

He'd asked her to do that before, and she had, to please him. But to do so now would take her back to that time with him—the closeness they'd forged driving the grid of streets, having sex in the empty day-lit parks where at night students gathered, negotiating with their money and their fake IDs and pharmaceuticals. She knew it would not take much to close the gap the years had formed between them.

"I really couldn't do that," she said.

"It's my name." He set one empty glass inside the other. "Why would it be a problem?"

"It's not who you are to me anymore," she said. "It doesn't feel right."

"What if I called you Mrs. Kinsey? How would that feel?"

She turned in her chair, crossed her legs. "I don't care how it feels. Call me whatever you want."

"Whore," he said, his face darkening, his voice low. "There's something."

She recoiled, the way you might if someone's injury had bloomed with blood. Her limbs felt hung with weights. Still, she managed to stand. Another woman who might have been her neighbor waited at the counter for her coffee order as if nothing were out of the ordinary.

Eva left the coffee bar, the door's bells jangling behind her, and began to walk toward her house. Other people were out walking, in groups or alone, with dogs on leashes or pushing strollers. The air blew, hot and thick, lifting her skirt. Oak trees swayed overhead, sending acorns down onto rooftops, onto car hoods. Dry leaves skittered across the sidewalk. The wind in the oaks was a sound like a hiss, a faucet left on, a leak in a gas line. She easily blended in—a resident out for a walk, not someone fleeing a man in a coffee bar.

She approached her house, its 1950s facade so benign, so unremarkable. When she'd been a college student seeing Dr. Harcourt she met another student and began to see him too. The boy knew about her affair with Dr. Harcourt, she told him everything—where they had sex, the positions Dr. Harcourt liked, the things he told her to say. The boy loved hearing the stories, and then he must have repeated them, and it was a small college and somehow Dr. Harcourt found out. He hadn't retaliated overtly, but now Eva surmised he must have been instrumental in her failure at school, the reputation she'd acquired, the accusations, the meeting with the dean who asked about her drug use, her poor grades, and who would not entertain her confession.

"Jim Harcourt?" he had said, twinkly-eyed and paternal, his expression bemused. He didn't need to say more. She would not be believed.

The Prius was there at the curb, and Dr. Harcourt waited at the gate to the front courtyard. She had cared for him in college. She'd had every intention of staying with him, assured his love for her was greater than that for his wife and it was only a matter of time before he divorced her. The other boy was just a boy, and she regretted ever spending time with him.

Eva edged past Dr. Harcourt, his coat's corduroy fabric brushing her arm. She opened the door with her key and stepped into the house, moved down the terrazzo hall to the living room and the wall of glass that offered its view of the patio and lawn, the wind-scalloped canal. She heard Dr. Harcourt enter behind her. He stepped alongside her and took her hand, gently.

"Let's not do this," he said.

"You should leave," she told him.

"You haven't gotten the tour yet. I promised you that, and I won't renege." He walked to the center of the room, his hands on his hips. "The scene of countless drunken escapades. Parties, dancing." He swiveled his hips, his hands holding invisible things: a cigarette, a drink. "Glass dish of peanuts." He mimed taking a handful, popping them into his mouth.

He took her hands and tried to get her to dance. He sang part of an old Barry White song. She felt the sharp press of the glass in her finger, and she tugged her hands away. He had told her the story to remind her of their time together, but he told her to frighten her too, knowing that what they'd done together would get mixed up in the story, that she needed to hear it, wanted it, much as the college boy wanted her stories of sex with a professor. Eva knew they all needed the stories for something.

"He came in here," Dr. Harcourt said, gesturing to the sliding glass doors. "It was wall-to-wall carpeting then. My mother favored white." He crossed the room to a door that led into what Eva and her husband had designated as an office. "He hid in here, so when my father came in," he walked down the hall to the foyer, "and set his keys down, he was in direct view."

"Were they caught?" she asked.

"The body was found here," Dr. Harcourt said, his mapping of the room ending, the foyer the X.

"Who found him?" Eva said, her voice small and soft. "Was it you?"

He stared at the spot on the floor. "We made a mess of things back then, didn't we?" he said.

He stepped around the imaginary body and approached

her, the soles of his Converse squeaking. He put his hand on her shoulder and slid it down her arm. They had a history together, he said. "There's something really powerful in that."

D.P. Davis, the developer of the Islands, had died mysteriously in 1926. He'd fallen from a porthole on a sea voyage to Paris with his mistress—a former Hollywood actress. There'd been questions about the night he died, Dr. Harcourt had said. The man was a drinker, but he was also in debt. "Did he fall, or did he leap?" he had said. "Or was he pushed?"

She imagined the dead man in the foyer, the white carpet stained with blood, these same tree shadows moving along the walls, the quiet of the neighborhood its own sound. And then a rattling of keys in the door and the door opening on the scene. It might be this scene, she and Dr. Harcourt together, and it might be her husband coming into the house, calling her name. Was it always clear? Victim or criminal?

The tree shadows rubbed the walls, a delicate, inaudible friction. Dr. Harcourt dipped his face toward hers. Eva thought she might cry out, though from fear or desire she could not ever say.

TRIGGERFISH LANE

BY TIM DORSEY

Palma Ceia

They keep coming to Florida.

People who maintain such records report that every single day, a thousand new residents move into the state. The reasons are varied. Retirement, beaches, affordable housing, growing job base, tax relief, witness protection, fugitive warrants, forfeiture laws that shelter your house if you're a Heisman Trophy winner who loses a civil suit in the stabbing death of your wife, and year-round golf.

On a typical spring morning, five of those thousand new people piled into a cobalt-blue Ford Aerostar in Logansport, Indiana. The Davenports—Jim, Martha, and their three children. They watched the moving van pull out of their driveway and followed it south.

A merging driver on the interstate ramp gave Jim the bird. He would have given Jim two birds, but he was on the phone. Jim grinned and waved and let the man pass.

Jim Davenport was like many of the other thousand people heading to Florida this day, except for one crucial difference. Of all of them, Jim was hands down the most nonconfrontational.

Jim avoided all disagreement and didn't have the heart to say no. He loved his family and fellow man, never raised his voice or fists, and was rewarded with a lifelong, routine digestion of small doses of humiliation. The belligerent, boorish, and bombastic latched onto him like strangler figs.

He was utterly content.

Then Jim moved to Florida and something quite unnatural happened: he made strange new friends, got in disputes, and someone ended up dead.

But none of this was on the horizon as the Davenports entered the second day of their southern interstate migration. The road tar at the bottom of Georgia began to soften and smell in the afternoon sun. It was a Saturday, the traffic on I-75 thick and anxious. Hondas, Mercurys, Subarus, Chevy Blazers. A blue Aerostar with Indiana tags passed the exit for the town of Tifton, "Sod Capital of the USA," and a billboard: *Jesus Is Lord . . . at Buddy's Catfish Emporium.*

A sign marking the Florida state line stood in the distance, along with the sudden appearance of palm trees growing in a precise grid. The official state welcome center rose like a mirage through heat waves off the highway. Cars accelerated for the oasis with the runaway anticipation of traffic approaching a Kuwaiti checkpoint on the border with Iraq.

They pulled into the hospitality center's angled parking slots; doors opened and children jumped out and ran around the grass in the aimless, energetic circles for which they are known. Parents stretched and rounded up staggering amounts of trash and headed for garbage bins. A large Wisconsin family in tank tops sat at a picnic table eating bologna sandwiches and generic cheese doodles so they could afford a thousand-dollar day at Disney. A crack team of state workers arrived at the curb in an unmarked van and began pressure-washing some kind of human fluid off the sidewalk. A stray ribbon of police tape blew across the pavement.

The Aerostar parked near the vending machines, in front of the *No Nighttime Security* sign.

"Who needs to go to the bathroom?" asked Jim.

Eight-year-old Melvin put down his mutant action figures and raised a hand.

Sitting next to him with folded arms and a dour outlook was Debbie Davenport, a month shy of sweet sixteen, totally disgusted to be in a minivan. She was also disgusted with the name Debbie. Prior to the trip she had informed her parents that from now on she would only go by "Drusilla."

"Debbie, you need to use the restroom?"

No reply.

Martha got out a bottle for one-year-old Nicole, cooing in her safety seat, and Jim and little Melvin headed for the building.

Outside the restrooms, a restless crowd gathered in front of an eight-foot laminated map of Florida, unable to accept that they were still hundreds of miles from the nearest theme park. They would become even more bitter when they pulled away from the welcome center and the artificial grove of palms gave way to hours of scrubland and billboards for top-less donut shops.

Jim bought newspapers and coffee. Martha took over the driving and pulled back on I-75. Jim unfolded one of the papers and read aloud: "*Authorities have discovered a tourist from Finland who lost his luggage, passport, all his money and ID, and was stranded for eight weeks at Miami International Airport.*"

"Eight weeks?" said Martha. "How did he take baths?"

"Wet paper towels in the restrooms."

"Where did he sleep?"

"Chairs at different gates each night."

"What did he eat?"

"Bagels from the American Airlines Admirals Club."

"How did he get in the Admirals Club if he didn't have ID?"

"Doesn't say."

"If he went to all that trouble, he probably could have gotten some kind of help from the airline. I can't believe nobody noticed him."

"I think that's the point of the story."

"What happened?"

"Kicked him out. He was last seen living at Fort Lauderdale International."

The Aerostar passed a group of police officers on the side of the highway, slowly walking eight abreast looking for something in the weeds. Jim turned the page. "They've cleared the comedian Gallagher in the Tamiami Strangler case."

"Is that a real newspaper?"

Jim turned back to the front page and pointed at the top. *Tampa Tribune*.

Martha rolled her eyes.

"Says they released an artist's sketch. Bald with mustache and long hair on the sides. Police got hundreds of calls that it looked like Gallagher. But they checked his tour schedule—he was out of state the nights of the murders."

"They actually checked him out?"

"They also checked out Gallagher's brother."

Martha looked at Jim, then back at the road.

"After clearing Gallagher, they got a tip that he has a brother who looks just like him and smashes watermelons on a circuit of low-grade comedy clubs under the name Gallagher II. But he was out of town as well."

"I hope I don't regret this move," said Martha.

Jim put his hand on hers. "You're going to love Tampa."

Jim Davenport had never planned on moving to Tampa, or even Florida for that matter. Everything he knew about the state came from the *Best Places to Live in America* magazine that now sat on the Aerostar's dashboard. Right there on page seventeen, across from the feature on the joy of Vermont's covered bridges, was the now famous annual ranking of the finest cities in the US of A to raise a family. And coming in at number three with a bullet—just below Seattle and San Francisco—was the shocker on the list. Rocketing up from last year's 497th position: Tampa, Florida. When the magazine hit the stands, champagne corks flew in the Chamber of Commerce. The mayor called a press conference, and the city quickly threw together a band and fireworks show at the riverfront park; the news was so big it even caused some people to get laid.

Nobody knew it was all a mistake. The magazine had recently been acquired by a German media conglomerate, which purchased the latest spelling and grammar–check software and dismissed its editors and writers, replacing them with distracted high school students listening to music on headphones. The tabular charts on the new software had baffled a student with green hair, who inadvertently moved all of Tampa's crime statistics a decimal point to the left.

The Davenports got off the expressway and Jim threw a quarter in the automatic toll booth, but the red light didn't change. He drove through. A wino scurried from the underbrush and pulled a quarter out of the plastic basket, where he'd stuffed a rag in the coin hole.

The family van headed into south Tampa. None of them had seen their new home yet, except in pictures. The deal was prearranged and underwritten by Jim's company, an expanding Indiana consulting firm that had asked for volunteers to move to new branch offices in Phoenix, San Antonio, and Tampa. Long lines formed for Arizona and Texas. Jim wondered why he was all alone at the Florida desk.

Jim checked street signs as the van rolled down Dale Mabry Highway. "I think we're getting close."

Anticipation built. Everyone's faces were at the windows. Antique malls, dry cleaners, Little League fields, 7-Elevens. Just like neighborhoods everywhere, but with lots of palm trees and azaleas.

Jim made a right. Almost there. Martha liked the sound of the street names. Barracuda Trail, Man O'War Terrace, Coral Circle. When they got to Triggerfish Lane, Jim made a left. Their mouths fell open.

Paradise.

The sun was high, the sky clear, and children played catch and rode bikes in the street. And the colors! Lush gardens and hedges, bright but tasteful pastel paint schemes. Teal, turquoise, pink, peach. The houses started at the bayfront and unfolded chronologically as development had pushed inland. Clapboard bungalows from the twenties, Mediterranean stuccos from the thirties and forties, classic ranch houses of the fifties and sixties. It used to be a consistent architectural flow, but real estate in south Tampa had become so white-hot that anything under two thousand square feet was bulldozed to make way for three-story trophy homes that now towered outside both windows of the Aerostar. Half the places had decorative silk flags hanging over the brass mailboxes. Florida Gators flags and FSU Seminole flags. Flags with sunflowers and golf clubs and sailfish and horses. Jim pointed ahead at a light-ochre bungalow with white trim. A restoration award flag hung from the wraparound porch.

"There she is."

Martha's eyes popped with elation, and she spontaneously hugged Jim.

The moving truck was already unloading in the driveway

when they pulled up in front of 888 Triggerfish. A grinning realtor stepped down from the porch and walked to the van carrying a jumbo welcome basket of citrus jams, butters, marmalades, and chewies, wrapped up in green cellophane.

"Welcome! Welcome!" The realtor pumped Jim's hand, then Martha's. "Gonna love it here in Florida. Couldn't live anywhere else!"

Jim went out on the lawn and triumphantly pulled up the *For Sale / Sold!* sign.

A boy on a skateboard stopped at the end of the driveway. "You bought a house on this street?"

The realtor grabbed Jim by the arm. "Let's go inside."

"What did that kid mean?"

"Guess what!" said the realtor. "The cable's already hooked up!"

Despite the serene surface appearance of the street, there was an unexpected amount of drama on Triggerfish Lane. Much came from the juxtaposition of family homes with mortgages and rental houses with itinerants.

For instance, across the street from the Davenports, a rental sign had recently been pulled up from the lawn by a tall, wiry man accompanied by a shorter, plump companion. Serge and Coleman, the ultimate odd couple. And fugitives.

Coleman wasn't the brightest bulb but was otherwise normal, except for his unabated substance intake that left him uniformly blunt and inert at all hours. Conversely, Serge was highly intelligent. And criminally insane. Part of his mental illness was the contradiction of possessing a rigid moral code, and some of his most heinous acts were the result of the noblest of intentions. Complicating matters was his consuming curiosity and savant penchant for improvised mechanics dating back to childhood. More than once, his elementary school science projects prompted responses from the local fire department. Psychiatrists believed Serge could lead a virtually normal existence with daily cocktails of mind-numbing medication, which he refused to take because it made him too foggy to seize every day for maximum value.

And there lay the pair's combustible dynamic: Coleman wouldn't stop taking drugs, and Serge wouldn't start.

Weeks passed after they moved in, much of their time spent relaxing on the front porch, respectively consuming sparkling water and whiskey. And watching their neighbors across the street.

One evening the Davenports stepped onto their front porch and Jim cheerfully waved across the street.

"What are you doing?" asked Martha.

"Waving."

"Why?"

"Because he waved at me," said Jim. "It's only neighborly."

"Jim! There's something seriously wrong with them!" said Martha. "The fat one is always wasted, and the other one is just weird!"

"You're imagining things," said her husband.

Across the street, Serge was showing Coleman a *National Geographic* article about a tribe in Africa. "Check out how they make their necks really long with metal neck coils."

Coleman popped another beer. "We should get some neck coils."

"I have an idea."

They walked over to the hedge and Serge pulled out a long garden hose, the collapsible flat kind full of pinholes that inflates with water to irrigate flower beds. Serge started wrapping it around his neck. "Okay. When I give the signal, turn on the water, and I'll have neck coils."

"Right," said Coleman, pushing his way through the hedge to the faucet.

"You're overreacting," Jim told Martha.

"Those men are deranged!"

"Maybe they're just simple," said Jim. "Wouldn't you feel bad if you found out that was the case and you'd been talking like this?"

"They're not retarded! They're dangerous!"

Jim and Martha heard something across the street. Serge was flopping around the front yard, turning blue and fighting a garden hose wrapped around his throat like an anaconda. Coleman thrashed drunkenly in the bushes, trying to turn off the water.

Coleman finally cut the pressure, and the hose deflated. Serge unwrapped his neck and sat up, panting.

Jim turned to Martha. "I don't think you're supposed to use the word *retarded* anymore. It's offensive or something."

Coleman pointed across the street. "Are the Davenports looking at us?"

"Yeah, they are." Serge smiled and waved again.

Jim waved back again.

"Will you stop that!" said Martha.

Serge rubbed his neck. "Another close call. I think God is trying to tell me something."

"Like what?"

"I think I'm going to try going straight."

"You?" Coleman laughed. "That's a hoot!"

"I'm serious."

"What brought this on?"

"We've been staying here a few weeks now, and I've been

watching Jim over there. I've decided to pattern my life after him."

"You mean that wimp who never does anything?"

"Don't you dare call him a wimp!" said Serge. "His gig may look mild from our perspective, but talk about living on the edge. Guys like him never get any glory. They've just quietly put away childish things to face the relentless adult responsibility of taking care of their children. We've been in a lot of close scrapes over the years. Car chases, knives, gunfire. But I think I'd crack under the kind of pressure Jim deals with every day. He's kind of become my hero."

"You've got to be kidding."

A week later, a '76 Laguna with chrome hubs screeched up in front of the Davenport residence. A young Debbie Davenport and the shirtless driver got out and kissed.

"Hey," Jim yelled at the driver, "I want to talk to you!"

Jim ran down from the porch as fast as he could, but the Laguna took off again. Jim stood in the middle of the street, in the middle of swirling worry.

Suddenly, a voice from behind: "You're Jim, right?"

Jim spun around. "Uh, yeah."

"We haven't been properly introduced. I'm Serge." He extended a hand to shake. "You're like my hero."

"What?"

Serge nodded hard. "The brutal stress you constantly face. And I think I just witnessed some of it. What's going on?"

"Nothing."

Serge wrapped a consoling arm around Jim's shoulder. "Come on, you can tell me. We're neighbors after all. It's about the fabric of the community! So my new hero buddy, what's burdening your soul?"

"It's just my daughter Debbie."

"Yeah, I saw her get out of the car and go in the house," said Serge. "How old is she now? Sixteen?"

"Next month," said Jim.

"Then that guy in the car is way too old for her."

"I know. I've forbidden her to see him, but she's rebelling. I need to strike the right balance of discipline or risk damaging our relationship."

"Then attack the problem from the other end," said Serge. "Just leave that guy to me. I have these friends and some base-ball bats—"

"No. I have to handle it myself. I'm her father. I heard her talking on the phone with one of her friends. I think his name's Scorpion. He's twenty-two. And what was the deal with his underwear hanging out like that? Didn't he realize it was showing?"

"I think that's on purpose," said Serge.

"Really? That's what they're doing these days?" Jim pointed toward Serge's front yard, where Coleman was bending over to drink from the garden hose. "So your roommate does it on purpose too?"

Serge shook his head. "That's not fashion. That's con-genital."

Tires screeched in the distance. Serge and Coleman looked up the street. A '76 Chevy Laguna tore around the corner and down Triggerfish Lane.

Serge stood up on the porch and yelled: "Hey! Slow down! Kids play around here!"

"He didn't hear you," said Coleman.

The driver pulled up in front of the Davenport residence and honked the horn.

Serge yelled again: "Go up to the door and knock like a human being!"

"Why are you so upset?" asked Coleman.

"That guy's pushing my buttons. And he's much too old to be going out with Debbie."

"It's Jim's business."

"I know," Serge said with resignation. "I promised I wouldn't interfere."

Debbie never came out of the house, and the Laguna took off up the street.

"What I'd like to do to him!" said Serge.

"Remember, you're going straight."

"I know, I know. What would Jim do in a situation like this?"

"Look," said Coleman. "He's turning around."

"I'll have a talk with him. I think his name's Scorpion." Serge jumped off the porch and ran down to the corner. He waited at the stop sign.

The Laguna screeched to a halt.

"Hi," said Serge. "Would you mind driving just a tad slower around here? We have a lot of children who play—"

The driver raised his middle finger. "Fuck off, pops!" He peeled out.

Serge walked back to his porch.

"Did you talk to him?" asked Coleman.

"Yep."

"Well?"

"It's a start. You have to begin the healing somewhere."

Coleman pointed. "He's coming back."

Serge ran down to the corner again. "Excuse me, Mr. Scorpion," he said, "I was trying to point out that we have a lot of little kids—"

The driver flicked a cigarette at Serge and sped off.

Serge returned to the porch.

"How's it coming?" asked Coleman.

Serge was looking down at his chest. "He threw a ciga-rette at me."

"It made a burn mark."

Serge scratched the spot with his finger. "This was one of my favorite shirts."

There were more tire sounds up the street. The two men turned and looked.

"I can't believe it," said Serge. "He's coming back."

"And look. There's Jim's car right behind him."

"Maybe I can stop them both, and we can all sit down and have a civilized talk."

Jim Davenport was heading home from the grocery store in the Aerostar when he pulled up at a stop sign behind a '76 Chevy Laguna. The Laguna turned left onto Triggerfish, and Jim turned left behind him. In his stress, he accidentally honked the horn.

Jim saw brake lights on the Chevy. The driver got out and ran back to the SUV. "Don't you ever blow your fucking horn at me!"

"I wasn't—"

Before Jim could finish, the Laguna's driver had opened the door and pulled Jim into the street.

Serge and Coleman jumped to their feet: "Road rage!" They sprinted for the corner.

The driver was sitting on Jim's chest, delivering a flurry of punches.

"Hey! Get off him!"

Scorpion looked up and saw Serge and Coleman running down the street; he jumped in the Laguna and took off.

They got to Jim and sat him up. "Are you okay?"

He was far from okay. His shirt was torn. Gravel filled his hair, and blood and mucus ran down his neck. His lower lip was split and both eyes were starting to swell.

"Let's get you back to your house," said Serge.

They helped Jim up the porch and into the living room. Serge and Coleman ran around frantically for ice cubes, peroxide, and Band-Aids.

Jim stared at the floor. Serge returned with a washcloth full of ice.

"Look up," said Serge.

Jim didn't look up.

"You'll have to look up."

Jim was breathing hard. "I don't want them to see me like this."

"Nobody's going to see you like anything," said Serge. "I'm going to fix you up like new."

"Are you kidding?" said Coleman. "With shiners like that?"

"Shut up, Coleman!" Serge turned back to Jim. "I have to see where to put the ice."

Jim slowly raised his face. He looked worse than Serge had expected. He bundled up the ice and showed Jim how to hold it against his eyes.

Jim's lower lip started to vibrate.

"No!" said Serge. "Don't! You better not!"

The vibrations increased.

"Stop it! Stop it right now! Don't you dare!"

Jim couldn't stop.

"I'm warning you! Stop it this second!"

Jim leaned forward and put his forehead down on Serge's shoulder and began shaking with quiet sobs.

Serge took a deep breath and put his arms around Jim's back and began patting him lightly. "There, there. It's going to be all right."

The front door opened and Martha walked in. She screamed when she saw Jim's face. She ran up to Serge and began pounding him on the chest with her fists. Serge let her.

"What have you done to my husband? Get out of our house! Get out! Get out!"

Serge opened his mouth to say something, but he changed his mind and left.

Two a.m.

Floor buffers hummed inside the local twenty-four-hour home-improvement store. Serge pushed his shopping cart down an empty aisle in the electrical department. He grabbed a box of security lights off the shelf.

A stock clerk came up. "Finding everything all right?"

"Got a question," said Serge.

"Shoot."

Serge held out the box. "Is this right? Only $19.95 for a motion-detector floodlight?"

"The bulbs are extra," said the clerk.

Serge put two boxes in his shopping cart. "Where are the bulbs?"

"Aisle three."

"Glass cutters?"

"Two kinds. What kind of glass are you looking to cut?"

"Floodlight bulbs."

The clerk looked at Serge.

"Just tell me where both kinds are," said Serge.

"Aisles seven and eight."

"Gas cans?"

"Twelve."

"Orange vests for highway construction sites? Reflective signs?"

"Thirteen and fifteen."

Three a.m.

The driver of a Chevy Laguna flicked another cigarette out the window and bobbed his head to the stereo. A baffled expression appeared on his face. Something shiny in the road up ahead. He turned off the stereo and leaned over the steering wheel.

"What the hell?"

The driver hit his high beams. He thought he was seeing things. Someone was sitting in the middle of the road in a lawn chair. He wore an orange vest and held up a crossing-guard stop sign.

The Chevy rolled up slowly, and the man in the vest came around to the driver's window.

"What are you, some kind of lunatic?" said Scorpion.

"Yes," said Serge, sticking a .44 Magnum in his face. "Now tuck in your fucking underwear."

Four a.m.

Scorpion was standing in the middle of an aluminum shed in a darkened backyard. It was the shed behind a college rental, used to store tools to take care of the yard. Nobody had been in it for months.

Scorpion's wrists were bound tightly, and another rope stretched his arms up over his head and tied his wrists to an eyebolt in the shed's ceiling. His mouth was duct-taped.

Serge sat cross-legged at the man's feet, tongue sticking out the corner of his mouth in concentration, wiring the motion detectors. He had one detector on each side of the man's feet, eighteen inches away, facing outward.

Serge looked up at Scorpion and smiled. "These new low-watt bulbs are incredible. The filaments will burn almost forever in the inert gases inside . . ."

Serge continued scratching away with the glass cutter until he had made a complete circle. Then he held the bulb upside down over his head and tapped the circle lightly with the butt of the cutter. The round disk broke free.

"Of course, if the bulb's filament is exposed to the oxygen in the atmosphere, it'll sizzle and burn out in seconds." He screwed the bulbs into the motion detectors. Then he unwound the security lights' power cords and plugged them into the shed's utility socket.

Serge reached behind some plywood and pulled out a Hula-Hoop. "You know who invented summer?"

Scorpion didn't move a muscle.

"The Wham-O Corporation." Serge held the Hula-Hoop in one hand and the gun in the other. "Step into this."

Scorpion lifted one leg, then the other. Serge raised the hoop up to the man's waist. He pressed the Magnum to his nose.

"If I give this thing a spin, do you think you can shoop-shoop Hula-Hoop?"

Scorpion nodded.

"Marvelous. You seem a lot more cooperative than when I talked to you before. I knew I had caught you on a bad night. That's my motto: *Don't be quick to judge others.*"

Serge gave the Hula-Hoop a healthy spin, and the man began moving his hips.

"Hey, you're a natural! You should see some of the kids around here with these things. You'd think they had them in the womb . . . Oh, but I already told you about all the kids we have playing around here. Remember? When I was saying how cars really should go slow? And while we're on the topic, Debbie's way too young for you. What's the matter with women your own age?"

The hoop continued rotating, and Serge continued pointing the gun.

"Let's see how long you can keep that thing going. I remember when I was a kid, the neighborhood record was like two hours."

Serge grabbed a metal five-gallon gas can and slowly poured the contents across the shed's concrete floor.

"If the Hula-Hoop falls, the motion detector will pick it up and turn on the floodlights. But they'll only be on a moment. That's how long it'll take for the filaments to ignite the gasoline vapor. It's the vapor you gotta watch out for, you know. The stuff explodes like you wouldn't believe."

Serge sniffed the air.

"In fact, it's starting to smell pretty powerful in here right now. I better get going. By the way, concrete is porous, so there's a slight chance that if you can keep the hoop going long enough, the gasoline will seep in and the fumes will dissipate. It'll take hours, but it's theoretically possible. And I wouldn't try to kick the detectors out of the way because that will set them off instantly . . . Well, toodles!"

Scorpion was young and fit. After the first hour, it looked like clear sailing, and he became almost cocky. Then something happened that he hadn't counted on, though Serge had. Muscle cramps. Lactic acid was building up in the tissue. Try as a he might, the hoop rotated slower and slower, and his eyes grew wider and wider.

The plastic ring fell to the floor.

PART II

BLOOD IN THE WATER

ONLY YOU

BY LISA UNGER

Clearwater Beach

Y ou. Long limbs graceful, incandescent in the moonlight. The surf, lapping lazy and warm against the sugar
shore. The sky. A void. Stars dying, galaxies spinning,
light-years ago, their glimmer reaching us only now when it's
far too late. Our toes disappear in the silken sand, salt on our
skin. You're so still, so near. But always out of reach. Even now.

"You shouldn't have come back here."

Was it just a week ago now? You. Surprised to see me.

"Why would you come back here, Scottie?"

But you already knew the answer. There's only ever been
one question, one answer between us. Silly, isn't it? When
the universe is so vast. That the only important things are so
small.

This place is apart. A world separate from the rest of it.
Didn't it always seem like that to you, even when we were
younger and we didn't know anything else? We'd never been
anywhere, really. We were just Florida kids, living in bathing
suits and flip-flops, always dragging a damp towel, or a fishing
rod, or a bucket filled with shells, or some long-suffering sea
creature we promised to return to the wild, and sometimes did
and sometimes didn't.

You, a sylph in a simple black sheath that draped off your
thin shoulders. The gossamer strands of your haircut blunt
and elegant, shaping your jaw. Your eyes a question at first,

an almost-pleasant memory lingering there, and then a final, sharp accusation.

That night, just a week ago, you weren't happy to see me.

He walked up behind you, broad where you are narrow. Dull where you are bright. That possessive hand at the small of your back. You turned and smiled at him, the glare you had for me all but fading.

"Oh, honey," you said, voice going soft, pleasing. "You remember Scott, don't you?"

His smile seemed earnest, blue eyes slanted as if searching memory. "Oh, right. From the summers. Hey, good to see you, man. You look great."

That's right. From the summers.

We all grew up here. Your father and his—founding members of this yacht club. My father the bartender, forever. These days maybe we'd call him a mixologist. But then, he was just Brian—the slow smile, the easy way he had with that shaker, the guy who could make anything they wanted and happily would.

"Wait a second," he said, reaching out a hand.

Vineyard Vines oxford, Brooks Brothers blazer, Rolex dangling. Oh please. All the stories we try to tell each other with our possessions.

"Scottie Rayder, right?"

I waited for him to add, *the bartender's kid*, or, *the camp counselor*—something like that, something to make me small. They always try to do that. Make you less than who you have become. I readied myself with a polite smile, returned his firm grip.

"Holy cow," he said instead, running a hand over the close crop of his blond hair. "I heard you're killing it. Your software company. Gaming, right? *Enigma* is the big one, isn't it? The puzzle."

His openness, his sincerity. It took me aback.

"That's right." I offered him a nod. "And you. A surgeon, right?"

A smile I recognized, a faux-humble squint.

"Hey, you need a new hip, I'm your man," he said with a grin that was almost—almost—self-deprecating.

"I think I'll try to hold onto the originals," I answered, patting my pockets. I'm a big fan of the light banter that's always been so easy here. Words slip off the tongue, polite laughter bubbles like sparkling wine.

"That's a good plan," he said with a practiced chuckle.

This conversation or one just like it has been uttered a thousand, a million times within these walls. The bar top glistened, the music—jazz, Charlie Parker maybe—ambient. Glasses, bottles stood sentry on shelves. Jewelry dangled on delicate necks and ears, wrists, glimmering.

You. Stiff, shoulders tense. Your smile was brittle. Your eyes glazed with impatience. Body turned just slightly toward the door. You couldn't wait to move away from the conversation.

"Good to see you again, Scott," you said. "I'm afraid we're late to join our friends."

Just shy of rude. Cold, certainly. Not like you at all.

He looked at you quickly, questioning, then nodded. The well-trained husband. Your fingers laced through his, and he gently led you away, casting a glance back. I offered him a farewell wave. Bradley. The one you married.

I wonder if he remembers, or if he ever knew, that you and I were in love. Once. About a light-year ago.

The house. The one I'm building here. It will be the biggest—by far—in the county, directly on the sand of North Clearwater Beach. Nine thousand square feet, ten bedrooms, eight and half bathrooms, a thirty-three-foot-high entry foyer, five balconies. A gym, a meditation space, a formal dining room that has more square footage than the house where I grew up just miles away. A gleaming state-of-the-art conference room. The master suite will overlook the infinity pool, which will appear to flow seamlessly into the ocean waters beyond. A restaurant-grade kitchen with gleaming Sub-Zero/Wolf appliances, another smaller "family" kitchen, the impractical but oh-so-gorgeous marble from Italy for all the countertops. Sauna, steam room.

It's obscene really, absolutely bloated. It will be nestled here in this tiny gated section of the beach where gigantic homes sit, oblivious to the state of the planet, on a tiny slip of land between the Gulf of Mexico and the Intracoastal Waterway.

"I thought you were a minimalist," mused my father, in his late seventies now. He's long retired, living comfortably nearby. He loaned me $200,000 to start my business and let's just say it was a good investment for him. My mother didn't live to see what I've made of myself; she passed, as you know. That's the last time I saw you, at her funeral. I saw you in the back of the crowded church, dabbing at your eyes. You loved her, and she you. You offered your condolences, stiff and distant.

"I *am* a minimalist," I told him. "It's the only house I'll need."

"Other than that apartment in Manhattan?"

"Well."

I tried to get him to move in. But he wouldn't.

"I don't want to live in a museum, son."

The old man is so practical, so down-to-earth. I think the house actually embarrasses him.

"It's so much, Scottie. Why do you want it so big?"

Because, honestly, that's all some people ever understand.

Tonight, the bar and dining room fill, volume swelling. Exuberant, loose. One booming voice in the corner draws eyes filled with respect. That shock of snow-white hair, those crystalline-blue eyes, presidential jaw, a good three inches taller than everyone else. His slim wife in attendance, smiling, sculpted blond bob, face pulled taut in that way of older wealthy women who've had too much work done. Your parents. I've yet to say hello.

"And I told him . . ." I don't hear the rest, just the boisterous, conspiratorial laughter that follows.

"I remember you."

She shifts into the seat beside me, where I hold the corner over by the wall, watching, my martini waning. Raven hair, a smattering of freckles, full cheeks, and a pouty mouth. Veronica. She is poured into that blush-pink dress. The diamond on her hand is the size of a Volkswagen.

"Good to see you, Ronnie," I say. It is. She always made me laugh.

"Scott." A nod. "Home visiting your dad?"

"Actually, I'll be around for a while. I'm building a house."

The bartender, crisp in white and black, wild jet curls pulled back, smart goatee, brings a glass of something sparkling in a flute that she didn't order.

"Mrs. Roth," he says easily. "The usual."

"Thank you, Sean." She smiles at him, friendly, familiar. "You're good to me. Since when do you call me Mrs. Roth?"

There's none of the distance between staff and members that there used to be here. Now it's all hugs and handshakes. The walls have come down, haven't they? The lines blurred.

"Since you got married," he says.

"Oh, so—I'm suddenly worthy of your respect?"

"You're an old married lady now."

"That's right." She sips from her glass and winks.

"Scottie here is building a house," he says. "He tell you?"

"He was about to say. When we were interrupted by the help."

"Ouch." He winces but then grins.

She tugs at his cuff.

The three of us used to get high together down on the beach. After the members left, the tent erected on the beach for events maybe still up, lit underneath by glittering strands of tiny bulbs. We'd light up and talk about—nothing. Which member was the biggest asshole, how hot it was, how heavy the chairs were that we had to carry down to the water's edge, what we were going to do with our lives. Then we'd strip down to our underwear and swim in the black warm water. North Beach flows up into Caladesi Island, a nature preserve. No ambient light at all, so the sky was—is—alive with stars. The world would sway and sing. Sean always had weed back then, the good stuff. From the peaceful glaze in his eyes, I'd say he is still up to his old ways.

"Why would you come back here?" she asks. Blunt. Always says exactly what she means. You never realize what a lovely quality that is in a human being until you discover how exceedingly rare it is. "Aren't you like crazy rich now? You could be anywhere."

She glances about the room and sees you. Her eyes linger, maybe on the line of your neck, the sweep of your black skirt. There's a dance on her face, a wiggle of her eyebrows, a flash of something in her eyes. Then she presses her mouth into a tight line. What is it between the two of you? Always a subtle antipathy.

"Oh." She rises, lifts her glass to mine. "Some things never change."

When she walks away, Sean stands drying a glass with a bright white cloth, shaking his head.

"Wanna get high later?" he asks, not looking at me.

"Sure."

You. Dancing. Having a good time, or so you'll have them all think.

I could be anywhere. Except I'm always here, waiting for you to see me.

It's only my second visit to this old club since I came home, but Sean already knows how I like my martini. Which is to say ice-cold Grey Goose vodka, one olive, a whisper of vermouth. I love this place—it smells of Old Florida, wood and salt, a hint of musk, candle wax, something else—sun-bleached memory. It's all towering ceilings and crown molding, wainscoting, walls and walls of windows that look out onto the serene mangrove bay. Nearly a century of commodore photos line the walls, all men, all white. Thick-carpeted stairs, solid-wood banister, gold finishes. It's run-down, a little, in a way that only makes it more beautiful.

Sean puts another martini in front of me, number two. I catch my reflection in the mirror, pale white skin, black suit, hair slicked back. Long fingers on the stem of my glass. Nothing about me communicates my extraordinary wealth, except perhaps an aura of indifference. The energy of needing nothing.

Enigma, the game I developed. A small robed figure, hooded, faceless, with a red heart on his chest, tries to find his way through a web of city streets, underground tunnels, forest-scapes, twisting canyons, mountain paths. The color palette is gray scale with jewel accents—bloodred, jade, sapphire. Enigma is searching for his heart's true home, the hearth fire burning, the embrace of loved ones, the place where he is understood. There are demons—dragons, ghouls, life-draining wraiths—with which he must contend. When he dies, it's a bloody affair.

"I still haven't figured it out."

There's a young man next to me now. A stranger. He has the look of someone yoked by expectations. It resides in the dark circles under his eyes, his cuticles raw and bitten.

"What's that?" I ask.

"The game," he says. "I've been playing for years. And I still haven't figured it out. I give up, go back to it. Give up again."

When they do figure it out, they can't believe it.

"You will," I say. This may or may not be true. "Just keep trying."

"Any hints?"

"The answer is closer than you think."

I drain my glass and walk outside. Summer has waned, the heavy blanket of heat and humidity lifted, the salt air cool on my face. The high moon colors the cumulus clouds silver, in a velvety blue-black sky. A great blue heron stands in silhouette, long and elegant on a piling to which is tied an enormous yacht. There are other more dramatic places—the elegant squalor of Manhattan, of course, the wild light show of Shanghai, the self-satisfied beauty of Paris, the cool gray loftiness of London. But there is nothing quite like this place, nature's canvas, peaceful and unassuming.

A gleaming, brand-new, fifty-foot Hatteras—the most self-indulgent of all luxury items, an absolute gas guzzler, an insult by its very existence to world poverty, the environment, good taste—sits tied off on multiple pilings. It's mine.

I feel, more than hear, you come up behind me.

"This is where I kissed you the first time," I say.

You blow out a breath. Disdain, something else.

"And where you broke my heart," I go on into the silence.

"Looks like you got over it." Your voice is tinny, distant.

"Is that what you think?"

"I don't think about you at all." It sounds like the lie that it is.

"Come by the house later," I say. Does it sound easy, casual? "Sean and I are going to get high."

"I'm married," you say. "I have a child."

There's a tightness to your voice, as if you've taken offense; as if you can't imagine I'd suggest such a thing. The good wife. The pretty mother. I know well the lovely little story of your life, the one you post about daily on your Facebook page.

"You were always good at slipping away," I say, turning to you. "As I remember."

You soften, laugh a little; we share a storybook of wild memories. Our misspent youth.

"Betsy Lynn." Your husband; he's come looking. You are the jewel in his coat. "Hon, you ready?"

"Of course," you say. "Let's go."

"Night, Scottie." Another robust handshake from your handsome Bradley. "Good to see you again, man."

But this time there's an edge. He does remember me. He knows what I was to you. I smile.

"Good night, Brad."

"They're never going to accept you, you get that, right?" Sean blows out the gust of smoke he's been holding in. His eyes glimmer with mischief, smile wide and peaceful.

Accept me? As if. My membership to this yacht club where I used to work was easy to secure. Just a phone call from my attorney, and the doors swung wide. No trial membership. No seeking of sponsorships. Just a nice big check, the golden key to any lock.

Accept me? People will bow at your feet if they think you can help them with something, anything—donate to their causes, buy their properties, use their contracting companies, drive off in one of their new cars. Acceptance is not the goal here. Acceptance is what people think they want.

We're on the bow of the Hatteras, still at the dock, the club closed and empty now of members and staff. The pool glows chlorine blue; the lights stay on. This was when it was ours, at night after everyone left and the pool was clean, the camp room tidied and the kitchen closed.

"Can I say something?" asks Sean.

"Sure."

"I don't get it. Your game. I don't get it. It's not that fun. It's not like *Fortnite*. That shit's epic, man."

I have to admit, I've always been pretty chill. I think I get it from my dad. These days more than ever, I just don't give a shit.

"It's not for everyone," I concede.

He takes another long drag before handing the joint off to me.

We drift along the Intracoastal, easy. Moonlight glinting on the black water. It's high tide and we know these waters, how shallow they get, how fast. Right outside the channel, a snowy egret balances on one leg, delicate, its clawed foot just barely beneath the surface of the water. Its white feathers glow, its gaze impervious.

Sean is easy at the helm. Kayaks, skiffs, bow riders, opti sailboats, big yachts like this one; we've done it all. We used to run the big ones home for drunk members. Sometimes member kids with a little too much freedom would invite us for pleasure cruises.

Once—do you remember, Betsy Lynn?—you and I ran your father's boat aground. Making out, not paying attention, we wound up in the shoals by one of the tiny barrier islands. There was hell to pay. But not really. We got a lecture about trust and responsibility. And: "Scottie, you should know better. You grew up on these waters. This is a million-dollar boat, son, not a bath toy." Your old man liked me; he grew up with my parents. If that historic prom night had gone a little differently, he liked to quip, I might have been his son.

Sean steers the boat to my new dock, so close that the club is still visible as he effortlessly brings the monster to a halt. I'm living on it until the house is done. Our house. The kind we used to dream about.

Edna Buck—white-haired, besuited, bejeweled gossip columnist—has already done her piece for the local paper. Hometown Boy Makes It Big, Comes Back to Roost. And you thought your kids were rotting their brains with video games! Just look at tech billionaire Scottie's new beach bungalow!

You. Standing on the dock, hands in the pockets of your white shorts. Blue and white–striped T-shirt, topsiders. Hair back in a high ponytail. You didn't dress for me. You never had to.

You're one of those women. Effortless. Creamy skin and golden hair, the symmetry of your face, the magnificent proportions of hip to waist to bust. You're the trophy. The prize that goes to the right man for a job well done.

I think you could have been more than that. Don't you?

"Sleep in one of the state rooms," I say to Sean.

He hops from the stern to the dock. You step back, barely acknowledging him.

"I gotta get back," he says. "Mom waits up."

"Give her my best."

"Great night, man," he says with that old smile. "Glad you're home."

"Me too."

Home. It is—this sleepy beach town, now overrun with tattooed Airbnb tourists from the sticks, aquarium, beach day crowds. Tiny motels leveled, giving way to towering behemoths with hundreds of rooms, surf shops, parking garages. No matter where I go in the world—isn't it odd? I always want to come back here and feel that humid salt air on my skin, watch the palms sway. Florida is the butt of a national joke, ripped to shreds by the intellectual elite. But those of us who really know it, we keep the secret of its savage beauty.

You climb aboard and I show you around. Your blue eyes don't register anything but vague acknowledgment.

"Same layout as my dad's," you say. "Much newer, of course."

"He still has it?"

"No." It comes out as a scoff. "They got tired of it—all the work, the expense. They're downsizing these days."

There's a note. Something wistful. "That's what happens, I guess."

You run a tender hand along a silver cleat.

"Get and get and get," I say.

"Then purge," you finish. "Free yourself."

You turn to the hulking shadow of the house. It's a dark mass, dwarfing the other large houses around it, houses that glow with lit landscaping, warm lights burning in windows. They fought the construction of the house, my neighbors. Too big, they complained. A monstrosity, more rooms than a B&B. But I won. Of course I did. I don't lose often. Except when it comes to you.

"It's huge," you say, staring at it. Your back is to me and I can't see your face. So I imagine it as it was earlier this evening—a little angry, suspicious, something else.

I climb down the stairs and step off the swim platform of the boat onto the dock. We walk across the silent street that separates the dock from the property, pass the house. We stroll across the wooden walkway that leads to the beach. You always loved those, remember? The more rickety and overgrown with sea oats, the better. Then the jewel at the end, the sugar sand, the silky blue-green of the ocean.

The gulf is usually lazy, languid, with waves that can barely be bothered to lap, much less crash, against the shore. But there's a storm out at sea, a no-name, threatening Texas and Louisiana. So the surf is wild. We stand a moment side by side. It's a time warp; we're twenty-two again, everything ahead of us.

I try to take your hand, but you pull it away.

"What do you want, Scottie?"

Your eyes are sad. I see it now, the disappointment in it all. All the things they tell you you're supposed to want. How once you have it, you're left to wonder what, if anything, comes next.

The world is crumbling. The planet dying, people diseased by greed, by technology, medicating to avoid the pain of their empty lives. But here we are, all the same.

"I want to go back to that night. I want you to make a different decision."

You just laugh. You were the one with the brains, the real

talent for code, for numbers, for science. I was just a Florida cracker in flip-flops and board shorts. You did my math homework while I snorkeled, raced the optis with the sailing students.

You should have been the one to go, and I the one to stay.

"Betsy."

We spin to see his thick shadow at the base of the walk. The soft reverence, the sweetness, are gone from his voice, replaced by the timbre of the bully he always was. You draw in a breath and start to move toward him, but I grab your wrist.

He moves quickly until he is in front of me, you between us, pushing back on his chest. He's a steamroller. You're a blade of grass. But he stops.

"Betsy, let's go." Voice granite-cold.

"Who's with Piper?"

"Your mother."

"You called my mom?"

She won't be happy, a stern, cold woman. Never kind to you, a drunk. One of those who drinks slowly all day just to feel normal. It never shows until after dinner when the five o'clock cocktails take it up a notch. She never liked me. I saw right through that patrician facade to the piece of white trash she was at her core. The cruel, careless things she said to you. How you used to cry.

How they all conspired to keep you here with them. She by undermining your self-esteem since childhood. Your dad, a titan in business, a weak enabler of her dysfunction at home. And him, Big Brad the college football star, golden, reflecting back to you the person you thought you should be. Hypnotizing you with your own warped, subliminal expectations.

"Don't go," I whisper.

But you're already gone, disappearing into his shadow.

* * *

The next day while I idle at the club, I see her with a gaggle of her tween friends. Piper.

She's your very image. And then as I stand there watching her drink a milkshake, laugh at something her friend said, another piece of the puzzle falls into place.

When he comes to the boat later that afternoon, all his polish, that bright smile, has rubbed away. He has an aura of wild desperation, hair mussed, tie loose, the purple shiners of a sleepless night.

I've seen this look before. The man about to lose everything. I saw it in grad school as people flailed under the mammoth workload. I saw it in 2007 when the market crashed. When my company went public. Dropouts. Debtors. Naysayers, short sellers proved horribly wrong. How I love the bitter truth, the authenticity of that look. I feel it in my gut. We all know what it feels like to lose, to fail. The agony of defeat.

"Drink?"

"You left them," he says from the dock, not climbing aboard. I sit on the aft bench, cross my legs, and lean back. "You can't just come here now."

The truth is, I didn't know.

You never told me.

That night on the dock, you said that no, you weren't coming to MIT. Your father needed you to help with the business. You mother was ill; she was fighting breast cancer then. You were, in fact, staying here, you said—to be near them, to be with him. We couldn't be together anyway, you told me, as cold and stern as your mother ever was. We were too different. Surely, I could see that.

All of it lies.

You two. Betsy and Bradley.

Married with a baby before I could blink the bitter tears from my eyes. I was too stupid, my ego too gigantic, swollen, and injured to understand what you did.

You let me go. Let this little town keep you here.

I wept over the wedding pictures on Facebook like a love-sick teenager. How happy you were.

How stunning. You were so tiny, you didn't even show. Maybe if you had, I could have done the math. Figured it out before it was too late. I decided to hate you instead, hate myself for not being the man you wanted to marry.

Enigma. There are seven layers to the game. He is a traveler, lost and far from home. They say it's addictive, that people lose sleep and days at work, make themselves ill trying to get Enigma back where he belongs.

"That's true," I say to Bradley now. "I left."

He nods as if we've come to some agreement. He turns back to look at the house, then back to me.

"You could have gone anywhere," he said. "Why would you come here?"

People say that a lot, the folks who never left, those who think that there might be something else, somewhere else. Something better. A thing they missed. I want to tell them that there's nothing out there that you don't already carry within you. But that's not a thing people want to hear. They'd rather believe that there's something more and they simply failed to find it.

"I'm just back to take care of my dad," I say. "He's sick. Did you know?"

"No." He looks a little less ruffled. "I didn't. I'm sorry."

"Thank you," I say.

The niceties, the phrases that roll off the tongue, a verbal dance designed to keep things shallow and easy. It's a relief. That's how people like it mostly, surface—not too deep.

"Just—just," he says, working for it, remembering why he came. "Just stay away from them. That's my family."

When we were young he was bronze, with flashing-white straight teeth, a surfer's body—lean and muscular, fluid. Nice enough on a good day, but with that blank entitlement of privilege, so blessed that he didn't even know it. He was easy with boats, on a board, he had a way with the weather—knew when a storm was coming. He's a dimmer version of himself now—softer around the middle, a little gray in the hair, tiny lines around the eyes. Still beautiful, of course, still broad and well-built. I feel bad for him, though I'm not sure why. He was the kind of guy I wanted to be—not the skinny, bespectacled nerd that I was, the son of the club bartender, the camp counselor, but not the child of a member.

He stands a moment, waiting for my response, which is just a vague nod I've mastered. It implies consent without being a commitment. He seems satisfied, if a bit confused by my calm, then walks off. I text you.

Biff was just here. Warning me off.

That's what we used to call him, remember? When you used to make fun of guys like him. I watch the little dots pulse on the screen, but you don't answer. You never do.

A few minutes later, there's a text from Sean.

Wanna go to a party tonight? Should be fun. At Ronnie's.

We've fallen back into the ease of our childhood friendship. It's like putting on an old baseball glove. It's as if I've been around the world, and I have, been to hell and back—that too. Then in a box in the garage of my childhood home, I find it. When I slip it on, that old glove, the grooves of my hand are worn in deep. I never left.

Sure.

Will you be there, Betsy Lynn? I'm betting you will be.

A towering "Mediterranean-inspired" McMansion—barrel-tile roof and terra-cotta walls, a double-height outdoor foyer with a wrought-iron lighting fixture hanging overhead. We ring the bell and it chimes deep inside the home; after a moment Ronnie's at the heavy wooden double doors.

She looks back and forth between us. She slits her eyes at Sean.

"Scottie," she says, turning to me, fake smile, "I didn't know you were coming."

"Thanks for inviting me," I say, though I'm guessing from her demeanor that she didn't.

I hand her a bottle of Veuve, which I know to be her very favorite.

"How sweet," she says, accepting it and standing aside. "Welcome."

Her eyes linger on me, something unreadable there. Then she glances back into the crowd. I don't see you. If you're not here, I'll beg off quickly. This is not my scene.

The place is packed, lights dim, music loud. EDM throbs from mounted speakers in the corners. There's a bar set up by the pool, with a hip, goateed mixologist dispensing something pink in martini glasses. The room is a field of smartphones, faces turned as often to those screens as to each other. People crush together for selfies; laughter is raucous, conversation a dull roar. Sean lights up a joint, hands it to me, and I take a deep drag. The hard edges of my awareness soften.

Enigma travels alone through the layers of the game; he has no friends, no allies. On level four, he might earn a lavender pouch and in it there are various weapons—a wand that hypnotizes, a cloak that makes him invisible, a watch that turns back time just ten seconds. The place where most people lose over and over is at the disco, a glam nightclub where a strobe flashes and beautiful creatures whisper and stroke, wind their lithe bodies around him. They offer mysterious drinks and plates of cakes and if he can't avoid them or ward them off, this is where he'll stay until his lives run out, the player powerless to save Enigma from his own appetites.

I wander away from the party and down to the dock. The water whispers, lapping against pilings, the halyard on the sailboat across the water clangs. Homes on the Intracoastal glow all around me—the typical Florida hodgepodge of towering new construction and flat split-level ranches from the sixties. Modest bungalows like my parents' place, in the shadow of gigantic modern additions to this man-made island. I can see in windows, sliding doors—a man and woman recline on a couch watching a game. Some kids gather around a firepit, tossing rocks into the water. A woman sits at a kitchen counter with a glass of wine, staring at her laptop.

Voices. Loud. They lift over the din of the party. And then someone's storming down the path leading to the dock toward me. A couple others trail behind, reaching.

He was always an ugly drunk, the kind who got nasty after that third beer. I saw the bruises on your arm the other night, the way you folded your arms across your middle when you saw him approach us on the beach.

"So this is what you do?" he asks when he's in front of me. "You just show up where you're not invited?"

"Stop it," you say, holding his arm. "Let's go home."

You are exquisite tonight in white—a simple top, jeans, silver thongs on your feet. The golden wisps of your hair. I only see you, in all of this. Your eyes rest on me—there you apologize and plead.

I'm so focused on you that I don't even see the blow coming. It lands squarely on my jaw and I go down, the world wobbling and tilting, the dock hard and splintering under my palms. More yelling—from Sean, and Ronnie's husband. Then some other guy I don't know pulls Bradley away as he struggles, roaring. He's drunk, obviously, all his darkness right on the surface. You and Ronnie bend and help me up. My hand comes away from my mouth red with blood.

"You shouldn't have come here, Scottie," says Ronnie. Her brow is creased with sorrow and concern. She touches my arm. "Please go."

I nod. Yes, that's obviously best. The pain, it's not that bad, not compared to other pain I've felt. Later it will hurt, though. My teeth are intact, I think. Ears ringing. I'm not much of a fighter, not in that way.

"I'm sorry," you say.

He's yelling your name. Everyone's staring, come to gather on the patio to look at us.

"Come with me," I say softly.

You look back at the party guests, who now avert their eyes. Whispering. Muttering. Someone issues an uncomfortable laugh. We can still hear him yelling.

You take my hand and we run around the side yard to my waiting car, a black Tesla gleaming like spilled ink. I don't feel bad about leaving Sean; he'll understand and Uber home. It is the unwritten rule among men; if she says yes, it's okay to disappear.

I make a smooth turn in the cul-de-sac. I expect to see him run out after us. But no. You cry softly in the passenger seat.

"Why didn't you tell me?" I ask, my voice low in the dim leather interior.

You look at me a moment, almost blank with disbelief.

"Why didn't you guess?" you say. "How could you not have known?"

You're right, of course.

"You always wanted me to read your mind."

"But you never got the hang of it."

You lace your fingers through mine, hand shaking, a tear trailing down your face. We're back there on the dock, that moment when you told me to leave. And I, angry, hurt, let my ego drown out my instincts. The truth is that I never believed someone like you could love someone like me. I always thought you'd leave me for someone who came from money, who won that genetic lotto of beauty. You were just saying what I had been expecting to hear all along. If I'd just asked a few questions, who knows what path we'd have walked together.

Enigma. All he does is choose paths—the lighted way, or the dark one, the high or the low. He knocks on doors and sometimes they open. More often they don't. If the player makes it to the final level, everything he needs to know about the game has been revealed, all the tricks and pitfalls have been navigated. He must draw on what he's learned to find his way. The stakes are highest here. One misstep and he has lost. He must begin again, all progress erased.

On the beach, our beach, the place we fell in love, where I made love to you the first time, where we've logged hours hand in hand, where we likely conceived the daughter I have never known, you fall into me. As easily as if we have not been apart for the last thirteen years. Thirteen years that passed in a blur of aspiration and acquisition, a kind of blindness, an emptiness of heart and spirit that looks to most people like outrageous success. Every gift and luxury falling to me like rain from the sky. And all of it ash until this moment.

When Enigma finally finds his way on that last level, he walks down a long tunnel which morphs into a forest path. He passes a still, glistening lake that sits surrounded by towering pines. The sun dances on the water, and the soundscape is dominated by wind and birdsong. When he comes to the final door, he finds it locked. Surprisingly, this last moment is where many people stay stuck. They can't figure out how to open the door. They look all around the scene for a clue, something that might act as a key. But the area all around them has stopped interacting—there are no more doors, or hidden passages, no more buried treasure, or wands, or bags of tricks.

It is only a very few who come to realize, in that final phase of the game, that the heart on Enigma's chest holds the key to the last door. When the player clicks on it, the key— golden and shining—floats into the air and hovers a moment. Then it's in his hand. He fits it in the lock, looks back at the player, and disappears. There's little fanfare, just a swell of music and he disappears inside the door. Some people rage at the simplicity of it all, the utter anticlimax. Others describe feeling a profound sense of peace, of accomplishment. *Enigma*, I have come to understand, is all about what you bring to it. Some people don't like that idea very much.

On the sand, my jacket laid out beneath us, we make love under the silver full moon. The warm gulf water laps languid and sweet. And the shell tree—a fallen tree that reaches out over the water, on which people hang their collected shells to make a wish—seems to sway and glow. Your skin, your hair, your breath, the feel of you in my arms. This, sad to say, is the only thing I ever really wanted. You always kept your eyes on me when we made love, your hands in my hair, on my back. Our legs wound together like wicker.

It's the first time; we own ourselves now. Choices are ours to make. I'm still unworthy of you. But this time I'm staying anyway.

Afterward, you pull on my shirt and we sit, staring at the black clouds that drift like wraiths in the night sky.

"Now what?" you say.

"I don't know," I admit. It's complicated. Even I can see that, he who has had no complications in his life—just wanting and getting. "We'll figure it out. Together."

You smile and issue a little laugh; it's a sad, knowing sound. Nothing will be easy moving forward. But maybe, when the dust settles, we'll be happier than we've ever been.

"That's what you always said. As if the world should bend to our will."

"And why shouldn't it?" I say. "Eventually."

This time your smile is wide and free, like it used to be, with a whole new path ahead of us.

I don't see him until it's too late, a figure slipping from the darkness. He must have walked up the beach after us. Now he's a towering shadow, breath labored. A ghoul. A monster.

None of us say a word.

The gun glints in the moonlight as he raises it and fires. I shield your body with mine.

How many shots?

The sound is deafening, drowning out the world. I walk through the blue doorway of your eyes. There's only silence.

You. Long limbs graceful, pale in the moonlight. The surf, lapping lazy and warm against the sugar shore. The sky. A void. Stars dying, galaxies spinning, light-years ago, their glimmer reaching us only now when it's far too late. Our toes disappear in the silken sand, salt on our skin. You're so still, so near. But always out of reach. Even now.

EXTRAORDINARY THINGS

BY STERLING WATSON

Pass-a-Grille

Lee Taylor had seen extraordinary things. Not wars, earthquakes, or tidal waves, not the biggest things, but the small ones, some of them delights, some so coincidental that they defied all but his own capacity to believe, and some of them dangerous. He had seen the green ray, and manatees mating, and there was the time the two joggers, beautiful young women, had stepped on the corn snake and their tanned skin had gone instantly pale. And the time he'd stood on the bluff above Troy Springs at sunrise and seen the giant alligator gar, a living torpedo, slip out of the dark water of the Sewanee River into the crystalline spring, and then back into the dark.

It had been his fate, he told people, to see these extraordinary things and have no proof of them because he saw them alone. He told the stories. At parties, to friends, sometimes to women he was interested in at least temporarily. Politeness reigns, mostly, so most people listened politely. When he noticed the onset of boredom, a yawn, he'd say, "No, really, this is true. It really happened." And polite people, good people, would focus on Lee and his tale, and hear him out to the end.

The woman had called Lee and asked him to meet her. She'd said her name was Helen Trenam, they'd met before, and she thought he'd recognize her when he saw her face. "Would you meet me? Please."

There was something in that *please*, a breath of excite-ment, a hint of *come hither*.

Excitement had been missing from Lee's life for some time now, and so, although the strangeness of the woman's call put him on his guard, as it would any sane man, he said he'd meet her. He made his voice as neutrally pleasant as an excited man could, and said, "Well, sure, all right. I'll meet you. But . . . I assume you'll explain all this a little more fully when I see you."

"Of course," the woman said. "You have a right to a full and complete explanation."

With that, she had him. The thing about Lee's right to an explanation sounded a little lawyerly, and Lee's country grandfather had told him to fear God, women, and lawyers, but she had him. This was already an extraordinary thing, and it only promised to grow in that direction.

Lee parked on Pass-a-Grille Beach and looked up at the Hurricane roof bar. Up there, the potted sabal palms waved their fronds in the famous gulf breeze, and the copper parapet reflected the gold of another memorable sunset. Memorable because a volcano in the Yucatán had erupted and the air-borne debris was doing something to the light. The volcano had been dormant for seven thousand years.

Laughter and music drifted down. The music was easy listening, but the laughter was high and giddy and desper-ate. It had been bottled in frozen Detroit and windy Chicago and flown to Florida to be released in pricey hotel rooms and restaurants and bars, and now suddenly, late on a Sunday, it had to be rationed. Lee crossed Gulf Way and took the eleva-tor up to the roof.

He didn't see a woman who looked like she might be looking for him in the naked-as-you-wanna-be crowd. A man the size of a sumo wrestler sat at the bar in a brown polyester suit. Empty seats on both sides of him. Lee took one of them.

The man turned, smiled, extended a meaty hand. "Hey there, buddy, how you doing? My name's Frank Dross."

Lee had learned a long time ago that people who sat alone in bars were expected to talk to any and all who might sit near them. Though by no means a chronic habitué of bars, he was often a man alone, and he'd learned the ropes, how to keep it friendly, avoid politics and religion, and offer nothing too personal. He'd told some extraordinary stories to strangers in bars.

Lee shook the man's nine-pound hand. "I'm fine." *Although not your buddy, not yet anyway.* "Name's Lee Taylor." He shifted on the barstool so he could keep an eye on the elevator door.

The bartender brought Frank Dross a second bourbon. "What's your poison?" Dross said to Lee. "Let me stand you one."

Lee thanked him and ordered Bacardi and lime. It came with a paper umbrella. The bartender was a trim, cheaply handsome kid with a copper-penny tan and a seen-it-all expression. His name tag said, *Fred. Tacoma, Washington.* The Hurricane's policy was that everybody in Florida came from somewhere else, and they had a lot of name tags to prove it. Lee's would have read, *Lee Taylor. Vanished, Florida.*

Lee and Frank Dross talked small for a while, Lee only half-involved, one eye on the elevator. They stopped talking when a cheer erupted from the crowd. The T-back bikinis and Speedos parted and a guy in a sandwich board—and very little else—moved into the center of the Hurricane. The board was white with black lettering. The shoulder straps could have been old seat belts. The guy was about thirty-five with an average face. He'd spent enough time making love to his NordicTrack to look pretty good in a pair of Calvin Klein silk boxer shorts, a paisley bow tie, flip-flops, and the sandwich board. The boxer shorts still held their packaged-at-the-factory creases and an *Inspected by Number 17* sticker.

"It's like when you go to the doctor," Lee said to Dross. "You go to the Hurricane in your sandwich board, you wear your new Kleins."

"Bet you he's wearing a jockstrap under those shorts," Dross said. "Bet he ain't swinging under there."

Lee said, "Courage has its limits."

The guy in the sandwich board was pulling it off. His embarrassment was crimson, even in the falling light of a memorable sunset, but he was managing a sort of determined, boyish grin. The grin was killing women all over the roof. Lee could see that plainly enough.

Thongs and sarongs drifted toward the guy, forming a circle. Men were backpedaling toward the copper parapets, looks of confusion or grudging admiration on their faces. Hoping the guy would flame out, but thinking, *Hell, he might set a standard we'll all have to meet.*

A fortyish redhead in a lobster-red bikini was the first to step forward. Her thighs had somersaulted through the pep rallies of yesteryear, but now they'd grown some cottage cheese. She started reading the sandwich board aloud in a Joan Rivers voice.

Dross turned to Lee. "It's brilliant," he said. "I pronounce it brilliant."

Lee had to admit it was the best idea he'd seen in months. Maybe not brilliant, but very damned good.

A hand-lacquered résumé, the sandwich board told the guy's life story. It was entitled: *The Visual Aid of Love*. The perfect antidote to the nauseating small talk of life-seeking-life in the temperate zone. The text began: *What's my sign? I'm an Equestrian. If you get the joke, I want to talk to you.*

It gave the guy's job (CPA, *small firm, specializing in corporate tax accounts*), his salary (*middle six figures*), his car (*Lexus, understated off-white*), his hobbies (*board sailing, jet skiing, jogging, good literature—Patterson, Ludlum, Nora Roberts—and long walks on the beach at sunset with YOU . . .*). There was some stuff about his philosophy of life. (*I believe in maximizing my potential, minimizing my negative effect on others, and letting YOU do the same thing. I believe we can work this out together.*) It ended with his address and phone number and . . . (*I'm secure in my masculinity. Anyone want to buy me a drink?*)

The bouncy redhead finished reading the résumé aloud, and the crowd cheered again, even the guys.

Frank Dross turned back around and faced the rows of glittering bottles. "Thing is," he said, "you can only use it once. Guy comes in here tomorrow night in that thing, the women'll throw his ass over the side. What's he gonna do for an encore?"

"He's got imagination," Lee said, watching three women offer to buy the guy a drink. "He'll think of something."

"Expecting somebody?" Dross raised his glass and gestured at the elevator. "The way you keep looking over there."

"Maybe," Lee said. She was late. He was beginning to think maybe not.

Across the bar, a whippet-faced brunette lifted her chin sharply when Lee said *maybe*. Dross shot the cuffs of his brown polyester coat and winked at her. She peered at him like she might have to speak to the management. Then Dross said,

"Look at that one," gesturing his glass again at the elevator door.

Lee looked. She was beautiful in ways that only a few women could ever be, and she was the type who kept it forever. Someday she'd be ninety-five, and all of the women in the assisted-living facility would hate her for the glory of her bone structure. But that would come later. Now she looked late thirties, about Lee's age, with honey-brown hair, long legs, and big brown eyes. And she was staring right at Lee Taylor. "I'm looking," Lee said as the woman walked toward him through the maelstrom of sex, alcohol, and thwarted expectation that was the Hurricane roof bar on a Sunday at sundown.

Lee gave Dross a last glance as the big guy lifted himself to offer the woman his pew. Lee heard ice clatter against Dross's front teeth but didn't see him fade away into the crowd.

The woman sat next to Lee and delicately pushed Dross's empty glass aside. The cheaply handsome bartender asked her what she'd have.

"White wine, Chardonnay," she said without looking at Lee.

The youth glanced at Lee's umbrella. Only partly cloudy. "Come on, man," he said, "justify my existence back here." Lee smiled, gave the umbrella a nose nudge, and poured the sweet hot Bacardi onto his tongue.

The woman turned her wineglass on the bar in the wet ring left by Frank Dross's bourbon. Still not looking at Lee, she said, "Don't you recognize me?"

Lee examined the side of her face. From any angle, she amazed. The polite thing to say was, "Well, you do look sort of familiar."

And then a door opened in his mind, opened just enough so that a little light shone on the past, and then opened wider.

In full brightness Lee saw his chemistry class, freshman year. It was one of his extraordinary stories.

The lectures were held in an amphitheater that seated two hundred. Numbers were painted in ominous black on the backs of the seats. Each number represented a student. A bored graduate assistant sat at the front of the room taking the roll by recording numbers not obscured by the bodies of aspiring young chemical geniuses. In chemistry, Lee was far from a genius.

At the University of Florida you had to have a major, or at least you had to answer the question, "What's your major?" when asked by a fellow student. As a freshman, with no idea when or how he'd actually declare a major, Lee had understood one thing: "I'm majoring in premed" sounded good to girls.

He'd made the mistake of announcing this to an academic adviser at registration and the guy had put him in this teeming chemistry class. The guy had Lee's high school transcript in front of him, and he'd explained to Lee with a stern and worldly expression on his face that Lee's record was spotty at best. So the guy had stuck Lee in this cattle-call chemistry class where Louis Pasteur could not have found a legitimate premed major.

Lee was never sure if his adviser had reposed faith in Lee's ability to mature in his understanding of the periodical chart of the elements or if the guy had just played a little joke on the freshman from Panacea, Florida. Whatever it was, soon enough Lee saw that he had no particular aptitude for chemistry. The lectures were showy demonstrations of explosions and beakers of liquids that changed colors dramatically when they were mixed. The showman lecturer was, Lee later learned, a drudge whose research career had fizzled years ago, but the guy knew how to dazzle.

Lee and the other two hundred students were assigned to discussion groups taught by grad students. So it was the big show on Mondays, and then the small group meetings on Wednesdays and Fridays where the mysteries of explosions and lurid liquids were analyzed in detail. Lee never caught the analysis, failed the weekly quizzes, and barely made the deadline to drop the class before receiving a well-earned failing grade.

After that, dropping things was easier, and he drifted through classes he didn't get, some he got but cared nothing about, and discovered Gainesville's bars and strip joints. In the middle of the spring semester, he left Gainesville after declaring himself a building-construction major, and with that credential in hand, went home, then drifted down to St. Pete Beach to work as a carpenter's helper in the construction trade.

But the extraordinary thing was what happened one day early in the fall down in the pit of the big amphitheater where the students gathered after the lectures, some to ask questions of the lecturer, most to chat with friends or, lacking friends, to try to meet someone.

Lee was standing in the crowd of fifty or so eighteen-year-olds when a girl approached him. She was pretty, well dressed in the mode of those days, and should have been happy for all she had won in the genetic raffle. She was not happy. Her first angry words to Lee were, "You said you weren't coming."

After all these years, Lee did not recall much of what he had said during their brief encounter. He recalled his embarrassment, his face reddening, his palms suddenly moist, as the girl came closer until her face was inches from his and he could feel her sweet breath on his lips. He'd probably managed only fragments of sentences that, had he finished them, would have meant, *I have no idea what is happening right now. I have no idea who you are. I am beginning to think I have no idea who I am.*

Her fists clenching and unclenching at her sides, the girl kept saying to him, "You promised me you wouldn't come! You promised!"

The girl's anger and the volume of her voice had cleared a space around them so that, like two dancers of exceptional skill, they stood at the center of a circle, their faces close together while the girl repeated her strange accusation, and Lee backed away sputtering his confused innocence. He remembered searching faces in the crowd for the sly smile or laughing eyes of an accomplice. Some gesture that would tell him that others were in on this, that it was some kind of prank. Maybe this was some sorority or fraternity foolery. But even as Lee considered this, his young mind objected that it was too early in the semester for the traditional rush. If this was a prank, it was the invention of freelance deviants.

The girl repeated her complaint—that Lee should not be here, that he had broken a promise—for what seemed a long time but really could not have been more than a few minutes. Then she stopped as abruptly as she had started and, face bright red, eyes streaming tears, turned and shoved her way through the crowd.

Lee never saw her again. Not in the chemistry class or anywhere else.

Later, back in his dorm room reflecting on the incident, he had rung through the possibilities.

There was the prank option.

Or the girl was just, well, nuts.

Or *he* was nuts. His fevered mind had sent him on a trip to a mad fantasyland.

Or this was some sort of acting exercise designed by the theater department.

If it was theater, the girl was the best teenage actress in America. Lee had heard that actors lived their roles, but he couldn't convince himself that the girl was acting. Her anger and her fear were real, and someone had caused them, someone she had cared about a great deal. Lee's reflections always led him to the same conclusion. There really was a boy out there somewhere who had promised this girl he would not be here, and she had believed Lee Taylor was that boy. The most extraordinary and the most frightening explanation was that Lee Taylor had a double.

Years later, when late one night he had told this extraordinary story to a stranger in a bar, the man, a scholarly type with the weary manner of those who had looked unabashed into the mysteries of the universe, had pulled off his glasses and rubbed his tired eyes with a thumb and forefinger. "My friend," the scholar said, "you ought to look into the myth of the doppelgänger."

"Oh yeah," Lee had said, baffled, "I should do that." He borrowed a pen from the bartender and asked the scholar to spell the word. Lee wrote it, doppelgänger, on a cocktail napkin and tucked it into his pocket. Then the scholar said, "In the myth, it's sometimes true that the doppelgänger is a menacing figure."

The woman beside him at the Hurricane bar sipped her wine and turned to face him. "It's been a long time, but I thought you'd recognize me. I was pretty sure you would."

Lee looked at the glittering bottles across the bar. For a couple of months now, maybe three evenings a week, he'd found himself sitting at this polished zinc bar drinking something with a paper umbrella in it and watching the sun set memorably. Happy to think of himself as dormant. Waiting to see what the next phase would be. Maybe this woman, Helen Trenam, was that phase.

He had picked the Hurricane for this meeting because it was too loud and too young for anything too serious. It was unlikely that here a meeting with a stranger could get out of hand. He membered Helen Trenam saying she owed him a full and complete explanation. "That day in chemistry," he said, "you were just messing with me, right?"

"Oh, no," she said, "far from it. I was as real that day as anything that's ever happened to you."

A lot of what had happened to Lee Taylor had been of questionable provenance, but now was not the time to go into that. Now was the time to fall into this woman's unfathomable brown eyes and drown.

She stared into Lee's eyes for a while, not blinking, certainly not afraid of anything she saw in them. She set her glass on the bar with a delicate finality. "You'll see when we talk some more, but not here. Let's go for a walk on the beach. It's been awhile since I've had sand between my toes."

Lee found that the prospect of seeing her bare toes, and maybe even more of her, was more than enough to get him up off the barstool, and headed for the elevator.

They walked across Gulf Way and through a gap in the low retaining wall that the city fathers believed would stop a mild tidal surge. Then on down a sand pathway through clumps of sea oats to the beach. It was fully dark now and Venus was rising out of the gulf, her brilliance shaming the pale stars of the early dark. A warm land breeze had begun to blow, and Lee knew it would grow stronger as night deepened. He followed Helen Trenam to the waterline where she leaned down and removed her sandals. Her knee-length turquoise silk skirt ruffled in the wind, and her feet, small and shapely, were the treat Lee had promised himself. She pulled her white cotton blouse from the waistband of her skirt, unbuttoned the bottom of it, and tied the shirttails in a knot, exposing a band of tanned flesh to the night wind. She waved her hand vaguely toward the south, the jetty at the end of the beach, and said, "Let's walk that way. It's nice out here tonight, don't you think?" Her voice was low and calm, strange for a woman who had called a man she had seen only once for a few minutes years ago and asked for a rendezvous.

"Sure, it's nice, very nice, but, uh, shouldn't you tell me what this is all about?" *Give me that full and complete explanation?*

She stopped walking, turned to him, moved close, their bodies almost touching, and gripped his upper arms with her strong little hands. "You're right. This has been a mystery for too long. That day in chemistry . . . was a cry for help. Didn't you know that?"

"No, I . . ."

"I was in trouble. I went to you for help, and you didn't . . . you didn't do anything."

Reason failed Lee. What could he say to this? "Why didn't you *say* you needed help? What was happening to you?"

"I couldn't. He was watching. He was there."

"You said I promised I wouldn't be there. What did that mean?"

She let go of Lee's arms and started walking again along the surf line. Lee glanced behind them at her small footprints in the sand.

"I know it's strange. You must have thought I was crazy."

"Yeah, I considered that, and that I was too. But I finally decided the best explanation was that you really believed I was some guy you knew. Some guy who had promised not to come. Believe me, I had to work through a lot of possibilities to get to some certainty—I mean, you know, provisional certainty—about that."

She laughed quietly. "Yeah, provisional certainty. The times we live in, right?"

"Right." They walked maybe ten paces before Lee said, "So there was this guy who looked, I mean, he looked exactly like me?"

"Oh, yes," she said quietly, a little shudder in her voice. "There is this guy, and he looks exactly like you."

"You said *is*. You said there *is* this guy."

"That's right. I did. Guys like him, they don't die young. They last, and they keep on doing what they do."

"What does this guy do?"

"He hurt me. That's what he did to me, and he liked it. It started when we were in high school, and it just kept happening even though I loved him and he loved me and I tried every way I could to make him stop."

"Wait a minute. Let's go back." But Lee wasn't sure what to go back to, or how far, or where this might take them. He knew now that he looked exactly like a guy who liked to hurt people. And he knew, he thought he knew, that he was not that kind of guy. So the resemblance was exact only as it pertained to the outsides of two men. Lee had been stupid, for sure, but he had never been a hurter, and especially not of women, unless usually being less than they expected him to be, hoped he was, was hurting them, and come to think of it now, here on this beach, he supposed it was.

"So," he said, "you're saying I let you down because I didn't realize when we were eighteen years old that *You promised me you wouldn't come* meant this guy was hurting you?"

"I didn't say it was fair, I just said it was true."

"Jesus," Lee whispered.

"He didn't help me either. I prayed to him a lot in those days. What I said to you, I said it because he was there, he was watching us. He wasn't a student. He kept that part of his promise. He never went to school anywhere after we graduated from Leesburg High. And he stayed home and worked on his dad's farm for a few weeks after I left, but then he followed me. When I said those things to you, I was speaking . . . to a symbol. I saw you the very first day in chemistry, and of course I thought you were him. Then I realized you weren't, and I thought I could use you to get him away from me. I thought maybe when he knew he had a double, he might take it as, I don't know, some kind of message."

"A message?"

"You know, like God or fate or something telling him to get out of my life. Showing him that there was another one of him, a good boy, a boy who wouldn't hurt me, right there in the same class with me. There by the grace of some power that was bigger than his hurting."

It had been a long time since anybody had called Lee Taylor a good boy. It hurt him now to realize this. "So you thought I'd do what, say what? I'd somehow . . . decode this message, know I was a symbol, and come after you, find you, and help you?"

"I guess I did. I thought if God had made two of you, He had the power to send you to me. I was desperate. You probably don't know what that's like."

Lee didn't know. Not really. His life had been a series of jobs he did pretty well but cared little about, a lot of time in bars, a few friends but no one he could depend on in a pinch, and those disappointed women who always saw enough in him to stay for a while, and always saw too little to make it last.

"No," he said, "I guess I don't know about that, not really."

Up ahead Lee could see where two sets of footprints came from the low dunes to their left, went to the waterline, and then headed south the way he and Helen Trenam were going. When they caught up with the footprints, he saw that one set belonged to a man who wore shoes. The other feet were bare and small, a woman's or a child's.

"So how did you finally get away from this guy?"

She said it so quietly that he asked her to repeat it: "I didn't."

"You mean . . . ?"

"I mean I've been with him ever since, and he's hurt me one way or another every day of my life. Every day since I appealed to you in chemistry class."

In spite of his sympathy for this woman, Lee felt that he had to defend himself. "Look, is that really fair? I mean, how could I know what you were saying? What you wanted me to do? And anyway, what did you *want* me to do? What could I have done back then? I was just a kid. I didn't know up from down."

Afraid to look over at her, he saw only the tips of her fingers in his peripheral vision. She was pointing ahead of them at the thin strip of beach by the old jetty.

"Look at that," she said. "Isn't that something lying on the beach?"

Lying? "Yeah, I see it. What is it?"

"I don't know. We'll see, I guess."

"Maybe we shouldn't—"

"We have to, now. Now that we've seen it. We can't just turn back."

"I guess you're right."

They walked on, Lee looking down from time to time at

the footprints they followed, a man's and a woman's, bare-footed. When they got close enough to see that it was a man lying on the beach near the surf, his head below his feet, Lee looked back at the four sets of footprints behind him. The two sets of barefooted prints were identical. *It's been awhile since I've had sand between my toes.*

"Hey," he said, "I think maybe we ought to—"

Two men stepped out of the shadows at the base of the jetty and walked toward them.

The big one was Frank Dross. The other one was Lee's double. The man at their feet was obviously dead. Even in the sparse light from a streetlamp on Gulf Way, Lee could see that the man's face was black from the blood that had run to it because his feet were elevated. Blood leaked from a wound in his chest. Frank Dross drew a gun from the pocket of his brown polyester suit coat. "Hey there, my buddy Lee."

But Lee was staring at the man who looked exactly like him. It was more than extraordinary. Even in the face of Dross's gun and with a dead man at his feet, Lee stared, searched for any difference that the years since that chemistry class might have made between himself and this man whose name he didn't know.

Helen Trenam said, "I brought him." Her voice sounded tired, not even the smallest revelation of sorrow or guilt or triumph in it. Nothing but the sound of years of hurt.

"We see that," Lee's double said. "And we appreciate it."

Helen Trenam took four steps to the side, as though to get out of the way of something.

Frank Dross pointed the gun at Lee. Lee's heart shrank to a dead black dot in his chest. It was all he could do to keep from falling to his knees. Somehow, to keep standing was a small victory.

"Well," Lee's double said, "we have to hurry. This beach isn't big enough for four people and a dead man." Even his voice sounded like Lee's.

"Tell him, Barry," Frank Dross said. "He deserves an explanation."

"I was about to, Frank." Lee's double pulled a gun from his back pocket and pointed it at Lee's chest. "Maybe you've already figured this out, Lee. You look exactly like me, and for reasons that don't really matter to you right now, I had to kill this man here, and a very good way for me to get away with this crime is for you to stay here with him."

"Stay here?" Lee heard his own voice quaver.

"Yeah, I'm afraid so," his double said. "It's obvious, isn't it? The cops find you here with this guy, and they find two guns, and they figure the obvious."

Lee's mind flailed. "But what about those footprints."

"What footprints?"

"Those, them. All of them." Lee pointed to the beach behind them, then at the sand along the edge of the jetty where footprints came from Gulf Way. "They'll know you were here."

"Correction, buddy. They'll know *somebody* was here. They won't know who. They'll just figure that some, uh, citizens came upon this unhappy scene and decided not to call it in. You know, the old don't-get-involved thing. Very common these days."

Lee's double pointed his gun at the center of Lee's chest. Helen Trenam took two more steps to the side. She had seen something like this before.

Lee said, "But I can't just . . . disappear."

"You won't," his double said. "You'll be me."

Lee's eyes caught the beginning of a flash, and his mind had only the time to say to him, *Extraordinary, but you'll never tell this story.*

LOCAL WATERS

BY Luis Castillo

Indian Rocks Beach

A bel Rivera had just printed his name on the dry-erase board and was midway through the date when he heard, "Friggin' homo."

The marker's felt tip squeaked to a halt. His back was to the class so he couldn't say with absolute certainty that he'd been the intended target, but a chorus of "oohs" left little doubt.

He narrowed his eyes and turned to face second-period Intensive Reading. A small class, perhaps a dozen or so students, and every one of them seemed to enjoy the sight of anger on his face. He lingered on a blond, stocky kid with cigar-shaped dreadlocks who was fist-bumping a boy next to him.

Abel picked up the attendance sheet. Right now figuring out who some of these kids were seemed to be a more pressing need than the assignment. Cody Kimball was the kid with the blond dreads. Abel pegged him as a surfer-stoner type and the guy who delivered the homo-blast. An Indian Rocks Beach local himself, he usually fared better with that crowd.

He thought he'd be subbing for Advanced Placement English, but when he showed up this morning at Gulf Beaches High he was informed of a change in plans. Instead, the school secretary assigned him to be today's floater and sent him off with a class-coverage schedule plus a thin stack of report cards and instructions to pass them out at the end of second period.

He'd been a floater here before. It was an awful assignment, crisscrossing campus after each period only to arrive at the next class moments before the bell, short of breath while searching for anything resembling a lesson plan.

After taking roll he returned to the board and finished writing out the date and assignment. As he hyphenated *Section Review 2-2,* an object cut through the air. It was a paper ball weighted with a penny inside. He'd been on the receiving end of one of these before. Judging from the force of the throw, the kid who nailed him had an arm.

His eyes raced around the room to get an AP down here pronto, but he'd only stepped inside a few minutes ago and he didn't know where the call button was. As he scanned for the intercom, he once again locked eyes with Cody Kimball.

The kid met Abel's gaze and held it long enough to make his point: *Prove it.*

Abel wanted to respond that this would be countered with a swift, harsh measure.

"Okay, class, let's not throw things." He raised the paper ball, shook the penny inside. "Technically, this is battery . . ."

"Nah, dude. A battery hurts way worse." Cody's timing triggered another burst of laughter. A couple of kids really put their lungs into it.

Abel's toes curled. He marched over to Cody. A bored expression spread across the teen's face. He played with the fluorescent-orange golf tee he'd fashioned into an ear gauge. Abel got to within arm's reach.

"Look, Cody," a mild shrill weakened his tone, "I'm going to need a little more respect and cooperation from you if you're going to be allowed to stay in here. So Cody, this is a yes-or-no question. Are you going to cooperate and not interrupt when I'm trying to explain something?"

"Listen, dude. Let me explain something to you. I don't

like you getting up in my grill. You smell like some bad burrito and I kind of freak when people I don't know stand close to me." He sprang from his desk and headed for the door. Near it, he raised both arms and flashed double-V victory signs. "Peace, my brothers. I'm out."

Abel could have sworn he heard *epic, owned, how'd that taste*, under Cody's classmates' breaths.

"Okay. Moving right along," was his reply. He tried to make this sound light-hearted, but knew it landed like a brick.

A few minutes later he found the intercom, but no referral forms. If he buzzed the office now to inform them that Cody had just dressed him down and walked out of class, they would simply tell him to write the kid up, and he wasn't about to announce that he didn't have anything to do that with in front of this bunch.

Cody was out of the class, not a half-bad consolation prize, but Abel was still seething. He slouched behind a computer monitor flanked by file trays and stacks of paper on the teacher's desk.

Despite his attempts not to, he kept staring at a couple of pictures near the American flag. A brightly colored poster read: *Our Kids Are Worth Whatever It Takes*. Taped next to that was a piece of notebook paper with a student's drawing of a dog dropping. It also featured flies with motion-depicting lines and came with an assumed laudatory caption—*Mr. Angelo Is the Shit*.

He substituted *Abel* for *Angelo* and omitted the *the* when he thought of Saturday and the spring luau at his daughter Emma's new school.

He'd bought tickets for the event and thought that gesture alone would be enough, but she later explained that they had to sit at the tables near the stage. The dinner was sponsored by the school's Tongan society, and the entertainment would be dance performances. Because of the way the hall was laid out, it was tough to see from anywhere but up front. That was where her two new friends, Lita and Elena, would be sitting.

Not wanting to disappoint his third grader, he said he'd get the VIP seating but discovered that you had to make a donation to get the upgrade. The news at the car line was that Lita's parents had paid for a suckling pig. Elena's had donated Hawaiian punch and the rum supply for the cash bar. Abel had just paid this month's bills and didn't have the funds for a suitable gift or donation. The bottom line was that he'd have to tell his wife and daughter they weren't sitting up front with Lita and Elena.

A bell rang and the students told him it was time for morning announcements. *Dolphin Daybreak* played from a mounted television set. Through the din came details about "a troubling development at GBH." Someone had broken into the Dolphin Store and stolen donated prom dresses for the upcoming spring dance. A fifty-dollar gift card would be awarded to anyone providing information on the theft.

His ears perked up, but fifty bucks still seemed a little light for the seat upgrade.

"Care less, bitch," a skinny surfer called out to a plus-sized girl. "They wouldn't have your size anyway."

The two looked as if they were about to come to blows, but the dismissal bell seemed to break it up before Abel had to.

He realized as he left that he'd failed to pass out the report cards. They were in a folder he'd set near the computer monitor. The kids didn't exactly strike him as the types to be excited about bringing them home. There wasn't much he could do about it now. Angelo could pass them out tomorrow, he guessed.

Maybe that's what set Cody off. Report card day could be

a bitch for the likes of him. Abel went back inside and snuck a peek. Below Cody's address, *1489 Sea Breeze Lane,* the grade column confirmed his hunch.

In fifth-period Woodshop, a message on the blackboard greeted him. *Students Not Allowed on Machines—Liability Issues/ Movie or Study Hall.* Abel found the DVD on the desk. The playback deck was coated in a layer of sawdust, but thankfully it worked. The jacket cover description promised extreme surfing action.

"I've seen this before," someone called out in a nasal drawl. "The soundtrack shreds."

This back-row endorsement seemed to be shared by most of the class, and Abel immediately sensed the spirit of cooperation that had been sorely lacking in second period. These kids might actually stay in their seats and not try to run anyone's hand through a belt sander.

The class buzzed with chatter about a cold front moving into the area. The system would move out by tomorrow night, but for a brief time the gulf would have waves. He'd seen an item in today's paper about an early spring storm fouling airport traffic in the Southeast. The only time the gulf had surf was when it sucked for someone else. Like the Labor Day when Katrina clobbered New Orleans. He had tried not to think about the Big Easy going under as he boogie boarded on some of the best waves he'd ever seen in the area.

Abel made a quick tour of the shop, sidestepping lumber strips, lathes, and table saws. Cabinets labeled *Student Projects* were locked. He inspected the craftsmanship on an unvarnished Adirondack chair before venturing back to the classroom section and sat near a tanned, flannel-clad freshman. Power chords accompanied surfers hopping up on their boards and gliding into huge barrels.

"Hey, Mr. Sub," the boy said, "I like your shirt."

A Hawaiian print his wife had given him on his birthday. He liked its baggy comfort, plus, he had to admit, the busy pattern could camouflage food stains.

"You surf?"

The question unexpectedly lifted his mood. This was more like the vibe he usually got from the Gulf Beaches High surf crowd. He was tempted to fib, but why spoil a gift?

"I boogie board," Abel said. "I thought about checking things out after school."

"Cool. It'll probably be blown out, tomorrow might be better." Then the boy asked, "Do you think I could borrow a dollar?"

Ah, the joys of this job. Did a day ever go by without a kid hitting you up for money or saying you smelled? Abel put a pause in their little chitchat and got up to stretch his legs.

Subbing was his way of testing the waters of a second career. The television production company he'd worked at for eight years had folded a few months ago and he was still adjusting to his new freelance status. From what he'd gathered, competition was steep in the market. But he'd told his wife that money was put away for times like these. The problem was, as his current checking balance bore out, he'd damn near exhausted the rainy day funds.

Tucked in the corner of the shop, he saw a surfboard and a skim board, both apparently in the middle of some refurbishing. Perched on a couple of saw horses next to them was a stand-up paddle board in the early stages of construction. A tableau of surfing hierarchy—surfers, paddle boarders, skim boarders. Boogie boarders, or spongers, were at the bottom of this food chain. He'd never stood up on a surfboard, never mastered the arm push-off with synchronized knee-tuck, then the pop-up that took one from the prone to pouncing position. He caught his waves lying down.

Back at the instructor's desk, he noticed some referral forms under a cabinet-making manual. The *Disrespectful or Discourteous* box seemed a little light for Cody's morning performance and there wasn't much room in the teacher comments section either. He'd have to choose his words carefully to adequately describe what went down during second period. He'd be lying if he said he hadn't been looking for these earlier in the other classrooms he'd been in. Word was that teachers here hid the forms from subs in an effort to cut down on the inevitable infractions. He'd also be lying if he didn't think there was more to Cody's performance than his report card. That prom dress business seemed like the type of mean-spirited prank that was right up his alley. Maybe Cody got wind that they'd be talking about it during the morning announcements and wanted to make it look like he had a good reason to bolt before anyone in class started pointing a finger at him. Abel decided to just stick to the facts: *Student said substitute smelled like a bad burrito and walked out of class.*

The movie's closing credits scrolled. A dull ache began to run up the base of his skull. As if a small act of kindness might blunt his headache, he chipped off a buck to the kid who had sucked up to him earlier and asked him to take Cody's referral to the office.

Abel's horror stories from subbing had led his wife to suggest they pull Emma from their zoned elementary and put her in private school. The luau was the first function his family would take part in at St. Cyprian's. He was keenly aware of the importance of getting off to a good start. Subbing was all about the first five minutes. A bad takeoff on a wave could be brutal. For Tori and Emma's sake, he wanted their coming-out party to go well.

* * *

At home after school, Abel let Emma watch the Disney Channel when she'd finished her math and spelling. Tori was at the gym. Tonight was his turn to fix dinner. She'd be home a little after five and liked eating before six.

She and Emma seemed so happy with Emma's new school surroundings. A welcome change to his wife's glumness over the holidays; Tori had turned forty in November and didn't seem too happy about it. With her uptick in mood, she seemed to be putting in more time working out and was quite proud of the ten pounds she'd shed since the first of the year.

Abel flipped a switch and the ceiling fan in the kitchen clicked on, its loud droning motor yet another reminder of something else he couldn't afford to fix right now. He pulled out a package of chicken breasts and gave it a smell test. It was past the due date. Iffy at best; he set it on the counter.

In the back of the freezer he found a box of fish filets and considered other instant options. He glanced over at the bad chicken. There was always the chance Emma or Tori could come down with some bug and they'd have to miss the luau. He'd gladly eat the tickets.

Emma busted Miley Cyrus moves in front of the television. Did he actually just think that? He tossed the chicken out. A whiff of something foul escaped from the garbage can. Tori entered the house from the attached garage. Above the strains of "Party in the U.S.A.," she cried, "What smells in here? Did someone forget to Febreze?"

Part of their new dinner routine since switching schools was Emma leading them in prayer.

"From-thy-bounty-through-Christ-our-Lord, amen," they mumbled in rapid-fire unison.

Abel had traded in his knee pads some time ago but was

dusting them off tonight, asking that the calls he'd made to every business contact he could think of would bear some fruit.

"Daddy," Emma said, "on announcements they told us they're still looking for donations. Me and Lita laughed at that. We said it sounded like they were looking for donuts."

"Donuts." He hoped they didn't detect his unease. "Cute."

He sensed his wife's disappointment with dinner, but complaining when he'd gone through the trouble of fixing something wasn't her style. She pushed back from her plate and declared that she had a surprise in her car. She took Emma's hand and led her into the garage.

"Tell your daddy to close his eyes."

In a few minutes the two appeared back at the dining table in matching outfits. Hawaiian shirts knotted at the waist. Tori looked great in her white denim shorts, which were shorter and tighter than Emma's. She twirled for inspection.

He tried not to spoil the moment and smiled and marveled.

Tori grinned back. "Emma, let's take these off before we get something on them."

"Thank you for the present, Mommy."

The two disappeared to change. *Front-of-the-room threads*, he thought.

At bedtime, after reading to Emma, he lay down and tried to relax while Tori brushed her teeth.

"Have you given any more thought to the school service hours at St. Cyprian's?" she called out from the bathroom.

"Not really." Although he knew they were subject to a fee if parental involvement hours weren't fulfilled.

"The Pot of Gold in April sounds good," she said.

"The ol' Pot of Gold."

Repeating her words rather than saying something he might regret was a technique he had often used in production meetings to tread water. He'd seen *Pot of Gold* marked on the kitchen calendar. At first he thought it might be a new restaurant she wanted to try. It fell on a Saturday in April, which coincided with a job he was hoping to get crewed on.

"I was planning to talk with Lita's mom at the luau about us getting involved with the event." She began to undress. "I hear the cool parents work it and she's the chair." Down to her underwear she added, "I'd rather do that than the Lenten fish fries."

Perhaps he should tell her now about the luau. She slid out of her bra and panties.

"Sounds good to me," was all he could manage.

"How 'bout this?" She struck a pose. "This sound good too?"

He tried to manufacture enthusiasm to match his wife's, but the more she tried, the worse it went for him. She was kind enough to give it a rest without asking, *Is anything wrong?* Perhaps it was because he'd been considerate during her sullenness after her birthday, when part of their agreement was to "go easy on each other for a while."

He kissed her forehead, relieved she didn't press him further, but he was ashamed by his lack of performance. He padded lightly to the spare bedroom-slash-office. After a while he moved to the couch in the living room, trying to shake spasms of worry. Worry about the freelancing and the added burden of private school. Worry that he didn't think he could hack it in the classroom. Worry that in three days he would blindside two people he loved with the embarrassment that they were sitting in the back of the parish hall at the luau.

The image of Cody paid an unwelcome visit as he tossed and turned. Abel fixated on that golf tee dangling from his ear.

* * *

At five in the morning he called the sub-finder system. What he didn't need was another floater assignment like yesterday's, one that left a something's-gone-terribly-wrong-in-your-life feeling. Unfortunately, everything offered seemed worse. Today, Tori was working a shift at the cell phone kiosk in the mall and he had to pick up Emma by three. But he also knew it would be a bad idea to be in the house when Tori and Emma got up. He wasn't up to answering, *What are you doing here?*

By eight they'd both be gone. He left quickly, quietly, and waited for the nearest Starbucks to open.

When Abel returned home, he found that Emma had left him a hand-drawn card on the dining room table. It had beautiful shapes of orchid-like blooms, pineapples, and a picture of an angry-looking island god with an evil smile on his face. She signed her name and added, *Our class made a picture that looks like this.*

He thought, *No dad wants to tell his little girl no, but this has gone far enough.* He would tell them today instead of springing it on them at the last minute. This, he had to get right. Maybe not subbing and running the risk of wearing defeat from another lousy day was a good idea. So too was getting his blood pumping by catching some waves. A little exercise couldn't hurt, could it?

He grabbed his wet suit, fins, boogie board, plus a water-sport hood and gloves for the chilly conditions. He also grabbed Emma's card before tossing everything into his truck.

The lot at 12th Avenue was full of cars sporting surf-brand decals as well as Gulf Beaches High parking stickers. He was lucky to find a spot. Beneath the shadow of a high-rise condo, he suited up in the bed of his pickup. Embarrassed of his middle-aged paunch, he thought of women putting on shape-wear as he stepped into his wet suit.

Wind rustled palm fronds overhead. He removed the truck's door key and stashed the clip with the ignition and house keys in the glove box along with his phone. A strong gust of wind blew Emma's card out. He retrieved it and stuffed it in his backpack.

Near the sea oats, he kicked off his flip-flops and set his stuff down. He was heartened to find that the waves had enough shape to propel a middle-aged boogie boarder forward, and pulled on his fins at water's edge and wrist-leashed his board. The break was better off to his right but he wanted to stay clear of the traffic, a small pod of surfers, no doubt skipping school.

Taking in a breath of tangy air, he watched youths glide across shoulders of waves. He waded out. A burst of cold water seeped into his wet suit as he ducked under a shore-pounder. He found a sandbar about seventy-five yards from shore where his feet could touch bottom and he could catch the inside break. A wave three feet higher than his shoulders approached. He hoped he was good enough not to waste this gift. A honed sense told him when it was time to take off, and there was no changing his mind after deciding to go. The wave began its bend. He lunged forward and angled down the face. The swell's force lifted his legs then dropped him, leaving it to him to maintain balance or taste defeat. Teeth clenched, he landed with a light bounce and got a face full of water. He rode the wave all the way in and beached it like a kid. The bottom of his board scraped the shore, his arms extended forward, feet in the air, as if he'd just slid home headfirst with a game-winning run.

The bigger sets were about 150 yards from shore near the

boat buoys. He paddled out and waited. A dolphin's dorsal fin rolled above the surface and disappeared in almost the same instant. In the next, the unforgiving energy of the gulf was on him. He panicked. Unsure if he had the time to dive under. The bending crest collected him up to the lip and dislodged him. He rolled over twice before he could regain his balance. He kicked up to the surface and discovered that his board was still attached, but it strained the leash, waving on top of the water, as if motioning for him to go in.

Yet he was just getting started. He continued to kick into the wind swells. His habit was to count the number of good rides versus wipeouts. Usually he had to be in double digits before calling it a day.

At about wave number five, a surfer encroached from the north. The hooded figure had his head down. Abel figured the guy would drift past, but he stopped and paddled into the wave Abel had been setting up on. He pounced on his board and aimed the nose at Abel's temple. Abel dove under and steeled himself for the skeg to rake his back. He held his breath until he sensed it was clear to pop up. The surfer rolled away above the froth, not kicking out, dismounting instead and jogging to shore with his board under his arm. Abel gave chase, but the clumsy wide ends of his fins dug into the gulf bottom. The rubber buckled and he tripped. One arm tangled with the leash as he dragged his boogie board forward. Abel got within a few feet.

The surfer reached behind his neck and grabbed the frill of his hood. "Sub dude," he said, as tentacles of blond dreads sprouted. Cody tossed his board down. "I thought that was you falling over on your face. Figured I'd come over and say hello." He snapped his hair back, directing the spray toward Abel. "I wanted to say thanks for writing me up yesterday."

Abel's knees felt watery.

"Ain't nothing but a slip of paper," Cody said.

A *slip of paper*. Abel spit salt water from his lips and walked away, hoping Cody would follow, but he didn't. As the kid had just demonstrated, anything in the water could look like an accident.

As Abel faced the horizon, it dawned on him that it was about this same time yesterday that Cody had hit him with the homo-blast and paper ball. That smile on his face reminded Abel of the one Emma had drawn on the angry island god. The water inside his wet suit sent a chill as he paddled back out in search of wave number five.

After reaching double digits, he took his fins off in the shallows and jogged to shore. The beach was void of tourists in the unwelcoming weather. He stepped up the incline where the heavy surf had dug into the sand. The coquina was rough against his feet as he walked to where he'd left his belongings.

He looked around but didn't see anything but his flip-flops. In the distance, Cody and his group were back in the water. Abel wished there were some other explanation, like a huge seagull had flown off with his backpack, but he knew Cody and his crew had swiped it.

Paddling over to ask for his things back would be futile. He wasn't in the mood to be turned into a spectator sport again.

Abel tucked his boogie board under his arm and walked to the nearest gas station to borrow a slim jim. As if to silence the soggy slap of his flip-flops, he let his thoughts run and became more convinced of what he put together in woodshop yesterday. *If that kid had the balls to swipe my backpack while I was in the water, I know he thieved the prom dresses.* He had a pretty good idea where to look.

After breaking into his truck, he retrieved his set of keys from the glove compartment and headed back to the station to return the slim jim. He drove to a nearby McDonald's and, over a Big Mac, hatched a plan.

The house at 1489 Sea Breeze Lane was on a canal street two blocks off Gulf Boulevard in the north end of Indian Rocks Beach. The Kimballs lived across the street from the water-front properties. Chimes from an ice cream truck and the grinding pitch of a wood saw broke the silence. The truck's tune was somewhat familiar, but Abel couldn't quite place it.

Garbage canisters lined the streets. Collection day was either today or tomorrow. The Kimballs had a derelict lawn. Shrubs, but no gate or fence, separated the front and back yards.

His best hunches of where to find the dresses were either the garbage or the garage. He'd brought along some plastic shopping bags to put the prom wear in and the swim gloves he used when boogie-boarding. There was no telling what he might run into.

He walked to the garbage can in front of the house and opened the lid. Except for a rancid smell, there was nothing inside. He hoped one of the Kimballs might come out and ask what he was doing. He'd gladly welcome this jumping-off point as an opportunity to voice his suspicions about Cody swiping his backpack. In fact, he decided, he'd go to their door right now to have that conversation.

He knocked. His pulse raced as he listened for the scrap-ing of a chair or footsteps from inside. He waited and knocked again. No one answered. All indications were that no one was home. He walked over to the side entrance of the garage. If the dresses weren't in the garbage, maybe they were inside there along with his backpack, and he'd tell whoever questioned him about opening this door that he was here to get it back. With gloved hands he twisted the knob, but found it locked.

He readied a story and walked around back. Should a neighbor happen upon him, he would say that he was a snow-bird relative, down from Michigan, and was stopping by unannounced. The Kimballs had told him to let himself in and make himself at home.

He sidled past a hydrangea bush and into the backyard. Vinyl privacy fencing cordoned off the rear of the property. Grapefruit rotted on a dying tree near an attached lanai. Through mesh screening he saw that the Kimballs had left their sliding glass door open. He tried the flimsy screen door on the patio. It was poorly hung and gave a little, but it didn't open. An eye screw and hook secured it. Tugging again, he found there was enough room to wedge the blade of a pocket knife between the door and frame.

Above the power lines a turkey vulture rode the thermals. Abel took out his knife, pulled on the door, put the blade to the hook, and nudged it free. He placed the shopping bags over his shoes and entered the Kimballs' house.

Morning breakfast odors lingered. His plastic-wrapped footfalls crinkled on the terrazzo as he treaded through a rear living room area. The dining nook led to the kitchen. Through that was the garage.

He froze when he heard a bell peal. His eyes darted, looking for a place to hide. Near what looked like a family portrait in the dining room, he saw a grandfather clock and realized it was only the timepiece striking one.

He studied the portrait. In between two weathered-looking adults was a soft-featured Cody. Hair parted on the side, he looked to be about Emma's age.

Abel looked at the gloves on his hands, the bags on his feet. As if the luau wasn't bad enough, try explaining this? He nodded to the Kimballs. Going through the kitchen and out the garage seemed the safest route.

A strong whiff of gas and dead grass hit him as he stepped inside the garage. He flicked on the lights. Huge breasts strained a pinup's bikini bra on a poster above a workbench. He took in the rest of the garage. His eyes traveled from the door panels to an oil pan and stopped on a surfboard bag with the word *Dakine* on it.

Next to the board in the Dakine bag was a tri-fin Volcom short board. The one Cody had at the beach was different from these two. How many sticks does one kid need?

A low rumble trumpeted something heroic inside his head, like the opening music of the old *Hawaii Five-0* show. He followed images of a banquet procession. Burly Tongans in grass skirts and Hawaiian shirts hoisted a roasted pig, apple in mouth, on a surfboard that doubled as a serving tray. Sequined prom wear blurred. Hell, who's to say those dresses weren't already on their way to the landfill, or were never here in the first place? Why waste a gift, especially one provided by a kid who ripped off his stuff and almost did the same to his head. And Tori and Emma didn't need to know anything about it.

Making a note to relatch the eye hook and take those damn bags off his feet, he allowed himself to venture that getting up on a surfboard probably felt a lot like this.

Should anyone ask what he was doing walking out of the Kimballs' garage with a surfboard tucked under his arm, he'd simply say, *Cody let me borrow it and told me to come by and get it.* Hell, Saturday night, should his punk ass somehow happen to be at the luau and start asking questions, Abel would welcome the turnabout. It's not like there was only one Volcom tri-fin in the world. This time he'd be the one dishing the hard look that said, *Prove it.*

Tree limbs swayed in the cold front's last gasp as he strolled down Sea Breeze Lane. Then it came to him, the tune from the ice cream truck. Slightly off-key and at a faster tempo, but he recognized it as the theme to *Love Story.*

He drove to St. Cyprian's, parked beneath a twisting live oak near the auditorium, and phoned the front office.

"Do you still have front-row tables available for the luau if I drop off a surfboard as a door prize?"

"Sure, how thoughtful," came the response. "The surfboard goes so well with the theme. I bet it'll be one of the best raffle items of the night."

"I'm actually here at school. Would now be a good time to drop it off?" he asked.

The woman replied yes, and after taking down his name, she told him that the custodian would unlock the hall so he could put the board near the stage.

Inside the parish center, decorating had just begun for Saturday's dinner and floor show. Student posters hung near the stage were the first items in place. He found the one Emma's class had drawn.

He kneeled to set the board down and gave it a long last look, as if aiming everything he hated about himself onto it. What he felt instead were the eyes of the angry island god. Behind its evil smile he heard his daughter's voice.

Daddy, what are you doing here?

PART III

GRIFTERS' PARADISE

TALL, DARK, AND HANDSOME

BY ACE ATKINS

Westshore

Except for being really, really old, he was exactly what she'd wanted.

He was well dressed, navy suit with pressed white shirt, good teeth (that she hoped were real), and seemingly most of his own hair. They met, as had been arranged over e-mail, at the Hyatt on the Courtney Campbell Causeway. The restaurant was called Armani's, and she knew it was nice because they expressly stated that they didn't allow cutoff shorts and flip-flops. He ordered oysters Rockefeller. She ordered butternut squash soup. Her mother always told her not to eat too much on the first date or men might think you owe them something.

The view was amazing. Top floor of the hotel looking out at Tampa Bay, the sun going down across the water, streaks of black and gray against the orange sky. Real postcard stuff. The very reason she'd left Detroit, her third husband Frank, and a worthless job as a teller at Citizen's Bank in Bloomfield Village. Only yesterday, she'd mailed a postcard to her friend Judy reading: *You throw snowballs for me while I pick oranges for you. With love and kisses from Debbie Lyn.*

"Really something, isn't it?" he said. "Takes your breath away."

"When I lived in Michigan, my tootsies would get so cold," she responded. "I had to wear snow boots to work and then slip into my high heels. Every time I left the office, I had to change out my footwear. Ankle-deep in slush. That's really no way to live."

He smiled at her, all dark tan and silver hair, holding the gaze. "My God. You are simply the loveliest creature I've ever seen in my life."

"Oh, quit it."

"No," he said. "I mean it, Debbie Lyn. I think I mentioned to you that I used to work in the film business, and you have what they call a perfect face. Completely symmetrical. Wonderful blue eyes and the most interesting nose. They used to measure that stuff with rulers. Measure how far apart your eyes were. That's why the old stars looked so grand."

"I think my nose is too big."

"Hogwash," he said. "That's what they said about Barbra Streisand and she's done pretty well for herself with the *Yentl* and the Oscars and all that. I knew her in my other life."

"You kind of look like her husband," Debbie Lyn said. "James Brolin? The one who used to be on *Hotel*. And his son is that purple bad guy in those comic-book movies. My son just loves that stuff. All he does, reads comics and plays online games with his friends. *Star Wars: Battlefront. Call of Duty.*"

"How old is your son?"

"Twenty-five," she said. "I really wish he'd meet a nice girl."

"You never know when you'll meet the right girl."

"Stop it," she said. "You are a charmer, aren't you? Tell me what films you worked on."

"Oh," he replied with a flick of his wrist. "I was just a producer. *Major League. Tremors 2.* A little film called *Tango & Cash.* Remember Stallone and Kurt Russell driving that big monster truck? Spent most of my time arguing with the studio about the budget. You'll never imagine what it costs to have a rat wrangler on set. One little nibble on Jack Palance's pinky and you're shut down for two whole days. For a tough guy, he could be so precious."

He lifted his Rob Roy in a toast and she met him with her glass of rosé just as the sun hit the water, turning the darkness all gold and electric. Outside the windows, as he smiled at her, a slight wind kicked off the bay and rattled the palm trees. Debbie Lyn felt a little shiver at the base of her spine. This was it. This was actually happening. Tall, dark, handsome. Rich. All of it.

The waiter returned to bring another round. For the main course, she ordered the mushroom risotto, thinking, *My God, what a wonder to be on an actual date.* He had the bone-in veal chop with the cauliflower hash. The sun was gone now, and it had grown dark and calm across the water, a few pleasure boats heading back to the marina. Small white lights flickering across the countless piers. He kept on staring at her with a twinkle in his eye. She couldn't help but notice the thick gold chain around his neck and some kind of old coin hanging from it. He fingered at it.

"A good luck charm," he said.

"For what?"

"Finding the rest one day," he said. "We were so incredibly close before the storm."

She tilted her head, playing with the stemware. "What exactly is it that you do? I mean, now."

"Oh," he said, looking away, grinning. "A little of this. A little of that. I'm mainly retired. But certain interests and passions can draw me out. That's what happened to my last relationship. I was told that I didn't know how to relax, when to quit. Who wants to get old? Who wants to stop chasing their passions?"

Debbie Lyn beamed, wondering what scent he wore—sandalwood, bourbon, citrus, old suede. Over Christmas, she'd taken a job at the Art of Shaving at the International Plaza. She taught men how to apply the perfect mix of scent, rubbing it on their necks, chests, and even a dab behind their knees. Never overpowering. *Find your signature scent,* she'd told them. She looked across the white linen table as he continued to stare and smile, enjoying being with her, in her presence.

"Would it be too much, before our main courses have even arrived, to say I think I'm falling in love?"

He was playing with her. He had to be. Thirty minutes in and he was already in love? Either he was completely nuts or a hopeless romantic.

"Let's see how you feel after the veal."

"I'm even more in love on a full stomach."

They'd just met and already she could see how that new life might work out. Out of that crummy apartment on Gandy Boulevard and away from living out of boxes, eating Jenny Craig frozen dinners while watching taped episodes of *Days of Our Lives*, telling her empty living room that dumb Eric better get his life together and realize that Jennifer was the best thing that ever walked into his young life. Her ex-husband calling over and over. *Debbie Lyn, where the fuck did you put my chain saw and safety helmet?* Talking to those teenage boys at the shave shop about making the proper strokes, them laughing as she walked away.

He reached for her hand and squeezed her fingers. "This is only the beginning. Today starts our adventure."

Looking back at it, at that very moment, that man across from her looking so sharp and contrasted, white on navy linen, silver hair and gold coin, smelling of goddamn sandalwood, yep, in that moment, he would've been the very last person in the world she thought she'd shoot right dead center in the head.

But damn, thinking back on it now on her bunk at the Orient Road Jail, she was still sure of it. The son of a bitch had it coming.

"Why me?" Debbie Lyn had asked, lying there as uninhibited as a twenty-year-old and as naked as a newborn, except for a gold ankle bracelet, playing with his thick gray chest hair. "What was it about me? Surely you had plenty of women who responded to your profile?"

"Well, I have to admit it was your sense of humor."

"My sense of humor? That's funny. My last husband said I couldn't be funny. That I'd never been funny a day in my life. He called me Debbie Downer all the time. Debbie Lyn Downer."

"He was wrong. What was it you said to me? About being a sucker for a man and his boat, setting off on the seven seas?"

"I said I've always had a crush on Popeye," she answered. "Which is true. Those big forearm muscles, the way he always looked out for Olive Oyl and Sweet Pea. It was cute. Real cute."

"I can't wait to show you my boat," he said. "You will love it. Don't bring a thing except for a bottle of champagne and your skimpiest bikini."

"Bikini? How old do you think I am?"

"How old do you think *I* am?" he responded, setting his feet on the floor of his home on Bayshore Boulevard. Big Mediterranean Revival number, all stucco and barrel-tile roof. He said they'd used it as a set for some TV show back in the eighties about a nice family running a zoo. "Age is but a number."

"I would never say."

He winked at her, pulling a prescription bottle from his suit jacket and shaking loose a little blue pill. "Hold that thought. Let me grab a cool glass of water."

He wandered off in the dark, tall, nearly six foot five, wiry and skinny with not much of an ass to speak of, sloped shoulders and randy as a sixteen-year-old. Debbie Lyn leaned back and stared at the ceiling and then all around the room.

There was only the bed and a folding chair, the kind you'd find in the basement of a church. Come to think about it, she didn't recall seeing much at all as they'd gone inside last night, all kissing and hugging and dirty promises. There was a Jacuzzi, that much she was sure of, and a lot of laughter about the wild parrots in the trees and how one might come down to roost when he stood up—naked again—to refill their champagne. He'd played an old CD from her car in his little boom box—she had not seen one of those for a long, long time. "Red Red Wine." UB40 from nearly forty years ago.

He walked back in, clapping his hands together, erect as a starter pistol. "Ready, freddy."

"I can see that."

"Let's change up positions a bit," he said. "We've already done one and two. But I sure like four and five. Maybe work our way up to a six if my back holds out."

She looked up at him as she pulled open the sheet and again exposed herself, all the wrinkles, freckles, and sun damage, three children and twenty hard winters in Detroit. An ill-conceived rainbow tattoo on her hip bone from a girl's weekend in Vegas. She was exposed. "I hate to ask," she said. "Just what book are you following?"

"Does it matter?" he said, getting on his bony knees. "Just follow my lead."

In the daylight, sun streaming into the big master bedroom, she started to wonder how a man so successful could've lost his wallet. The meal cost her $382 without tip. If this didn't work out, she'd have to be dipping into her savings account.

"Ever watch a Western?" he asked. "Roy Rogers. Gene Autry. It's just like that."

"Who's the cowboy and who's the horse?"

"Giddyap," he said, falling onto his back and reaching his long skinny arms up to her.

So it was now a week—or was it ten days? Either way they'd been together day and night, every damn day, since that first meal on the causeway. By now, the not-paying thing was starting to niggle at her. Now, she was looking down at the check at a Ruby Tuesdays on Dale Mabry Highway, not too far from the Best Buy and Home Depot. He'd had two margaritas and a fruit salad, talking about a meeting he had later in the day with investors for the sunken-treasure deal that he just knew was about to come in. He said he already had a house on standby in Key West, two boats and a helicopter. Just like that, talking about old days in the Keys with Tom McGuane and Jimmy Buffet, some kind of wife-swapping action with the woman who played Lois Lane.

"Isn't she dead?" Debbie Lyn asked.

"Is she? I don't know. We quit speaking some time ago."

"Are you finished?"

"Yes."

"And no word on the wallet?"

"Ah," he said. "It won't be long. I'm having new credit cards issued that should arrive today. This whole thing has been a misunderstanding. So embarrassing."

"You knew Lois Lane?"

"We called her Marjie. She was a Libra. God. So much coke back then. Are you going to finish that?" He pointed to her half-eaten portion of blackened tilapia and wild rice. Her second day of calling in sick to work, nearly broke, and waiting for this mysterious cash to come in. It was so stupid. But still . . . maybe something.

"Tell me about this boat," she said.

"It's more than just a boat. It's a galleon. Sunk off the coast of Islamorada. Have you ever heard of Mel Fisher?"

"No."

"Really?" He stabbed the rest of the tilapia, looking less dapper than on their first meeting. Bright blue polo shirt with elastic-waist khaki shorts and blue Crocs! When she saw the Crocs she about died. *Maybe he's eccentric. Most rich people don't care.* They dress and live as they want to, her mother had always said. *But he's old. So damn old. Maybe his feet hurt. Fallen arches. Arthritic toes. Is there such a thing?* But he'd held out in bed, making a go of it ten, twelve times with the help of his magic blue pill. Making that off-to-the-races horn sound in his clenched fist.

"Interesting," he said, chewing. "This is so much better than Applebee's."

Most men didn't give a second thought about shaving. They had their Barbasol, a disposable razor, and horrible hacking habits. Yes, she was supposed to say *hacking at their face.* Didn't they know that shaving was a true art? That's how she'd get them started, maybe a nice guy looking at a straight razor or fancy silver handle for a safety razor, wondering if he might like to upgrade. She was taught to talk to him about it, not sell him, only consult him on what he was doing now and if he might like to upgrade the process. *What kind of facial hair do you keep?* That being kind of a dumb question if the guy had a big brushy beard or a Tom Selleck mustache or something like that. But mainly she got younger dudes. Guys her age shaved like her dad did, to get clean, but these young guys had shitty little beards or constant scruff to make them look cool and edgy. *What do you do to prepare your shave? You know, that's the most important aspect of getting a close shave—clean your face, prepare your face.* She might sell them on the less expensive products, see how interested they were in going all the way to a straight razor, brush, and shaving soap kit that retailed for nearly a hundred bucks.

Arranging a display of silver-tip brushes and mirrors, she turned right into the face of a husky dark woman. "He's a fake," the woman said, whispering to her. "A goddamn phony. You know this? Yes, you do. You are nothing but a meal thing to him. One of those things for a free meal."

"A ticket?"

"Yes," the woman said. "One of those."

She was short and looked and sounded Latin American, with lots of frizzy hair and a wide backside, pointing her finger right at Debbie Lyn's chest, speaking in a funny little accent that Debbie could never place—Cuban? Dominican? Guate-malan? The woman wore a flowing pink paisley shirt with a lot of silver rings and bracelets. She said her name was Delores. She was a good foot shorter than Debbie Lyn but weighed maybe twice as much. Not to judge . . .

"Delores," Debbie Lyn said, "not here. I'll meet you at the Starbucks in five minutes. Okay?"

"The Starbucks where I seen you with that rascal of a man, where he kiss your arms and your fingers?" she said. "He make me want to be sick. Make me want to shower myself."

* * *

The Starbucks was nice, big, and open-air, a wide kiosk right by the Neiman Marcus, a marble staircase winding up to the second floor. A gaggle of teenage girls took selfies on the landing, wearing short-shorts and cropped tops, looking for a million views on wherever they posted pictures these days. Their clothes, their manners, all of it so silly and foreign. She would never, not in a million years.

"Okay," Delores said, "don't you tell me. I tell you."

"About him?"

"Yes, about him. It's all about him. It's only ever about him. About him and the movies. All those big stars. Him and his big boats. His big cars. His cigars and money. Driving fast in the slow lane. All of it. He tell you about what he did with that man on television? That man from Australia with that knife? He say to me that he and that man were best friends. He say he come up with that line, about the knife. *That no knife. This a knife.* He say he the man who told that man and how that man go on to the Oscars. I should've known. I should've known." The woman hit her own head with her hand. "Delores, what'd you do?"

"Then who is he?"

Delores shrugged and blew at her coffee, although it was mainly froth, nonfat, extra-foamy, vanilla cappuccino. That of course Debbie Lyn paid for, back two days and already an hour's wage gone. But she was curious, so curious, with him lying on her couch when she left, forearm over his eyes from the seven-martini hangover. Ketel One, super dirty with extra olives. He called it a meal unto itself as if buying him seven goddamn martinis at Bar Louie would soften not having to buy dinner. Which she did anyway, drunk and stupid herself, opening up her safety Discover card for a Hawaiian hamburger and fries. He didn't even offer her part of the burger, the man making friends with half the bar, most them calling him *mister* and *sir*, clapping him on the back and wishing him luck with the big treasure hunt. They were all pulling for him.

"I would like to know," Delores said. "How about you?"

"What about me?"

"What he wants?"

"I have nothing."

"Of course you do," Delores said. "Or else he wouldn't waste his time. Sniffing your behind. Who are you, Miss Debbie Lyn? What do you have that I don't?"

"The house is being painted," he said. "Tons of fumes, it will make you sick. I nearly passed out just leaving the place this morning."

"Where's your car?" Debbie Lyn asked.

"In the shop."

"And what kind of car is it?"

"We've been through this," he said, picking at his breakfast sandwich at Pass-a-Grille Beach, egg and cheese on a croissant with black coffee for $4.99. "I don't want to brag. I'm driving the Aston Martin this week."

"I thought it was a Rolls." Debbie folded her arms over her chest, turning to watch a woman helping a small boy with a kite. It was February and warm, lots of blustery wind coming off the gulf.

He put down his breakfast sandwich on the Styrofoam plate and looked up. "I know what's really going on here."

Debbie Lyn turned back to face him, trying to gauge his expression, but his oversized Porsche sunglasses making it tough. He had on a Hawaiian shirt, sweatpants, and those goddamn Crocs.

"Delores found you."

Debbie Lyn didn't answer, turning back to the woman and the kid with the kite, the kid running like hell just as a blast of wind zipped that kite a hundred feet up in the air, the spool unwinding so fast, it burned his little hands. The woman picking it up as it skittered across the sand. This morning, she had seen on TV, Detroit got two feet of snow.

"I know you two have been communicating," he said. "I saw it on your phone when I came over this morning."

"That's my own personal business."

"It was on the counter. The message flashed on the screen. I can't believe you'd listen to such trash."

"Aren't we supposed to be at your house?" she said. "Picking out window treatments?"

"The fumes are awful. Just terrible. I have the worst headache right now."

"Sure," Debbie Lyn. "Exactly. Perfect. Swell."

He stood up and stretched, reaching down to touch his toes and then rotate back and forth with his lower back. She could hear his bones and cartilage pop, his smooth silver hair looking more white this morning, kicking up off his head like a rooster's comb. "Did Delores tell you that she's been institutionalized? Three times. Sad, really. The last time she believed she was José Martí, wanting to emancipate Cuba or some kind of nonsense. I'm sorry about that. I'm sorry you've so quickly become tangled in my affairs. I wanted to help her. I really did. But she grew paranoid. Dangerous even. Cuban women are the worst."

He began to unbutton his shirt, folding it neatly and placing it on the outdoor table near the beach café. A shapely young woman in her twenties wandered past them and began to shower the sand from her body. He watched her as she turned and lifted her feet, toweling off her little rump and heading off with a tote bag and straw hat in hand.

"Excuse me," Debbie Lyn said.

"I'm sorry. She looks just like my first wife."

"She could be your granddaughter."

He smiled at her, making her feel like she was jealous, like she'd been out of line just asking him a few honest questions and then expecting him to listen instead of gawking at a twenty-year-old wearing dental floss.

"The thing I like about shelling," he said, "is the exploration. The adventure. The discovery. You never know what you'll find if you keep your eyes peeled. Some shells wash up completely intact. Others are nearly perfect but broken off at the edges."

"That's what you want to do?"

"Isn't that why we're here?"

"Delores," Debbie Lyn said. "She said you're a fraud. That you're broke."

He reached out and offered his hand, the old gold coin swinging back and forth like a pendulum from his saggy neck. Debbie Lyn hadn't moved from the seat, staring up at him and then the beach, the kid now in control of the kite, the woman pulling it in some, showing him how to walk backward to keep everything nice and balanced. *Two steps. Two steps. Reel it in slow.*

"How's the shipwreck?" she said. Again, thinking of her mother. Nice girls don't pry. They let men talk and they listen. Men like good listeners. They like to feel important.

"Just amazing," he said. "Let's walk and seek and I'll tell you all about it. The story starts off at the beginning of the seventeenth century. The ship was heavy with gold, treasures from the New World, when it sailed from Havana. Dark skies on the horizon . . ."

Damn, she loved to hear him talk.

* * *

"According to him, it's you who's crazy," Debbie Lyn said, not knowing who or what to believe now. After the beach, he'd taken her to another home he said he owned, this one in St. Pete along Sunset Drive. It had a long wrought-iron fence, lots of palm trees, and a lovely view of the water. He called it one of his properties. But like the one on Bayshore, this one seemed to be under construction too. Only letting her visit the kitchen, where he kept a small table, a few mismatched chairs. He reheated half of a Papa John's pepperoni pizza with black olives and served her some white Zinfandel from a box.

"Me?" Delores said, standing by an aging Mercedes Coupe in a Bob Evans restaurant parking lot. "Me? Crazy? Sure, I'm the crazy one. Crazy for believing his bullshit all the time. Me who is crazy for buying this man clothes and dinner and the fancy cologne."

Next door was some kind of sex shop, XTC Super Center, with a sign offering two-for-one on inflatables to *Make the Bedroom Great Again*. There were several cars parked outside but no one seemed to be coming or going from the front door.

"What kind?"

"I don't know," Delores said. "Some socks. Underwear. I can't be so sure."

"The cologne?"

"He call it sandalwood. He say he like it because it's dry and manly. Like I think of him before he stole my money and my pride."

"How did you know?" Debbie Lyn asked. "How did you know who he really was?"

Delores leaned against the trunk of her nifty little Mercedes, faded tan with a few rust blemishes. She pulled out a pack of cigarettes from her Chanel purse and lit one, blowing into the wind, nodding. "You sure you are ready?"

Debbie Lyn nodded.

"Come," Delores said. "Get in the car with Delores and she show you where this old man come from. So much shame. It will only bring you shame. I'm so sorry for this. But you must know."

The apartment was on the other side of the bay, in downtown Tampa, just off the Hillsborough River. A high-rise complex called Buena Vista Terrace, an institutional-looking building with small balconies overlooking the Crosstown Expressway and a parking lot. The place looked like it had been fancy-schmancy back in the day, with a dry fountain of a dolphin by the entrance and intricate terrazzo floor showing the settling of old Tampa.

"Third floor," she said. "You will see. You will see who this man is all about. You meet his friend. The man he lived with. His name is Jack Russell, like the little dog. The man is older than dirt. But he remember things. His mind is sharp. He know. He know the kind of man we deal with here. This man. This man we think we love. Who we take to our beds. He stole this man's microwave and the scrotum of a tiger."

"Excuse me?"

"You will see," Delores said, punching the button on the elevator. The elevator clanking and moving upward, Debbie Lyn having to hold onto its side. "Jack Russell collects such things. This man know it was valuable and he took them. The scrotum of the tiger was to keep tobacco. A pouch he got in the war. It was very special to him. It gave him strength, he say."

* * *

Jack Russell was a chain-smoker in a wheelchair, oxygen tubes running up his nose, wearing a Vietnam veteran ball cap. He leaned sideways into his chair, scruffy and potbellied, as he looked Debbie Lyn up and down and said, "Yep, he's a phony all right. Let me know if you find out what happened to my tobacco pouch. I carried that thing through the jungle. Brought me vigor and luck."

"He lived here?" Debbie Lyn said. "With you?"

"We were roomies for two months," Russell said, nodding over at Delores, who'd sunk into a La-Z-Boy, flipping through a *Guns & Ammo*. "Don't be ashamed. He promised me all sorts of things too. Said that once that pirate ship, or whatever it is, paid out, he'd hire me to watch over all his vehicles. I could wax 'em from my chair. Said it would do him proud to put a disabled veteran to work. Saluted me and everything."

"Could he be telling the truth?" Debbie Lyn said. "About some of it?"

"That man swore up and down he was a fighter pilot in the war. A goddamn Air Force colonel. But you ask him a few questions. About planes and such, and the son of a bitch didn't know an F-4 from *F Troop*. Delores, you told her, right? About all those other women? The ones before you and after you? I don't know how he does it. Is it the silver hair or is it the tan? If it's the tan, someone please push me on out to the parking lot to get some sun."

"It's true," Delores said, licking her thumb and flicking the page. Hand cannons, Smith & Wesson M19s, new Combat Magnums. "So many. He probably have that VD. He use his ding-dong like old men use metal detector on the beach. You know, *beep-beep-beep*. Sweep it left to right to look for silver?"

"Oh God," Debbie Lyn said, laughing. "Oh God."

"Say," Russell looked her up and down again, "you got protection, right?"

She thought he was asking about prophylactics, but he wheeled over to his bed and pulled out a little black gun, so small it looked almost like a toy. He kept feeling under the bed until he got a magazine and slid it in place, grinning.

"You got to protect yourself, ma'am," he said. "None of us know who this man is. What he does. One night, he said he was some kind of CIA assassin. Here, put this in your purse. Just promise me to get me that tiger pouch back. Bastard had no right."

"I feel like a million bucks," he said nearly a month later. A whole entire month of Debbie Lyn being quiet and polite, a good girl who didn't ask questions and let the man do the deciding. She wanted to say something or do something, but she'd been having such a lovely time. They'd just gone to dinner, a nice little Vietnamese place off Treasure Island, and he'd spoken back and forth to the woman in French. Debbie Lyn was amazed, being reminded in some way of *Miracle on 34th Street*, Natalie Wood seeing that little Dutch girl singing "Sinterklaas," feeling happy for the first time since losing her family in World War II. He'd been back to himself, clean shaven, non-Croc'd in knit shirt, khakis, and broken-in moccasins, smelling nice. He'd worn a Rolex. He'd opened the door for her. He'd even paid.

Holding her hand as they brought over the fried green-tea ice cream, he leaned in and kissed her cheek. She knew. She knew. But every night had been fun. Every night different. An adventure, as he had promised. She quit her job and moved into the old estate on Sunset Drive, sending her friend Judy more silly postcards from the beach. A bummy-looking man poking up from an ice hole near a sign that read, *Thin Ice*, beside a picture of a good-looking woman swimming at the beach, palm trees on shore. Her sign read: *Pretty Nice . . .* He still didn't have a car. But she quit asking questions. He was on the phone constantly with the Keys. They had found something nearly a mile offshore. A candlestick. A gold bar. He said they had a big vacuum sucking up all that mucky sand until they hit pay dirt.

"How do you know French?"

"I lived in France some time ago," he said. "Back then, I was in marketing. We handled business for Kellogg's International. We did a lot of promotion for Frosted Flakes. I knew Tony the Tiger. The real Tony the Tiger. The original, Thurl Ravenscroft. Nobody could do a *They're great!* like old Thurl. Wonderful, wonderful deep voice. He's also the voice of Fritz at the Tiki Room at Disney. Did you know he was very religious? His lifelong dream was to record the entire Bible on tape. I'm talking the whole thing. Old and New Testament."

They were back at the mansion on Sunset Drive, sitting in the Jacuzzi with the doors open. She'd bought some Korbel champagne at Walgreens and they drank it from a couple of plastic cups he kept in the empty cabinets.

"Who really owns this place?"

"Who do you think?" he said. "I know. I know. Delores filling your head with all that nonsense. I know it's hard to believe, but I have had a pretty amazing life. I've worked in Hollywood and on Wall Street. I have been a millionaire but I also know what it's like to be broke. I have traveled across this world and hope to again. And yes, Debbie Lyn, I am a risk-taker. A rascal. A rogue. A treasure hunter. Someone who looks tough and weathered on the outside, but inside I'm just a marshmallow. I'm not asking a thing from you but to trust me. Just like you see people do sometimes, those trust-fall thingies, where you close your eyes and fall backward. Why don't we try and do that? Yes, let's do that."

"Fall backward in love?"

He laughed and laughed and reached for the champagne, filling it nearly to the top of his plastic cup with a University of Florida Gators logo. Chomp. Chomp. "Yes," he said. "Exactly. I guess I'm just like this old house. A real fixer-upper."

The house was big and empty, with a few broken windows, but so many bedrooms and bathrooms, seeming like the kind of place an old movie star could live. She could make that work. The palm trees and the beach made the old stucco, the empty swimming pool, and all that just fine. She could be happy to sit up here on the second floor and drink cheap champagne and watch the fishing boats come and go, feel the wind on her face, smell the salt air. This was at least something. This was something to work with. Eating Suki Hana alone at the International Plaza was a torture she'd rather not endure.

He smiled at her and reached for his pill bottle. Downed a little blue one. "Tallyho."

When the police came, the first time, she didn't even know he was gone. She was asleep in the master bedroom, a brand-new Sealy Posturepedic king they bought on sale on the floor, a swirl of blankets and sheets. Two bottles of Korbel and an empty prescription container scattered nearby. The police-woman shined a flashlight into her eyes and asked her for some identification.

"Excuse me," Debbie Lyn said, pushing herself up and covering her bare chest. "You can't just come in here. Bust in the door and hassle people. Just what in the hell's going on?"

The cop looked at her partner, a burly man, and didn't

say a word, just clicked off the flashlight, the room filled with early morning glow right before sunrise.

"The neighbors called about squatters," she said. "You do know you can't just break into any home in Florida and set up shop. Come on, lady. Get some clothes on. Get your stuff. Let's go."

"It's not mine," she said. "It's his. This place is his home. He bought it at auction. We're fixing it up."

"And who exactly is *he*?" the cop asked.

Debbie Lyn looked up as the cop tapped the flashlight against her leg, the room filled with that bluish-gray predawn glow. Her head throbbing from the night before, more Hawaiian martinis at a tiki bar on Treasure Island. Him doing a silly little dance, forming a conga line with some bikers down from Mississippi. Debbie Lyn touched a Tiffany bracelet he'd given her and twirled it on her wrist. "I don't really know," she said. "My God. How stupid does that sound? I really have no idea."

"I knew you would come to your sense," Delores said, speeding across Tampa Bay on the Howard Frankland Bridge in her battered little coupe, Harry Connick Jr. coming through the speakers. "The Way You Look Tonight." Rain pinging her windshield, her wipers tick-tocking.

"He left me there," Debbie Lyn said. "I was arrested but they let me go. I told them everything I knew about him. I'm not sure they believed me. I think they thought I was nuts."

"And he take your things?"

"Yes, he took my stuff. Boxes of my things. Some of my clothes. My television. He took my brand-new television. And my stereo and my CDs. My UB40. *Meet Me in Margaritaville*."

"No one cares about CDs no more," Delores said. "I play this man on my iPhone. This man, Harry Connick Jr., sing from his heart. He's a real man. He know what it is like to love and feel. I see him on TV and he says such things."

She pounded at her chest as she drove with her left hand, right wrist covered in an assortment of bracelets. Debbie Lyn felt at her wrist for the gift he'd given her. She pulled off the silver bracelet and held it up. "Do you recognize this?"

"Yes, yes," Delores said, taking the exit downtown. "That's mine. You keep it. It's yours. You earn it. I tell you what we do. First we find him. And then we kill him. You okay with that? He take your TV, your music, personal soundtrack to your life, and my bracelet. That man, Jack Russell. He take his tobacco pouch made from the tiger's privates. That's what we do. We kill him and take his pouch. I make a coin purse out of it. Not for big change, no. But for nickels and dimes. Small things to buy Chiclets and gumballs. He small time. He nothing to me."

"I couldn't kill a man," she said. "I couldn't kill him."

Delores shrugged, laughing but not with much humor, following Armenia toward Bayshore, past an old cigar factory and lots of restored bungalows and new trendy restaurants. She let down her window and lit up a cigarette. "You know where he go? He go where he always go. He go to that house where they make that TV show about a zoo. You see that zoo house where he feel safe and comfortable? Like an animal behind glass. That zoo house where he woo a woman, take her to bed for the first time. That man liking to do it in the Jacuzzi like a lizard, like a reptile at the Busch Garden."

Debbie Lyn found him in back, skimming the pool naked, a hefty blond woman in a cheetah-print swimsuit sprawled out in a lounge chair. He had his little stereo with him, playing her CDs. "Red Red Wine," just like from before. The woman passed out or asleep, gently snoring, not even lifting her head as Debbie Lyn came around back of the mansion. She had noticed a *For Sale* sign staked in the front lawn that she'd never seen before.

He stopped skimming and looked up. Son of a bitch. From the looks of it, he'd just taken the pill.

"It's not what it looks like," he said, dropping the skimmer and raising his hands. Debbie Lyn marched right up to him, tearing off the bracelet and tossing it toward him. "So many leaves at this time of year. And I hate tan lines. It's so much healthier for the skin, getting all that vitamin D."

"And her?" Debbie Lyn jacked her thumb at the hefty blonde. "Who is she? Did you fall in love with her too? Did you ask that she join in your adventure? Is she going to help you roam the beach for surprises and dive for pirates' treasure?"

"Where is Delores?" he said. "She put you up to all this. She filled your head with lies. Made you crazy. I told you that she's not well."

"She's calling the police," Debbie Lyn said. "They woke me up this morning. You asshole. You stole my fucking TV. And my music. It's *my* personal soundtrack. Not yours."

He stretched his hands out wide, looking in the harsh afternoon light like a tribal elder from a *National Geographic* film, all those folds and wrinkles like a hand-crafted wallet or a tobacco pouch.

"I was moving us," he said. "Over here. It's so much better over here. On this side of the bay. We can take long walks on Bayshore, gaze into God's sunset. I just didn't want to wake you this morning."

The blond woman, about Debbie Lyn's age or perhaps older, stirred, flipping over on her back and showing off the plunging neckline of the cheetah suit, a pair of ginormous breasts. "Honey?"

"And who is she? Or did she come with the property?"

"Nobody," he said. "She was just helping me with a few items of business. Don't let the nudity fool you. It's all very European. Don't let those Midwest morals your mother taught you cloud your mind."

And at that very moment, Debbie Lyn did think about her mom, up in a nursing home in Hamtramck watching reruns of *The Newlywed Game* and Frank futzing around their old house, cursing her for stowing away his tools. And she thought about those high school boys laughing at her at International Plaza when they got her to talk about *stroking it*. She looked at him, standing there on the diving board, and thought, *Gee, that old bastard could really use a shave*. The white whiskers made him look crummy as hell. She fumbled around in the purse slung over her shoulder and found Jack Russell's gun, closing one eye and aiming it right toward the right side of his face. You always started with the right, pulling your skin taut with the left hand, then started into a downward stroke. She would stroke that smile right off his face.

"Come on," he said.

"No, no, no!" Delores called out behind her. "I was kidding! I kid. Come on. He no worth it."

But he was so very worth it. He was worth every damn penny she'd spent on hamburgers and martinis and self-respect. Just a nick, just a quick shave. That would scare the living daylights right out of him. No more Debbie Lyn to woo and cajole and lie to, his penis erect and mocking like an angry finger pointed right at her.

Blam. Blam. One shot to the right cheek and another to the left.

And damn. She knew she'd screwed up when he toppled off the diving board, a dark-red period showing right between his eyes, his bony old body landing with a hard splash. Delores was screaming. The hefty blond woman was screaming. Debbie Lyn lowered the gun. She placed it in her purse.

She took a long, easy breath and smiled. Good. That was done. She'd done good, right?

Walking around to the other side of the pool, Debbie Lyn stopped the music and pulled out the CD. She placed it in the purse right next to the gun.

After all, it was hers.

THE MIDNIGHT PREACHER

BY SARAH GERARD

34th Street

The Victory Motors building was squat and run-down, some of the windows partially covered with thick Styrofoam panels painted electric blue, molding and crumbling. Others were covered in plywood or a crosshatched layer of plastic. A low overhang provided shade. Two long, narrow signs taped near the top of the windows read, *IN HIS NAME*, in a seventies color palette and retro computer font.

A sign on the door read, *No Trespassing: Violators Will Be Shot, Survivors Will Be Shot Again*. Another, illustrated with a human target, read, *We Don't Call 911*.

I was looking for the Live Crusade, particularly for Buck Hill, who used to have his studio in the back office of Victory Motors. The televangelist had disappeared from the airwaves and Internet without a trace two days after the election of Donald Trump, a week prior. I'm a freelance writer, and had convinced the *Tampa Bay Times* to let me look into his disappearance.

A stack of printed-out articles and e-mails sat just inside the front window, with a Post-it on it that read, *Trump stuff, file*. The article on top was dated 2013, and attributed to "Capitalist Evangelist" radio host Wayne Allyn Root, who had variously aligned himself with the Republican, Libertarian, and Tea Parties, and endorsed Trump in the 2016 presidential race. The front door was ajar.

At the sound of the bell, a tiny, frail-looking old man emerged from the back office. I assumed this was Clive Waters, owner of the car lot, whom I had read about in an old issue of the *Times*. Waters had donated the office space to Hill, explaining, "I like what he's doing. One-third of the population is up at that hour anyway. Better they find Buck than temptation."

There appeared to be no one else at Victory Motors that day, save for a longhaired cat, asleep on a rolling chair. I asked Waters if Buck was there. It took a moment for him to understand that I was talking about Hill.

"He hasn't lived in St. Petersburg or had his office here in several years," Waters said.

Indeed, there was no remnant of a production studio in sight. I informed him that Victory Motors was still listed as the Live Crusade headquarters.

"We collect Buck's mail for him and send it down to Naples," he said.

He looked at me suspiciously. I smiled to reassure him that, as an attractive young woman, I was no one to fear. Usually, a smile was enough to convince people to give me information. "Do you know why he stopped broadcasting?" I asked. I decided to follow this with, "Is he okay?"

Clive relaxed. "Maybe he's getting ready to do something big."

I looked around the Victory Motors office again. The state of disrepair suggested no one was doing business there anymore. I thanked Clive for his time and left, heat waves warping the asphalt back to my car, crosshairs at my back.

More interesting than where Buck Hill had disappeared to was why I wanted to know in the first place. I suppose I wanted to come face-to-face with hate.

* * *

In the days after Trump's election, like many, I spiraled. I started drinking again after two years sober. I broke up with my boyfriend, whom I suspected of voting for the wrong side. I locked myself inside a room at the Gateway Motel, which advertised Jacuzzis and free adult movies. I refused to answer the phone. I called in sick to my part-time barista job, claiming I had the flu.

Whenever I made eye contact with someone on the street, I wondered whether they were responsible for the rise of evil. I ate pickled pigs feet from the gas station, figuring, *If they want me to die, then I will.* I derived a sick pleasure from imagining someone discovering my body. It rained for days. Thankfully, the Gateway had wireless Internet. I couldn't tear myself away from the bad news.

I had never heard of Buck Hill until I saw his name on the Southern Poverty Law Center website. I had gone there trawling for hate groups I could infiltrate and explode from the inside; this delusion had become my lifeline. Live Crusade was listed among the sixty-three active hate groups in Florida. There was the Supreme White Alliance, the Daily Stormer, the Nation of Islam, and the New Black Panther Party. Then there was the Live Crusade, just a mile away from me, listed under "General Hate." Buck's anti-Muslim vitriol, racism, and homophobia had earned him the designation.

"It's sad, it's always sad when these things happen, whenever people have to die," he said. I was meditating on my encounter with Clive by combing Buck's old videos, which I had discovered on YouTube, looking for clues about his move down to Naples. He was a bloated white man broadcasting alone from a darkened room, his thinning, dyed-blond hair gelled into spikes, the camera tilted up at his face, illuminated blue as if from a laptop screen.

"But then you have to think, four thousand babies die every day in this country and nobody's upset about that. Nobody is pro-*choice*. Don't ever let anyone tell you they're pro-*choice*. You're either pro-life or you're pro-death," he said.

He leaned toward the camera and away from it, eyes darting wildly around the room. I wondered if he might be drunk, like I was.

"Don't let them confuse you with this weasel language—call it what it is," he said. "They're baby killers."

I'd had an abortion the year before. My boyfriend and I were stupid; *I* was stupid, taking my hormonal birth control pills when I happened to remember. I smirked at Buck and left him ranting in the background while I dove into the black hole of his web history. He had risen to prominence in the early days of the Internet with "the world's first full-service Christian website." At its height, he sent free *Worship War* newsletters out to more than two million readers each day. The newsletters, called "Battles," were part Live Crusade news and part sermon. Some of the most popular of them were addressed to Osama Bin Laden, Ann Romney, and Oprah. Buck had called Oprah a "new-age witch" and "the most dangerous woman on the planet." I appreciated his flair.

In 2012, he told his followers to write in Jesus on the presidential ticket. He equated a vote for Mitt Romney with a vote for Satan. I found this funny. It seemed no one was immune to his wrath. In 2010, he opened a "9/11 Christian Center" at Ground Zero in response to the construction of an Islamic community center nearby.

I was amazed that I had never heard of this asshole. He had been on the *Howard Stern Show* three times. He preferred to appear on secular media, he said—as an evangelist, he had been called to reach non-Christians with the Truth of God's

Word. It occurred to me that I was now a part of this secular audience. I opened another Magic Hat and looked at the clock. It was four in the morning.

At first, my interest in Buck was perverse: I enjoyed hating him. I scrolled through old news stories with a sense of awe— that someone who harbored such hatred could call himself Christian; that he had accrued such a following; that he had amassed such wealth as to now live in what I assumed was a shiny mansion down in Naples. Maybe I was jealous.

I lived alone in a motel on 34th Street, a segment of US-19, a large highway that ran the length of the state north to south. My neighbors were drug addicts and homeless families paying with vouchers. It was the most I could afford for now, living by myself as a newly single freelancer, if I wanted to have both car insurance and health insurance. There was no Medicaid extension in Florida and I couldn't find a full-time job, despite having a master's degree and plenty of student debt.

I was divorced and had sex outside of marriage. I fell somewhere between spiritual and atheist in terms of faith claim, and I voted Democratic and drank alcohol, so I was everything Buck Hill preached against, and he was everything I preached against.

And yet, even as I hated him, Buck was familiar. He was a midnight preacher of the kind selling plastic pouches of holy water on late-night television. I'd seen his like while channel surfing through my teenage insomnia. I would land on a broadcast that commanded me to surrender my immortal soul along with my allowance, and the rise and fall of the huckster's voice would soothe me to sleep on the sofa. It reminded me of my childhood when the only thing to do on a Wednesday night was tag along to a friend's Bible study. Buck was every pastor who had ever pulled me aside for asking questions, and the sound of the Christian radio station playing in my friend's mom's car on the way to school. Most preachers at least tried to disguise their hatred, though. Buck washed himself in it like the blood of the lamb.

He had been simulcasting daily on his website, YouTube, and the Walk TV until two days after Trump's election. Now his only signs of life were the Battles he continued to post on his website each day, which I quickly figured out were reproductions of previous Battles. He posted links to the Battles on his Facebook page, which only had a few hundred followers, most of them over sixty; the response was quiet. The posts received a handful of likes. He implored his readers, whoever they were, to "give generously" and "cover the ministry's past two months of shortfalls," at $65,000 each. He begged for one "ram in the bush" to cough up the $35,000 he claimed to need immediately, before month's end.

Given that he wasn't broadcasting anywhere, I knew that whatever pennies he was collecting on Facebook weren't covering operating expenses. I searched the open records of Pinellas and Collier counties and discovered that he was being evicted from his Naples mansion. The eviction notice was dated two days after the election—the day he'd stopped broadcasting. His rent had been $8,000 per month. He owed his landlord $64,000, the equivalent of eight months.

A notorious televangelist's fall from grace. His pitiful attempt at scamming people. Whether anyone was falling for the lie at this point was unclear. If no one were falling for it— if he wasn't bringing in any money from the Battles—there would be no reason for him to continue publishing them, unless it was for existential reasons.

"Our spiritual free fall would be less if God allowed Trump to become president over Clinton," he said in his last broadcast. I was eating my dinner from the gas station, watching the recording on my laptop. My dinner included beef jerky and a single-serving Häagen-Dazs strawberry ice cream. I made a tiny Ritz cracker–and–yellow cheese sandwich, and ate it with a mealy apple slice. Despite my greasy appearance, I was feeling gleeful. I had found someone worse off than I was, and more evil, and I was going to publicly shame him. "And that's what happened," Buck said. "The wrath and judgment is still coming, but I do believe it gives us a little bit of a reprieve."

His eyes cast wildly about the small room. Behind him, cheap-looking gold curtains hung pleated from a tall window. He talked in circles and sniffled, rocking back and forth. I simply needed to uncover the reasons for his downfall. He wore a plaid shirt open at the collar. He strained to fit the election results into the tiny framework of his limited belief system, grasping for any justification he could find.

He based his "final conclusion" on Trump's clean slate of a voting record and his recent reversals on the topics of gay marriage and abortion. He acknowledged that many believers considered Trump to be morally bankrupt, but explained that because Trump was in the entertainment industry, like God, we shouldn't seek to understand why he does what he does.

In the end, neither candidate could alter the "spiritual course" of this nation, he concluded—and though in the end, "Trump might be just as bad" as Hillary, "at least he might not be."

I called the number hovering at the bottom of the screen. Someone answered, then immediately hung up. I called back and stepped outside to smoke a cigarette on a folding chair chained to a dead planter. The rain had finally stopped and the air was now thick with foggy exhaust. The sky was a flaming sunset. Next door, a skinny girl leaned against a doorframe. The call went straight to voice mail. I left a message: "Hi . . . Buck? My name is Andrea Noble, I write for the *Tampa Bay Times* . . ."

My phone vibrated against my ear. I glanced at the screen. *What is it that u need?* it said. The sender had signed the text, *BH*.

I hung up the phone. *Thanks for responding*, I typed. *I'm wondering when Live Crusade will be back on the air.*

Hopefully back on tv in Sept . . . thnx, he responded.

Did you stop broadcasting because you're working on a new project? Clive said you had outgrown Victory Motors.

Who is this?

The skinny girl greeted a ragged biker in a leather vest. The vest had a Confederate flag on it. He asked her something and she shook her head and looked away.

Andrea Noble. I'm a reporter for the Tampa Bay Times, I said. *I'm wondering if you can tell me what motivated your move down to Naples.*

Email me so I have ur info, he said. *Will get back to u later in the week.*

The biker walked across the parking lot to the milky check-in window. The office didn't have a door on it, just the window, and someone saw you there or they didn't, and if they didn't, then you waited. There was no bell. The bell would ring all night if there were one. The illuminated *Gateway Motel* sign flickered like a moth against a lightbulb.

I asked Buck if he would be open to talking on the phone. *It may be faster, save you some time.*

Email me so I can work it into my daily schedule, he said. He added, *Thnx*.

I knew this would be the last I heard from him. I'd e-mail him and he'd never respond—he was ghosting me; it had happened to me dozens of times. He was hiding something.

So I said, *God bless.*

Buck had given his life to Christ while he was in prison, serving thirty months for insider trading. He'd been raised Methodist, and had planned to be a minister. Then in college, he had answered an ad seeking PC salesmen, and soon after got into selling fax machines, then got into investment banking. He spent eleven years running from God.

"Lying on my prison cot, I thought about my wife, Mi-Seon," he told Bay News 9. I was making my way through the videos posted on his YouTube channel. It had been twenty-four hours since I'd stepped outside the Gateway and every flat surface in my room was now populated with beer bottles stuffed with cigarette butts. Bags had appeared beneath my eyes, but it didn't matter since no one was looking at me, and I also wasn't looking at myself.

"We'd been married seven years and I hadn't been a good husband," Buck said. "She had every reason to leave me, and yet, that morning, she had vowed to stand by me. If my wife of flesh and blood could love another person to that degree, how much more must God love me?"

I had e-mailed my editor that morning with an update. *My hypothesis is that Buck's recent troubles stem from an illness brought on by his daily consumption of wrath,* I said. *I think I can have this story to you by the end of November. There are questions I still need to answer.*

Send when you can, he responded.

I knew he didn't care. I was not a priority—the paper was buried under postelection news. No doubt he'd forgotten about this quirky editorial. I couldn't even imagine which section he would put it in. Metro?

I was a shitty journalist, and this couldn't be argued. The drinking didn't help. I hoped there was a story in Buck, but I hadn't yet found it, and I couldn't be trusted with anything breaking.

After leaving prison, he'd earned his ministerial degree and had hit the road as an itinerant preacher, then accepted an invitation to produce Christian television in Florida. Neither was satisfying. Everyone he ministered to was already saved, and as an evangelist, he needed to reach souls in jeopardy.

In 1999, he launched LiveCrusade.com, the first place where people could go seven days a week, twenty-four hours a day for prayer. He answered prayer requests live on the air, broadcasting from midnight until two a.m. Within a year, seven hundred volunteer pastors around the country were responding to forty thousand LiveCrusade.com prayer-request e-mails daily. Within three years, Buck had secured a time slot on secular television. Though *Live Crusade with Buck Hill* reached national and international audiences for limited periods, his greatest impact was in regional networks throughout Florida.

He appeared on air in a suit and tie. His hair was cut and styled, bleached blond. He was charismatic, seated before a serious-looking bookcase, preaching on everything from divorce to gluttony.

Even back then, his sermons skewed political. He took particular aim at "baby killing" and "the radical homosexual agenda." After five years, networks pulled Hill's show under pressure from the Council on American-Islamic Relations. Among other things, he had called Islam a "1,400-year-old lie from the pits of Hell," and called the Prophet Mohammed a "murdering pedophile." The Koran was a "book of fables and a book of lies."

Americans United for the Separation of Church and State petitioned to have Live Crusade's tax-exempt status revoked. "I have every right to educate people on spiritual matters and deal with the pressing spiritual issues of our day, even those that transcend into the political arena," Hill told the *New York Times*, which broke the story. "Unlike many Christian leaders, I have never and never will endorse any candidate for public office. I have never told people who to vote for or who not to vote for."

The IRS launched an investigation into the Live Crusade ministry that lasted for nine years. This past March, Buck and his lawyer finally reached a settlement. I spent a day at the courthouse, wading through the filings. He owed $10 million in unpaid taxes. He owed $100,000 to American Express.

"He was very theatrical," said Shelly Zeno, his former publicist. I had found her on Facebook, living in Sarasota. To my amazement, she posted her phone number on her profile. It sounded like she answered the phone in her car. She invited me to come down to the lot where she was now selling Aston Martins. We borrowed a Vanquish Volante and followed the bay. She rolled the top down. Chrome clouds gathered over the water. She was a fast talker, peroxide blond, with oversized lips and enormous knockers. She had represented some of the biggest names in Christian media, including Buck's archnemesis, "prosperity pimp" Joel Osteen. I hoped she would give me some dirt on Buck's spending habits.

"I worked pro bono for him," she told me. "He never had the money to pay me. He wrote his own copy, and I just sent it to editors. I didn't always agree with what he had to say, but he was good at attracting attention. I liked his spirit. There was a time when he felt everything he was saying and doing was coming from a very deep conviction."

"You believe that?"

"Absolutely."

We pulled up to a streetlight and she smiled at the car next to us. Two men leered back. I could tell my plastic Walgreens sunglasses next to her Ferragamo's didn't make sense to them, much like her story about Buck's finances didn't make sense. Did she think I hadn't done my research? That I didn't know about his Naples mansion or his trouble with the IRS?

"If he didn't have the money to pay you, what happened to his donations?" I said.

"What donations?" she laughed.

"You're saying he never got any?"

"Not that I know of."

I'd read somewhere that he refused to sell trinkets on the air. "The Bible says the Gospel should be free," he'd said. But then, he also ran a "Souls of Gold" mail-in jewelry campaign offering only receipts and prayers in return for your family heirlooms. And the Ezekiel Project: a paid membership that offered prayers in return for the membership fee. Members of the Ezekiel Project were expected to sign up other members who were "committed to the Truth," like a holy pyramid scheme. Where did that money go?

"I looked him up about a year ago," Shelly said. "It made me sad. I could tell he wasn't doing well, that something had happened to him."

"What do you think happened?"

"I couldn't tell you. His website was rolling out old information. His appearance concerned me. It looked like he was in a dark, tattered room with the drapes pulled. It was just so not Buck."

"Did you talk to him?"

"I considered it, but I was afraid he would ask me for help." She wasn't doing Christian PR anymore—she refused. "You can't pay me to walk into a church now. By the time I left PR, I didn't feel like I was doing anything except making rich Christians richer."

I was driving on the Tamiami Trail when Buck called me back. I had been persistent in trying to get him on the phone since leaving St. Petersburg, wanting to make a plan to meet him in person. In my voice mails, I had expressed my concern for the future of Live Crusade given his recent troubles with the IRS. I was careful not to give him further reason to avoid me. I pulled out my recorder and steered with my elbows, praying that my car wouldn't veer off the road, since I didn't have the money to get it serviced, and hadn't in over a year.

"We've been jammed with so much, trying to get our TV show back on the air," Buck apologized. "I've just been so slammed with so many things."

I said it was no problem. The sun streaked past my passenger window. "What do you have to do to get your show back on the air?" I said. I figured entertaining his fantasy was the best way to ingratiate myself.

"Oh, just . . . when you're working with twenty-five syndicators, it's a daily grind to get everything set up," he said.

"That's a lot of syndicators. Can you name some of them?"

"We're going into eighty-some-odd markets," he said. "But I'll, uh, fill you in on everything. Just let me get through December and I'll talk to you, okay?"

"You know, I talked to Jim West from the Walk TV," I lied.

"He said he would be happy to have you back on the network, but that you owe them money, and would have to negotiate a new contract."

"We're dealing with another syndicator," said Buck. "One of the major networks."

"I thought there were twenty-five syndicators? Is there only one? Which one are you working with?"

"I'll talk to you about it in January, hon. Everything will be up and running by then."

"You know, I talked to your landlord, Carol, too. I know that you're in the middle of eviction proceedings, so I'm wondering what's going on with that."

"I'll talk to you in January."

"You owe her about the same amount that you're asking for in the Battles—$64,000. You're asking for $65,000 in the Battles. Is that related?"

He hung up.

I knew from Google Maps that his mansion sat at the end of a cul-de-sac in a double-gated golf course community. I parked across the street from the entrance and leaned on the hood of my car. There was no way I could drive up to it; I would have to sneak in. Given that Buck was dodging me again, showing up at his door now could seem like escalation, a threat. I decided to get a room and regroup. I expected him to e-mail me that night, anyway, since I had baited him. The truth was, his landlord had refused to speak with me. I wasn't surprised; I knew from social media that she was a Trump supporter. When I'd asked her whether she believed in Hill's work, whether she and Buck had a "personal friendship," she'd said it was none of my business.

No official motion had been made on his eviction in several days. This led me to believe that she didn't really want him out; she just wanted her money. Maybe she believed his lies about syndication. Maybe she agreed with his views on Muslims, Oprah, abortion, and salvation.

Some part of me was beginning to sympathize with Buck. I could almost ignore his hateful messaging and see him for who he was: an insolvent, weak, lonely has-been. I related to his moral certitude, but tendency to violate his own moral code. I related to his failure, but determination to keep trying against all odds. I almost, in spite of myself, felt like reaching out to him and saying, *Here, let me help you be less of a fuck-up.* Then again, he might not have wanted my help. Maybe he believed himself a martyr.

I checked into the Sunrise Motel, advertising fifty cable channels, a mini fridge, and low rates. A wreath of dead leaves hung above the bulletproof glass of the check-in window, beside an American flag. Next door was a liquor store that I planned to hit up as soon as I changed out of my dirty clothes. My car was one of two in the lot. The other was missing a back window. I needed a nap.

The walls of the room were concrete blocks, painted white and unadorned. The bedspread was the color of red tide. I was checking the mattress for bedbugs when Buck's first e-mail came in. I scrolled until I reached it—he had not waited for me to respond before sending others, each spiraling deeper. *Who are you?* he demanded. *First..I am NOT being evicted. Second..why would you be calling my landlord? Wht is your real goal? Issue?..If we are to move forward??*

His messages were riddled with snark and jabs at my intelligence, and sarcastic turns of phrase: *FYI, LOL, Obviously you are very ingenious.*

Outside, the sun was setting fast over a blighted intersection crawling with souls of little faith. I decided to hold off reading any more of Buck's e-mails until he was done being mad at me, but my phone kept vibrating in my pocket, and each time I felt it, my pulse quickened. I hated when people were mad at me, even people I hated. I asked the liquor store clerk where the Scotch was, and opened my phone in the back corner. *Interesting,* Buck said. *Spoke to Mi-Seon?..Spoke to Shelly?..Mike? Key $ man David?*

I took note of these names.

He insisted that the Live Crusade's monthly operating budget for the last nine years had been $65,000, that the bulk was balled bandwidth—though it was obvious to me, and anyone taking even a cursory look, that he was using no bandwidth.

I paid for my Dewar's and carried it out in a paper bag. Back in the room, I brought it to the bathtub, where the squawk of Trump's voice penetrated the wall from the next unit. A murderous fantasy overtook me and I thought about my ex-boyfriend, how proud of himself he must be now, seeing that horny toad's face every day. I hadn't even told him about my abortion. I'd paid for it with my own credit card and had lied about leaving town for two days to report on a story. "I'm a feminist," he had told me. "I just think that a man should have some say, if he's the father."

I smiled imagining telling him now, imagining stabbing Trump in the face and, as he died, holding up a picture of the thirteen-year-old he'd raped, tossing money at him for an abortion as I was leaving.

Buck was still e-mailing me.

...btw..throw Hinn...Jakes..and the rest of the prosperity pimps on Christian TV with Osteen, he said. *I would never worry*

about money again if I took their path to preaching/fleecing the choir…

Poor baby.

I actually live and believe all I teach..and one day..like each one..will stand before God..

Then, to my surprise, he said, *Chat with you in Jan…*

I went back to Buck's Facebook. The sun had set and the Sunrise was filling up, all of the windows coming alive. Next door, someone was getting fucked or murdered. I turned up the TV. Buck and I had a friend in common: the mother of a person I'd dated briefly in high school. The family identified as Messianic Jews, or "Jews for Jesus": ethnically Jewish, but evangelically Christian. This manifested in curious ways. One day, my boyfriend built a didgeridoo out of some old PVC pipe. He was playing it in the kitchen and his mom came to listen.

"After a while, it kind of puts you into a trance," said my boyfriend.

"Then you have to stop," said his mother. Her expression was fearful. "That's how the devil gets in."

Two years after we broke up, when my ex was seventeen, he married a fifteen-year-old girl from the next street over. Twelve years later, they were divorced with five children. His social media was now a scrolling advertisement for misogyny. *Ladies, this is how you take care of your man! Another woman coming at me!*

I often wondered why I was still virtually connected with him. Maybe I recognized his rage as suffering. I suspected the problem was an undiagnosed illness, though that seemed insulting to people with illnesses, and could be letting him off too easily. I knew via rumor that his ex had taken out an injunction for protection against him after he'd tried to strangle her in the shower. Afterward, he got another girl pregnant and beat her into having a miscarriage.

Now he lived with his mother. I unfriended him and messaged her to ask about Buck. I wondered whether she knew him personally or just followed his ministry.

I used to call his program for prayer in the late nineties, she responded. She asked me why I wanted to know, and I explained that I was thinking of writing a story about him. I asked her if she'd noticed that he was no longer broadcasting. She hadn't thought about him in years, she admitted.

But listen, Andrea, I hope you're doing an exposé that's compassionate, trying to find the answers, she said. *What could have contributed to this great man's fall? What were the factors? And you know what? He may tell you. If you say, "Listen, I really want to paint a vivid portrait of what can happen, and the pressures, and what led you to these decisions," he might tell you.*

The mansion was peaches-and-cream, bordering a golf course. In September, Hurricane Hermine had knocked the pool enclosure down, and it had yet to be repaired, so it sat crumpled in a heap on the deck furniture. A cluster of potted plants waited at the edge of the driveway beside bags of potting soil and an ash-gray Toyota Camry. The front door was open. I knocked on the screen. Mi-Seon appeared in a nightgown. She was a petite Korean woman with a kind, open face. She made no move to open the screen while we talked, so we spoke through it. She was convinced at first that someone had put me up to writing the story, and demanded to know who had tipped me off. I assured her that I was writing it as a matter of personal interest. She told me she didn't want to talk about Buck. "If I talk about Buck, I have to talk about myself," she told me. "And I don't want people to call me up and ask me about it." She told me they'd divorced. He was no longer living there. She'd been living on Buck's alimony payments, which he'd stopped sending. She didn't know where he was. "Nothing good can come of this," she said. "I know it's public record, but it's personal."

"Buck is a public figure," I said.

"He's been through enough." She smiled at me. I saw she was crying. I wondered about his new wife, if he had one—I suspected she would be the blonde I'd seen in the Souls of Gold infomercial. In it, she was dropping her old jewelry with French-tipped nails into a padded envelope, and walking it out to the mailbox behind me, at the end of the driveway.

"Do you think Buck has been persecuted unfairly for his beliefs?" I said.

"Well, he would say things, and people would get offended, but it's just his opinion." Mi-Seon told me again that she didn't want to talk about it. "If you're not Christian, you're against Christians." She began to shut the door.

"Wait, Mi-Seon . . ." I'd been attempting to make contact with her for days. She wasn't listed publicly and wasn't on social media. She no longer used e-mail. I told her that I had recently been attending church. "First Methodist, in Largo." This was a lie but it worked.

She cracked the door. She told me that life with Buck had led her to want to "cocoon." Pressure in the televangelism industry to maintain a facade had become exhausting. "People say they're your friends and then they turn around and they're not your friends," she said. She was a private person. The screen door didn't have a knob on it, I now noticed. I asked her if she found it hard to live in the public eye, given how opinionated Buck is.

"No, it's not that. I don't trust secular media. Buck paid a lot of money to the secular media and then they kicked him off. And you journalists pad the story, make it more dramatic, fictitious."

I reminded her that she didn't know what I would be writing.

"You print lies."

"The *Tampa Bay Times* has fact-checkers."

"I don't like the *Tampa Bay Times*," she said.

"Buck used secular media to reach nonbelievers."

"That's what got him into trouble. He made mistakes."

"What mistakes?"

"With money. And in his personal life," she said. They had separated a year into his investigation by the IRS. They'd been married twenty-six years. "He wasn't praying about it."

"How did you meet?" I asked, knowing my time was running short.

Mi-Seon smiled. She opened the door wider and stepped toward the screen. "He saw me at the mall. He approached me and spoke to me in Korean. Then he wrote my name."

"How did he know it?"

"He'd followed me."

I can't say I was surprised to see an Aston Martin parked at the Gateway Motel when I got home. The clouds had lifted, revealing a silver sun, and Buck sat in the folding chair outside my room with his hands in his coat pockets. I wondered which hand had the gun in it.

His red-ringed eyes were drunk and crying. I walked to the check-in window, though it was abandoned, pretending I didn't see him. I dropped my night's pay into the rusting mailbox. The skinny girl came around the corner, her face bruised. I asked her how long Buck had been there.

"All day," she said. "He rented the room next to yours."

"Did he say what he wants?"

"He asked me if I was a hooker."

I took out my recorder and turned it on, then tucked it into my pocket and thanked her. If he shot me, at least there would be a record of who had done it. He followed me with his eyes as I crossed the lot back toward him. He sat forward on the chair, a mordant smile on his face, then he rose and came into my room behind me without saying a word. I closed the door.

We sat at the particleboard table across from each other. I placed an ashtray between us. He reached into his coat pocket and my heart lit up, expecting to see a gun, but he pulled out a flask and offered it to me.

"No thanks," I said, "I'm working."

He shrugged. "The IRS will never see a dime due to the fact that I have nothing," he told me. He pulled at the flask. "The investigation into Live Crusade was started by Lois Lerner, former director of the Exempt Organizations Unit. Heard of her? In 2013, she was investigated for unfair probing of conservative groups applying for tax-exempt status. The IRS knew they would never see a dime. They knew the settlement would never be collected. They just wanted to ruin me. They pick and choose targets based on their own biases."

His face became red. I thought he would cry, but he didn't. He closed his eyes, as if praying. I looked away, embarrassed.

"Are you asking me to feel bad for you?" I said. "Because I don't."

"No, I'm asking you to leave me with some dignity."

"Why should I?"

"Because I have a gun."

He opened his eyes. My gut turned to liquid. I reached up

and pulled back the curtains next to us. The window looked out on the parking lot. I made eye contact with the skinny girl. She nodded.

"You also have a luxury car," I said.

"Don't be an idiot. I've had that car for six years."

"And?" I lit a cigarette. I ashed in the tray, blowing my smoke in his face. I didn't believe he had a gun. I chose not to, or was unable.

He cocked it beneath the table. I felt it pointed at my uterus. His forehead was wet with sweat. He got off on his power. "The *Times* isn't paying you enough to risk your life," he said.

He was right about that. The acrid smell of gunpowder filled my nostrils. The crack rang in my ears. The wall's plaster crumbled into my lap, and I laughed, but the laughter was my overwhelming sadness and fear.

"You're living in it now, aren't you?" I said, meaning the car.

But he was already gone, leaving the door open.

JACKKNIFE

BY DANNY LÓPEZ

Gibsonton

I finished packing my overnight bag and was about to head to the shelter when my phone buzzed.

"Wes?"

I hadn't heard Lisa Moon's perilous voice in over a year. Now she breathed deep into the speaker. "I need your help."

"Really, my help?"

"Please . . ."

I tightened my grip on the phone and fought the impulse to throw it against the wall, smash it to pieces like she'd done with our relationship, or whatever you call what we once had. But I was soft—a sucker. She had me wrapped around her finger. She knew it. I knew it.

"I'm sorry," she went on real slow. "I . . . I didn't know who else to call."

"What's going on?"

"I need a ride," she said.

"Where are you?"

"I'm at Jack's place in Gibsonton."

Gibsonton. It wasn't even a real town, just a few blocks of old houses and single-wide trailers that had seen better days. A depressing Florida suburb once favored by circus folk and carnies.

I held the phone away from my face, paced around the living room of my run-down Seminole Heights apartment. I could still hear the sound of the door slamming as she walked out of my life, the chain of the lock swinging, clacking against the dead bolt like a clock.

"Wesley?"

"There's a hurricane—"

"I know," she said. "I'm sorry . . . but I need help."

"What about Jack?"

"That's what I need help with."

"Jesus, Lisa."

"Wes . . ."

"This isn't a good time."

"Just say no, then. You can do that, you know?"

No. She knew I couldn't. So I took down the address. Just before I shut off the TV and walked out the door, the weatherman pointed to the image of the perfect round eye of the storm. Hurricane Lloyd was now a category four with sustained winds of 135 miles an hour. The shiny, well-groomed weatherman warned everyone to evacuate the barrier islands from Longboat Key to Cedar Key and seek shelter immediately from Sarasota to Tarpon Springs.

Gibsonton was right smack in the center of the cone.

I met Lisa Moon at the Mons Venus during one of my first gigs as a PI after I'd been forced into retirement from the Tampa Police Department. The Internal Affairs investigation into the shooting death of a well-known drug dealer destroyed my law enforcement career. I was canned for doing my job. About half a dozen of us responded to a call of suspicious activity that was soon upgraded to shots fired in Ybor City. Two suspects were dead. Turned out neither one of the victims had a weapon. The investigation found we followed proper protocol, but three of us got terminated because heads had to roll.

I started doing work for a bail bondsman I knew who did a little side investigation work for select clients. That's how I ended up following this sleazeball who'd taken out a second mortgage on his nice home in Bayshore Gardens and was using the cash to live it up while his wife stayed home with the kids. Every few days he'd hit the Mons and throw money at the strippers. He got lap dances, and on a number of occasions took one of his favorite girls to the Seminole Hard Rock Casino for a night of gambling and debauchery.

I sat away from the action at the Mons and observed. I took notes, some photos, maybe a little video for evidence. And every time it was Lisa Moon in her skimpy waitress outfit who came to take my drink order.

"Just soda water."

"For real?"

"Yeah," I said, "you have soda water, don't you?"

She shrugged and wrote the order down on her pad. "You on the wagon?"

"Does it matter?"

"You a cop?"

"What makes you think that?"

She gave me that little sideways smile. "I dunno. The Dockers, the shoes. You got the look."

"The look, huh?"

"You come in here a couple times a week and sit in the back, drink soda water, and never get a dance. What gives?"

"Nothing gives," I said. "You getting me my water or do I have to go to the bar and get it myself?"

I took my overnight bag. Hurricane Lloyd was less than a couple hours away. We were already getting occasional feeder bands. If rescuing Lisa Moon took too long, I'd have to find a shelter down in Gibsonton.

Traffic was hell. Every gas station had lines of cars that snaked out onto the street. I-75 was bumper-to-bumper heading north, but the southbound lane was deserted. I was the only crazy headed into the storm.

On my last visit to the Mons, my subject didn't leave until closing. When I walked out, Lisa was standing outside smoking a cigarette. She tossed the butt in the air and it flew across my path like a falling star, stopped me in my tracks.

"So where to next?" she said.

I had to smile 'cause she was too cool, wearing a pair of black leggings, combat boots, and a gray tank top. She looked totally different than the waitress I'd come to know at the Mons.

"Sleep," I said.

"What about the dude you're shadowing?"

"What about him?"

"You gonna follow him or what?"

"Nope. But when that son of a bitch wakes up in the morning, he's going to be looking at divorce papers."

"So, mission accomplished?"

I nodded.

"Right on. We should celebrate."

I looked behind me at the Mons. "Bar's closed."

She nodded to the side. "How about breakfast? My treat."

We walked to the Denny's down the block and took a booth at the very back. She had French toast and coffee. I had the All-American Slam. She talked. I listened. I don't know if it was the lack of sleep or that the last few months of surveillance work had destroyed whatever little social life I had, but that morning, as dawn turned the windowpanes a sad gray, I was captured by her bright-blue eyes.

Lisa told me she grew up in a small town outside Augusta. She dropped out of high school and escaped to Miami, where she found a job booking cruises for some online discount outfit.

"It wasn't as glamorous as I thought it was gonna be," she said as she drowned her toast in syrup. "I wanted to travel, so I stuck with it for a couple years. The dude I was living with at the time managed a club on Washington Avenue in Miami Beach. One day he tells me he's been offered a job running the London Victory in Tampa, so he splits. I followed only to find out his move had nothing to do with work. He was chasing some Cuban bitch with huge knockers."

"What'd you do?"

"I kicked his ass," she said all casual, "and moved to St. Pete and got a job at one of those trendy restaurants on Beach Drive. Three years and five jobs later, I ended up at the Mons Venus. I should've gone there from the start. Place is a gold mine." She stopped talking and eyed my plate. "You gonna eat that last piece of bacon?"

As predicted, we went back to my place.

The address Lisa had given me led me to the Fairfax—a trailer park across Riverview Drive from the VFW. The place was like a junkyard of eight or nine single wides in various stages of disrepair. My first thought was that I was in the wrong place. I couldn't see Lisa living in this filth. I couldn't see anyone living here. But still, I parked between a rusted orange trailer with a Confederate flag on the window and a dirty single wide whose roof was half covered with a blue-vinyl tarp and old tires.

I barely knocked when the door flew open. It took me a moment to realize it was Lisa—*my* Lisa. She had her long dark hair up in a messy bun, wore cutoff jean shorts and a pink T-shirt. But it was her eyes that struck me. They were big and jittery. She was scared.

"Wes!" She grabbed my hand and pulled me inside, saw the scar on my thumb. I pulled my hand away quickly. She looked to the side and back at me like she was waiting for something—or someone. Still, it felt good to be close to her again, taking in the sweet flowery smell of her perfume. I could've stood there for hours, but there was a hurricane coming.

"We should get going," I said.

"What?"

"The storm."

"Wes . . ."

"What happened to you?" It escaped me like a prayer. This was her life, where she lived—the nasty yellow shag carpet and the warping dark-wood paneling, the stink like burned Spam and cigarette smoke.

The Lisa Moon I'd known was tough. She dressed like Joan Jett and lived in a nice studio apartment in Palma Ceia and drove a bloodred Miata. She had it together like no one I knew. She was always in control. That had been our problem. We were two headstrong lovers with trust issues. Protecting our own feelings came first.

Now here she was, living like trailer trash—and in Gibsonton, no less.

"I don't know where Jack is," she said, and took a short step back. "I need to know he's safe."

"I'm sure he's fine." But I really didn't give a damn about her knife-throwing clown.

"No. I need to know. We need to find him. He's been gone three days. He won't answer his phone. And now this damn hurricane. He would never just go and leave me here like this."

"You sure about that?"

She slapped me.

Within the first couple of months of dating, I asked Lisa to move in with me. She refused. She said she liked her independence. She said she loved her little apartment with the white walls and gold crown molding. She said that if we moved in together it would ruin the magic.

By magic she meant sex. It kept us together, like a drug we had to get a fix of every few days. We often fought, but somehow we always ended up in the sack either at her place or mine. Sometimes it was rough. Sometimes it was soft. But it was always good.

Our problem was that I wanted to take care of her and she didn't need any taking care of. When I told her she should quit the Mons and get a respectable job, flatware flew across my apartment.

"What is it about men that you need to dominate us?" she cried. "I was fine before you showed up, and I'm fine now."

"I hate you working late nights around all those creeps."

"That wasn't a problem when *you* were hanging out there every night."

"I was working."

"And what do you think I do there?"

I was jealous. I worried she'd meet someone else. And she did. Jack the fucking Knife. And now here she was.

She never let me get close. I wanted all of her, body and

soul, but all she ever gave was body. All I could do was wonder if it was different with Jack. She'd been with him at least eight months, living in this tin can. She looked thin, dark circles under her eyes, haggard. Maybe she was on drugs.

I raised my hand to belt her one but stopped short. I promised myself I wouldn't do this. I wasn't going to be drawn into our usual game of love and pain. I was a new man.

"I'm sorry," she said after a moment, her lip trembling. "I love Jack. I'm not leaving without him, Wes."

"For all we know, he might be sitting in a cozy suite at some hotel in Orlando or Atlanta."

"He's not like that," she lamented, and pointed to the door. "He walked out that door three days ago and hasn't come back. He won't answer his phone."

"You go to the cops?"

"No . . . I—"

"Why not?"

"I don't know." She lowered her eyes. "I was scared. I didn't want him to get in trouble."

"An affair?"

"No!" She gave me a poisonous look. "He said he was meeting a friend. I don't know. Some of those guys he hangs out with are bad news."

"Drugs?"

"No, not him, but his friends. They're lowlifes. Carnies. You can't trust them."

"You think they did something to him?"

She turned away. Tears escaped her eyes. "I just thought it'd be better not to involve the police. Not yet."

"Okay," I said, and placed my hand on her shoulder. "Take it easy."

She shrugged my hand off and wiped her tears with the back of her wrists. "Can you help me?"

A strong feeder band from Lloyd swept in, rattling the aluminum roof of the trailer and bringing a wave of hard rain.

"We need to leave," I said.

"Not without Jack."

"We're not going to find him if we stay here."

She didn't move.

"Fine," I said. "Did he take anything when he left?"

"His knives."

"What?"

"He took his set of knives."

"That's it?"

"It's a set of custom Laguiole knives. They're worth a small fortune."

"Why would he take them?"

"I don't know!" she cried. "We were working on an act. He was in touch with a producer, someone who'd been in Hollywood and was looking for innovative acts. Things were looking really good for us. But then he started getting these phone calls. Last week he said someone was following him."

The racket of the rain on the roof died down.

"The man's a con, Lisa. I swear, you fall for these guys—"

"Don't—don't you talk down to me. I love Jack and he loves me. Get over it, Wes. You don't wanna help me, fine." She grabbed her purse and shoved past me to the front door. "You should've just said so before you came down here." She ran out.

I went after her. "Hold up."

She stood by my car with her back to me. The night was suddenly dead still.

"I came all the way down here . . . I'll help you look for

him. But the hurricane . . ." I pressed the unlock button on my key. The car beeped. Lisa lowered her head and ambled to the car.

Another feeder band swept across the Fairfax. The gust dragged a plastic trash can across the dirt road to the far end of the trailer. It came to rest next to a large round target, the kind you see at the circus with straps and a star and the outline of a woman painted on it. Part of Jack's William Tell routine.

I turned away from the rain and made my way to the car. I drove to the entrance to the trailer park and stopped. I knew we were not going to find Jack. I had to get us out of here, back to Tampa. Or at least find shelter. I had a quarter tank of gas.

I took a right toward the interstate.

"Where we going?"

"75."

"Can't we drive around a bit?"

"You think he'll be walking around in this weather?"

"Let's just take a quick drive. Ten minutes. That's all."

I glanced at her. She knew I would do what she asked. I took a left and we crisscrossed Gibsonton in a grid pattern through the narrow streets of this sad run-down town. The roads were deserted, shitty little houses boarded up with plywood. The feeder band passed and the night was suddenly calm again.

I kept asking myself why I'd fallen for her of all people. But I knew better. There was never any logic to love, lust, infatuation—they were all a mystery. They drove people to do crazy things. I was no exception.

Maybe I'd been lonely.

But I was lonely now—had been since the day she left. There was something about her. And when I learned she'd hooked up with Jack the knife thrower, it hit me in the gut. Bad. I knew I would never see her again if I didn't do something. And then she called. But what she wanted was him. She was willing to risk our lives in the storm to find Jack.

Just as my temper was about to snap, I saw the lights. Blue and red cut the darkness like a disco. Cops. They were camped at the intersection of Riverview Drive and 41. The railroad tracks. On the north side was a wooden shack like an old-time station, an abandoned depot covered in vines and graffiti. It was a circus: three police cruisers, an ambulance, the crime scene van, and two unmarked Grand Marquis.

"Must be the president," I joked. But I knew better.

Lisa covered her mouth with her hand. "J-Jack . . ."

"You don't know that."

"Pull over."

I did what she asked, eased the car to the side of the road where a uniformed officer stood directing the nonexistent traffic.

Lisa lowered her window. "What's going on?"

"Gotta move on," the officer said, and waved for us to pass.

"Is 41 clear to Tampa?" I asked.

He leaned in. "What do I look like, Bay News 9?"

I inched forward to the tracks and stole a quick glance at the abandoned depot. Detective Morano was standing to the side in a blue plastic poncho, hood pulled back.

I pulled over on the gravel.

Lisa looked at me. "What're you doing?"

"I know that cop," I said. "I'll ask him about Jack."

"I'm coming with—"

"No!" I placed my hand on her thigh. "No. Let me go. He'll be more at ease if I go alone."

She looked down at my hand. I pulled it away and stepped out of the car, made my way around the back of the car and across the tracks to where Murano was standing, tapping the screen of his phone.

"You updating your Facebook status?"

He glanced up and smiled uneasily. "Yo, Riley. What the . . . Last I heard, you were putting in hours as a bouncer at some hipster bar in Ybor."

"I'm a PI."

He put his phone in his pocket and offered his hand. "The hell are you doing here anyway?"

I shook his hand with my left. "Came to give a friend a ride." I pointed with my thumb over my shoulder. "What's the best way to Tampa?"

"You're better off finding a shelter." He nodded to the east. "Collins Elementary on Summerfield. You got maybe half an hour before it starts coming hard."

"What happened here?"

"Body. Or what's left of it. Guy was cut up into little pieces a couple days ago."

A cop poked his head out of the depot. "Detective, we're ready for you."

"You got an ID on the stiff?"

Murano shook his head. "Gotta go to work."

As I made my way back to the car, another feeder band swept in and almost blew me over. The rain pelted me like hail. When I finally got in the car, it was empty. Lisa Moon was gone.

Lisa had a tendency to disappear. She was, as they say, mercurial. We'd have a pleasant date, maybe drinks at a bar or a late-night dinner at the Mermaid Tavern or Esther's Cafe.

You'd think everything was roses. But when I drove her back to her place she wouldn't invite me up, or she'd insist on taking an Uber home. I wouldn't see her for weeks after that. Then she'd magically reappear acting as if we'd been hanging together the day before. Until she met Jack.

The wind and rain persisted. There was no sign of Lisa near the abandoned depot or up and down Riverview Drive. I worked my way toward the dense Brazilian pepper bushes and combed the area, but the ground was muddy from the rain and my feet sank deep in the muck. There was no trail or tracks anywhere. All I could think of was that she ran back toward the Fairfax.

I drove back east on Riverview Drive, told myself to forget Lisa Moon, head back to 75, find shelter. There was not a soul on the road. It was just the punishing rain and wind. As I drove past the Fairfax the weather turned like a switch—calm and dry. I stopped the car and backed up into the Fairfax, parked by the trailer. We'd left the door unlocked. But she wasn't there.

I didn't get it. She didn't deserve to live like this, in this mess, in this moldy, dilapidated can. She was better than this. She was better than Jack. I offered her a good life, even risked my own to come here and save her, and she ran away from me. Again.

I turned to the door and threw a punch at the wall. My fist went through the paneling like it was made of paper. I looked at my hand. The thin fresh scar that ran down from the ball of my thumb bled a few drops. I stormed back outside. The air was dead. The night had a dark, translucent quality. Gibsonton didn't look like Gibsonton. It looked fake, like a Hollywood set—a place made to look like Gibsonton.

I got in my car, started the engine, and tuned the radio to one of those all-news AM stations to get an update on the hurricane.

The monster storm was upon us. The cone was narrow and making landfall just north of Bradenton on a northeasterly direction. It was coming for Gibsonton.

I was out of time.

The wind picked up as I crisscrossed Gibsonton at random looking for Lisa. Road signs trembled, trees and bushes danced back and forth, debris dragged across the road, the rain fell in torrents, washing across the road in waves, then dying down, only to start again.

I passed the Fairfax for the fifth time and pulled up to the VFW building across the street. Certainly not a proper shelter, but it had to be better than staying in my car. I hurried to the front but the door was locked. I went around the back. Locked.

A transformer blew with a big fireball at the end of the block. Then everything went dark. That's when I saw the kid running across the field and into a small warehouse in the back of the property.

I dashed after him, pulled at the steel door. Three midgets, small people—whatever you call them—an older woman with long gray hair, a man with long pork-chop sideburns, and a younger one, blond, who was busy drying his hair with a towel. They stood around a large wooden crate with a lantern in the center.

"I'm sorry," I said. "I had nowhere else to go. I saw . . . I saw one of you run in here . . . and . . ." Behind them was a mountain of parts for a mechanical ride—flying elephants, cheap Dumbo imitations—and a trailer with a colorful sign for fried Twinkies. The walls were block and mortar, steel roof. "Seems like a safe place. I hope it's okay."

"It'll hold," the woman said. "You didn't happen to see Ricky or Jacques out there, did ya?"

I shook my head. The small person with the sideburns rubbed his forehead with the tips of his fingers. "I'm telling you, Gail, they must've gone with her."

"The girl ain't got no car, Kyle." The woman moved a small plastic chair up to the crate and sat. "We best just hope they didn't abscond and done left us here."

The younger small person with the blond hair nodded. He tossed the towel on the crate and climbed into one of the fiberglass elephant rides.

Kyle fiddled with a small transistor radio. Static. Voices, static. A seventies song. Motown. Then a voice came across loud and clear, rattling off statistics and the cost of previous hurricanes—Harvey, Katrina, Andrew.

"Whatever the storm does," Gail said, "bet you we don't see a dime of relief money."

"It's all a shell game," Kyle said.

"Look here." The woman leaned forward on her chair and squinted at me. "How come I ain't seen you around Gibsonton?"

"I'm from Tampa," I said. "I came down to help a friend, but I guess she found another ride."

"Yeah," Kyle said. "Welcome to the club."

"They kept sayin' the storm was headed to Sarasota," Gail put in. "Then it shifted at the last moment."

"But Gibsonton was always on the cone," Kyle said. "We just thought we'd be spared 'cause we always are."

"Not always," the woman sighed.

Behind her a sign with a colorful illustration of a giant Twinkie on a stick separated her from the bulk of the machinery. The place smelled of oil or lubricant. Outside the wind was howling. The rattle of the steel roof and debris came and went with each gust. I took a step back, sat on the ground, and leaned against the wheel of a trailer. I didn't want to think of Lisa Moon out there in this mess. It was my fault. It was a stupid idea. I shouldn't have come.

The blond small person sitting in the elephant shrieked with laughter. The woman glanced back at him, then at me, and touched the side of her head. "Foley's a little . . . you know . . ."

"Aren't we all?"

She laughed. "You're all right, Mister . . ."

"Riley. Wesley Riley."

She nodded. "Funny how the storm brought us together."

"You live down here full-time?"

"Born and raised," she said. "Met my husband Ricky when he came down for the Lobster Boy trial. He's a nephew of Harry Glenn Newman, world's smallest man. I was testifyin' against Christopher Wyant. I seen Mary talkin' to him 'bout shootin' Lobster Boy a couple weeks before he done it. Yeah, we're showfolks to the bone, ran quite a business for a time. Nine rides, two concessions, and half a dozen full-time workers, ain't that true, Kyle?"

Kyle stared at the ground and nodded, mumbled something about the financial crash of 2008.

"But we're gettin' back in the game. Tell'm, Kyle. Tell'm about the act."

The wind grew loud and ominous like a train rushing overhead. We fell silent and looked up at the steel roof shaking and rattling under the pressure of the storm.

"Kyle!" Gail broke our trance. "Tell'm."

Kyle's eyes went wide. He swallowed hard. "We have this new act with Jacques Couteau. A real famous performer.

Maybe you heard of him. Anyway, he's one hell of a talented knife thrower, and—"

"We been practicing all year," Gail interrupted. "Jacques and his gal Liz La Lune. She's a real pretty gal. Got real talent for show."

"It's built like a play," Kyle said. "We've got a whole drama. Foley here tries to steal Liz from Jacques and they start this back-and-forth dance, kind of like a jealous lover. So Jacques and Foley hate each other, but it's Liz who's playing them against each other. Jacques keeps throwing knifes—"

"No need to bore him with the details," Gail cut in again. "Point is, Liz and Foley keep runnin' round and Jacques keeps throwin' knives but keeps missin'. It's tragic and funny at the same time."

"We just signed with an outfit out of Chico, California," Kyle said.

"I'm gonna be in the circus!" Foley chirped from his perch on the elephant.

The freight-train sound shook my bones like a jackhammer. Then stopped. We looked at each other.

Foley hopped out of the elephant. "Is it over?"

"It's the eye," I said.

"*It's over!*" Foley sang. "*Over. Over. Over!*"

"No. It's just the eye," I said.

"You don't know that." Kyle was already at the door. Gail and Foley followed him out. Then me. We walked together to the middle of the field. The VFW post was standing but the roof had blown away. The whole field was littered with debris, a fallen oak. The plastic VFW sign had flown off and gotten snagged on the barbed-wire fence. There was no rain or wind, just this deep pressure. I yawned to pop my ears.

"Look!" Kyle pointed. Someone was running toward us. "Ricky!"

Ricky was tall and thin with long gray hair in a ponytail. He swooped up Gail and kissed her on the mouth.

"Did you find Jacques?" Kyle asked.

Ricky put Gail down and shook his head, then nodded toward the warehouse. "We better get inside before the storm comes around again."

We locked ourselves in the warehouse. Foley climbed back onto his ride and rocked back and forth in his perch while humming a song I didn't recognize. Gail wouldn't let go of Ricky's hand. They sat together and watched Kyle fiddle with the radio, but all he got was a station playing Mexican music. Then the train sound started again, faster and louder and harder. Felt like it was going to pull the roof and the lot of us out into the night sky.

When the noise finally settled into a steady drone, Ricky stood. "I have bad news. Jacques Couteau's dead."

Kyle jumped to his feet. "What?"

"Someone did a number on him with his own knives. Chopped him up into little bits."

"My God." Gail lowered her head. "Who . . . who would—"

"Liz!" Kyle snapped. "It had to be Liz."

"Cops found the body in the old train depot. Liz is with them. I think she's the one who told them."

"No . . ." I whispered. Jacques and Liz, Jack and Lisa. "He wasn't French," I said.

They looked at me.

"Well, he wasn't," I said. "And neither was Lisa."

"What're you talking about?" Ricky asked.

I looked down at the scar on my hand, the neat slice Jack's fancy throwing knife made when it caught his rib and buckled. He begged for mercy in perfect English. He told me he would go away. He wouldn't interfere. He swore again and again that he would leave. He would go to California and never look back, never contact Lisa—ever.

But that wasn't the point. Lisa had to do it on her own. She had to call me. She had to need me. Otherwise she would always be looking past me for Jack. And it was working. She did call. She needed my help. But then . . .

I walked out of the warehouse. It was pouring rain and the wind was blowing hard. I made my way across the dark field to the Fairfax. The trailers were torn, mangled, and crushed against each other.

I turned. Ricky and the small people were standing across the street as two cop cars cruised slowly down Riverview Drive and pulled into the entrance of the Fairfax. In the front seat of the second car I could make out Lisa Moon. She was crying, her face slightly distorted from pain or anger, her hand raised, pointing at me.

PART IV

Family Secrets

IT'S NOT LOCKED BECAUSE IT DON'T LOCK

BY LADEE HUBBARD

Lake Maggiore

Cedric and Gerard hadn't seen each other in five years, not since Gerard's mom got remarried and Gerard went to live with his father in Tallahassee. Then, out of the blue, just as Cedric was coming home from work one evening, the phone rang: it was Gerard calling to say he was back in town and wanted to know if they could get together. Cedric borrowed his sister-in-law's car and drove out to Gerard's mom's house to pick him up. When he got there a tall, heavy-set man was standing in the driveway. He didn't even recognize the man as Gerard until he started walking toward the car, pulled open the passenger-side door, plopped down next to him, and smiled.

"Look at you," Cedric said.

"Been a minute, huh?"

"What happened? You're like a foot taller than the last time I saw you."

"I grew up, man. That's all." Gerard smiled. "Thanks for giving me a ride."

"No problem. It's good to see you. Wish it was different circumstances."

Gerard reached around and fastened his seat belt and Cedric put the car in reverse and backed out of the driveway. They cruised at parade speed down 28th Avenue, rolling past hacienda-style houses with tile roofs and sprinklers shooting jets of water above well-manicured lawns.

"How's your aunt doing?" Cedric asked.

"Not good. She's in there with my mom now." Gerard nodded back toward the house. "Taking it pretty hard, you know. I think she feels like it's her fault."

"Well, you have my condolences. Really. I mean, I knew your cousin had problems. But still."

They wound alongside Lake Maggiore, views of the lake flashing behind the houses that lined the shore.

"She's not his real mom, did you know that? My mom had another sister but she died when he was a baby. He stayed with his daddy for a while but his daddy's crazy. They had a falling out. Aunt Darla's been keeping him since he was nine. She's the one who really raised him . . . She almost had a heart attack when she heard what happened to him."

"Damn. That's rough."

"Now she keeps saying how she thought he was getting better. You know, getting his life together. I think she feels bad she didn't do something, but I don't know what she could have done. It's like she thinks she should have seen it coming."

"Well, I imagine sometimes it's hard to see."

Cedric turned onto 27th and the car moved past New Beginnings Community Church.

"Wasn't that hard," Gerard said.

"What?"

"To see. Like you said, even *you* knew he had problems. My cousin always was a lot to deal with. Never made anything easy for himself or anybody else. Always been like that. Ever since we were kids. But he was still my cousin."

They reached 26th Avenue and Cedric put on his turn signal. He looked at Gerard, trying to find the boy he used to know. Gerard was only seventeen when he left. They'd played football together, been real good friends in high school, but this was the first time they'd actually talked to each other in years.

He switched gears. "Hey, you know what? It's good you called. Good you're coming out tonight. Sounds like you need a break. For real though. I know you have a lot going on with your family right now, but you should try to put it out of your mind for a little while." Cedric smiled. "Tony and Paulie are going to be there. I know they're really looking forward to seeing you."

"That's nice," Gerard said.

"A lot of people want to see you. Paulie said he would put the word out. Might be we could even get the whole team back together."

"What about Shaun?" Gerard asked. "He gonna be there?"

"Maybe. I don't know. Yeah, probably. Honestly, Gerard? Shaun and I . . . we're not as close as we used to be. Not like before. Don't really associate much anymore."

"No? Why's that?"

"Because he's crazy. Why do you think? You remember Shaun. Hasn't changed at all. Still acts like we're in high school. But I'm a grown man now. I got responsibilities, bills to pay. I don't have time for foolishness anymore. Everybody has to grow up sometime. One day he'll realize that too."

The light changed and they turned onto 9th Street. The car drove past a group of five children playing in a gravel-strewn driveway next to an old Ford truck. Across the street from them, a man in a robe stood behind his fence watering the grass in his yard as he smoked a cigarette, his robe fluttering around his shorts like a flag at half-mast.

"Last night she started talking about that robbery," Gerard said.

"What?"

"My aunt. You remember? Right before we graduated? That time my cousin got mugged? At least that's what he told my aunt. Someone beat the shit out of him, that's for sure. He wouldn't talk to the police and never properly explained what actually happened that night, so she just figured he must have been someplace he shouldn't have been, doing something he wasn't supposed to be doing. In her mind it was some crazy drug addict that did that, somebody high out of his mind. I mean, it had to be someone crazy, right? Doesn't make any sense beating someone up like that when he and his friend didn't have but forty dollars between them."

The car rumbled onto 22nd Avenue where the houses evaporated altogether, along with most of the trees. They were replaced by a gas station, a liquor store, and Atwater's Soul Food restaurant.

"Now she says she feels like he was never the same after that. She told me that for like a year after he wouldn't talk to nobody, and never even wanted to go outside after dark. He'd just go to work and then come home, eat dinner with her, and watch TV. Acting like he was scared all the time." Gerard shook his head. "Which is hard for me to picture. We didn't keep in touch after I left, but I remember my cousin. And he may have been a lot of things. But not scared."

The car turned onto 16th Street and they rolled past a man in beige pants and army boots sitting on a bus stop bench. He nodded as the car passed, then lifted a small bottle wrapped in a brown paper bag.

"She says it wasn't until a few months ago that he started acting like his old self again. Got his own place, a new job. Started going out with his friends again. And then this happens. Kind of makes you wonder if he didn't have a reason to be scared."

"You got to be careful out there, that's for sure," Cedric said. "Careful where you go, careful what you do. Make sure you know who you're talking to. Sometimes you got to watch what you say. Lot of knuckleheads out there, people looking for trouble. I mean in general. I don't really know what your cousin was into, so I can't speak on his specific situation."

"Someone strangled him," Gerard said. "In an alley, behind a dance hall. That was his specific situation."

They hit a red light and stopped next to the Blue Nile restaurant. Behind it was a brick building that had lost most of its front wall and stood carved open like an excavation site.

"Look, Gerard. What's up? You have something you want to say to me? Because I thought I was coming to see an old friend. Why are you bringing up something that happened five years ago? I mean, I'm sorry about your cousin. But I don't see what the two things have to do with each other."

A woman in a long red dress clutched a Bible to her chest as she strode past the black and charred remains of some of the buildings set ablaze during the riots. Gerard watched the woman make her way to the bus stop on the corner.

"You were there that night," Gerard said. "The night he got beat up like that."

"Yes, I was there. A lot of people were. Who told you? Cheryl?"

"My cousin did, right after it happened. I didn't understand what he was saying at the time. Didn't make sense to me, thinking about my friends doing something like that to my cousin. Thought it was like my mom said, that he didn't want people to know what he'd really been doing that night. I knew he hated Shaun and figured he was just trying to stir up some mess."

"It was five years ago, Gerard. We were kids. It was stupid

and I'm sorry it happened. But, like I said, I don't really see what it has to do with anything now."

"How come you never told me?"

"I don't know. It had already happened. I guess I didn't really see what good talking about it would do. We were about to graduate and then you were moving to Tallahassee. I felt stupid, just for having let myself get involved in something like that. And honestly? I think a part of me just assumed you knew."

Cedric shook his head and looked out at the restaurant across the street, where three teenage boys pounded their fists on the window of the kitchen. It slid open and another boy, plastic hairnet festooned to his skull, stuck his head out and passed them a large doggie bag full of leftovers.

"What did your cousin tell you?"

"He said y'all were having some kind of party at Tony's house. He said he wasn't doing nothing but walking down the street with a couple of his friends. And you and Shaun just started hassling them. Said it seemed like you just went berserk. Kicked the shit out of him while everybody else just stood around and watched."

"Yeah? That what he said? Because that's not exactly true." Cedric sighed. "Your cousin was provoking us. You know how your cousin was, know he used to provoke people all the time. He and his friends always strutting around in those crazy outfits, laughing all loud and talking shit. And we were all at Tony's celebrating because the school year was almost over and here he comes, walking down the street. Shaun made some joke about the way his ass swished when he walked, and he came back asking something like why Shaun spent so much time looking at it. People started laughing. Looked to me like your cousin enjoyed the attention because he just kept going.

Shaun warned him to stop but he wouldn't shut the fuck up. And now everybody was laughing at us. We had to do something, it was like he was giving us no choice."

Cedric looked out the window. "It was stupid. And I'm sorry about it, if that makes you feel better. I was sorry as soon as I woke up the next morning, soon as I realized what I had done. Over what? Some weirdo calling me a name? Saying something about me everybody already knew wasn't true? And here I am, about to graduate. Got my whole life ahead of me and I'm gonna risk blowing it like that?"

He shook his head. "I'll tell you the truth, Gerard. It's part of why I don't hang out with Shaun anymore. Because I learned from it. Realized I couldn't just be flying off the handle like that. Realized I had to know how to keep my cool, that I needed to be around people who kept cool too. Because if you think about it, the one who might have really gotten fucked up over it is *me*. My future. My chances in life. I mean I'm serious. I could have wound up in jail. Just for beating up some little freak."

Gerard stared out the window. A clean-looking kid in a white Camaro pulled into the parking lot of the restaurant. He watched the boy walk around and open the door for a pretty girl in a yellow tank top sulking in the passenger seat.

Cedric put the car back in drive. "I'm sorry it happened. But that was five years ago and, if nothing else, I learned from it. And, I don't know, when your cousin didn't press charges, I thought maybe he had learned from it too. Because it wasn't just me and Shaun acting foolish that night. Your cousin was not some innocent party. He provoked us. Was asking for it. And maybe you don't want to hear this right now but . . . truth? If you'd had been there that night, you would have been right there with me and Shaun. Because I know you. I mean, I remember how you were in high school. Know how mad you would have been if someone ever disrespected you like that. Just like I know that deep down you realize: a lot of the trouble your cousin had back then? He brought it on himself."

Gerard stayed quiet. The car continued down 16th Street where two elderly women in matching green dresses, gold lamé shoes, and leaf-shaped hats walked down the concrete steps of a small house, the thin breeze puffing their skirts into bell shapes, hems raised just enough so Gerard could see that their dark stockings were only knee-highs.

Gerard nodded. "My cousin always was hard. And like you said, he did have problems. You know how he came to live with my Aunt Darla? His daddy caught him trying on his mama's lipstick when he was nine. Come home from work and there's my cousin standing in front of the mirror in his bedroom with bright-red lipstick smeared all across his mouth. His daddy beat the shit out of him and kicked him out of the house. My cousin and I were real close back then, if you can believe it. Used to do everything together. I didn't even realize there was anything strange about him at the time. Because he didn't seem strange to me.

"When I asked him why he'd done that, he said he'd found it in the drawer and just wanted to know what her kisses felt like. Isn't that funny? I realize now he was probably lying about that, but you know what? At the time? I believed him. Somehow it made sense to me. I understood it and I didn't see why it was such a big deal. But then my aunt told some people at her church about it and somehow it got around at school. People started teasing him, calling him names, and laughing at him. And because we were always together, people started calling *me* names too. Got so bad I stopped wanting to do anything with him.

"Finally, I just couldn't take it anymore. Got tired of defending him, got tired of having to hear it. Told him I was embarrassed to be in public with him because he acted so weird all the time, when really he acted the same when we were alone at my house, and the stuff he used to do never really bothered me then. Truth is, I was scared. Scared of the way people made fun of him, scared people would start confusing him for me. And mostly I was scared because when he told me about kissing that mirror, I hadn't realized it was a big deal. Started wondering if maybe there was something wrong with me too, just for feeling like I understood it, for the fact that it didn't bother me the way it seemed to bother everybody else. It was like I got suspicious of my own understanding, the fact that, deep down, I never thought he was all that strange. I mean, not in a way that really mattered. And now when looking back on us in high school, I feel like I spent most of my time trying more than anything *not* to understand things. Didn't want to feel nothing because I was so worried what I felt might be wrong. I think that's really why I was so mad all the time. When people tried to explain to me why I needed to calm down, why I shouldn't be so upset or something wasn't a big deal, I would just look at them, suspicious. It's almost like I thought feeling something for other people was some kind of trick, because I believed there was something wrong with me and I didn't want other people to know."

In the rearview mirror, Cedric could still see the two old women passing slowly beneath a streetlight's glow.

"My cousin used to say he figured I stunted my own growth that way. One time he told me that, as much shit as he got from people just for walking down the street, the one he really felt sorry for was me, because at least he was being who he was. Said he thought it was pathetic how hard I tried to fit in with people like you and Shaun, that there was a beautiful person somewhere inside me but I had smothered it by being a coward. Used to say stuff like that to me all the time, and of course I didn't like it. Was provoking, just like you said. But now, when I look back at myself in high school, I figure he might have been telling the truth. That's how I know you're right. If someone had ever tried to disrespect me the way he did to you that night, I would have been right there with you. Except for one thing." Gerard reached into his jacket pocket and pulled out a gun. "He was my cousin."

"What are you doing?"

"That was my cousin. What the hell were you thinking disrespecting my family like that?"

"Wait a minute, Gerard—"

"You didn't have anything to do with what happened at that dance hall, did you? Someone jumped him that night—how do I know it wasn't you?"

"Me? No! Of course not. I don't go to places like that. I would never—"

"What about Shaun?"

"Shaun? I don't know about Shaun. I told you I don't have anything to do with him anymore."

"Well, maybe you do, maybe you don't. *Somebody* did it. Somebody got to pay for it. Might as well be you."

"But it wasn't me. I didn't have anything to do with what happened to him. And that thing at that party, that was five years ago. Doesn't have anything to do with now. Look at me, Gerard. I'm telling you I've changed."

"That's what I've been trying to explain to you. *I haven't.*" Gerard shook his head. "Why do you think I just told you all of that, about what my cousin used to say to me? I think he was right, I think I may have stunted my own growth somehow. Because I'm sitting here, listening to you talk about how you've changed, and how long ago that party was, and how I have no business being upset about it now. And I got to tell you: I don't understand a word of it."

"Don't do this, Gerard. Please—"

"I know. Pitiful, huh?"

They didn't even realize they had run a red light until the car braked suddenly and they lurched forward in unison. A station wagon roared through the intersection, the man in the driver's seat mouthing curses while two girls stared with their mouths curved into startled *Ohs!* and their palms pressed against the glass of the rear window. Cedric swerved to avoid hitting them and ran into a telephone pole. There was a loud crash and a hubcap popped off and rolled into the street. For a moment, the car sat stranded on the sidewalk, blanketed by a cloud of smoke kicked up by screeching brakes.

Cedric struggled to lift his head. He could feel blood gushing from his nose, spilling into his open mouth. When he opened his eyes, Gerard was still sitting next to him, a nasty gash on his forehead. There was blood running down the side of his face, spilling onto the front of his shirt. He looked like someone had just beaten the shit out of him. But he was still holding the gun.

"Now let's go see Shaun," Gerard said.

MARKED

BY GALE MASSEY

Pinellas Park

Callie stood at home plate in the first inning of the game, hoping for the right pitch, when she heard the crash. A breeze rustled the palm trees out past the left field fence. Overhead the sunset had turned the sky purple. The crowd in the bleachers fell silent waiting for the metal-against-metal screech to stop, but it went on so long that everyone knew it had been deadly. The dugout emptied onto the field, the players and coaches stood facing south where the train crossed Park Boulevard, even though that intersection was a quarter mile away and blocked from view by city hall and none of them could see a thing. Pinellas Park had been built after the railroad, and the tracks ran through the small town at a foolish angle. Callie rested the bat on her shoulder and scrunched up her face, but that thing people talk about, how you know in your gut someone close to you has died? That part never happened. After the game resumed the lights on the field came on, she swung at a fast ball, and was out. By the last inning her granddad had arrived to tell her the news.

It never dawned on her that her parents might've been in that car. They had said they wanted a few minutes alone and dropped her off at the field promising to be right back. It seemed they were always trying to get a few minutes alone, a thing she doesn't understand even now, two years later. The three of them were always happy enough, riding in the pickup with Callie squeezed between them, her father's arm stretched behind her back, playing with a lock of her mother's hair.

Burial expenses wiped out the equity on their small cinder-block house, so it went back to the bank. Her grand-dad, the town's widowed preacher, insisted on a four-foot-tall family headstone, had it installed beneath the ancient moss-draped oak at the grave of his long-dead wife, and bought two silk-lined mahogany caskets. Nothing less, he claimed, would serve the memory of his son. Callie saw the reasoning there, but when Granddad paid for three plots, one for each of her parents and one for himself, it bothered her. The old man ex-plained that when she grew up she'd have a husband, and when she died she'd have to be buried next to him, but it was a man and a situation Callie already knew would never exist.

On the day of the funeral the crowded church was swel-tering beneath the Florida sun. Halfway through delivering his son's eulogy, her granddad had a stroke that nearly killed him. He never walked again and soon his ability to speak van-ished. He went into the retirement home two blocks from the high school, and Callie went into a foster care group home. But in a town that was Little League crazy, the half-grown girl never got noticed by families looking to adopt.

The sudden upheaval in her life was a shock, though a well-meaning counselor at family services stepped in to teach her how to manage the anxiety that consumed her. The better help came from a large bottle of small blue pills that the house manager gave her at intervals throughout the day and when-ever she asked for another. The pills helped her breathe on bad days. On other days they kept her from biting her nails to the quick. The first year after the train wreck passed without lodging itself in her memory. She went through the motions of brushing her teeth and eating, but her mind was always at home plate, the bat resting on her shoulder, listening to the screeching metal.

With help from the pills two years crept by so slowly that her memory seemed like a movie about some other girl and some other family. After another year Callie couldn't trace herself back to a moment when she wasn't sliding toward panic. Approaching a window caused a small jolt of adrenaline to burst in her stomach. A door could leave her paralyzed. The house manager kept an eye on her, took her shopping sometimes at the Dollar Store at the strip mall in town just for the distraction of stocking up on household goods. Callie hated shopping. The store added dimension to the world when what she craved was something that would make it smaller. Shelf after shelf of canned and boxed food. Where did it all come from? Who had touched it? Had they washed their hands? Everyone knew about tampering, how it happened all the time.

Opening jars was the worst. Wondering what some stranger might have put in the applesauce or toothpaste. Anything could be tainted, especially products from the Dollar Store where the poor people shopped, yet the house manager refused to waste money across town at the more expensive Winn-Dixie. Callie stayed awake at night worrying that the food from supper had been contaminated by a disgruntled worker on a production line, amused at the thought of killing a stranger on the other side of the country. Callie took to slitting the tube to get the toothpaste out of the bottom. She'd use it a few times and throw it out, count herself lucky each time she survived. Eventually she stopped using it altogether because the counselor told her it was good to trust her intuition, and her intuition made her suspicious of Dollar Store toothpaste.

On the really bad days, when even four pills didn't help,

she used matches. She kept a pack with her because some days just holding the matchbook was enough, on other days the smell of sulfur was enough. On really, really bad days she had to feel the burn. The burn turned her mind white. It told her she was strong and had nothing to hide from because in the middle of a burn the only choice was to endure.

A girl at school had asked if she wanted to see a match burn twice and Callie had been intrigued. The girl struck the match, blew it out, and touched it to Callie's arm. She screamed as white light exploded behind her eyes.

The girl laughed and said, "Make your mark or the world will make it on you."

Callie saw her point. Right then she decided to make her own marks—a strip of burn scars down the inside of her arm.

The burn hit the back of her head first and wiped her mind clean. Nothing else existed while her head was lit up like that. The counselor noticed the scars. She made a note on Callie's chart and suggested she trade softball for basketball. The next day a new prescription showed up and was added to her morning medication. Callie studied the new pill. It was solid and harder to swallow and sometimes got lodged sideways in her throat and hurt until it dissolved.

Basketball was no more fun than softball. She couldn't run and dribble at the same time, she always got turned around on the floor and ran to the wrong net, but she was taller than the other girls and able to snag rebounds over their heads. The coach told her to plant herself under the net and stay there. It was a losing season and the coach cut her after the last game. The counselor told her sports weren't for everyone and signed her up for the Junior ROTC in the hope that she might develop responsibility and leadership skills, maybe start to see a future for herself beyond graduation.

Officer Sloan ran the Junior ROTC program at the high school. There was a rumor that he wrestled for money at the armory on Saturday nights, and she felt safer when he was around because no one was fool enough to start a fight in his presence. Halfway through the second semester he started taking the class to the shooting range to teach gun safety and get them some target practice.

The first time she held a gun she was surprised at its weight. The heft of it sent a charge up her arm all the way to the center of her stomach. The feeling didn't have a name, but as she stood there turning the gun over in her hand, she felt a shift inside.

Sloan came up behind her. "It feels good, right?"

It did feel good.

"The rules are simple. Keep the barrel aimed at the floor and never point it at anything you don't mean to destroy," he said.

He showed her how to open the cylinder and load the bullets. One by one she slid them into place, then flipped the cylinder closed. He took the gun and handed her earmuffs, pointed the pistol toward the target, and fired off a round.

She watched him, the twitch in his shoulder, the bullets shredding the paper target at the end of their lane.

"Now you," he said, and she reloaded.

He stepped behind her, adjusted her grip, and put his hand on the back of her right shoulder blade. She shuddered. It was the most human contact she'd had since sitting on her father's lap in church.

Sloan didn't notice. "You're going to feel the kick right here. Brace for it and pull the trigger."

When she fired, his hand caught the kick in her shoulder. The bullet tore a hole near the center of the target.

"I knew it," he said. "You're a natural."

He stepped back and she emptied the cylinder. It was like a wind sweeping through her bones. The gun was hot in her hand, her breath steady and even. Her spine straightened as though tempered by the strength of metal. Guns cracked all around her, up and down the firing lanes, and left an intoxicating smell in the air.

She got a part-time job at the range just to be near that noise, smell that smell. For the first time in her life she didn't mind waking early. One hour before school to empty the bins of shredded paper targets and sweep the lanes of used casings, saving the last ten minutes for practice. The rush from shredding a paper human was the medicine she needed most. Her first paycheck surprised her. She would have done it for free. She bought a necklace at the strip mall, a bullet on a chain that once she put on, she never took off again. Her enthusiasm pleased Sloan and earned her the honor of packing up the pistols and carrying them to the backseat of his apple-red truck each Friday after class ended.

Scared. She'd felt scared for as long as she could remember, but pulling that trigger made everything different. Holding a gun calmed her more than the pills, more than the breathing techniques the counselor had taught her, more than a match head on her skin. She didn't need to burn anymore and the counselor took that as a sign of progress. The weight of the gun, the smell, and the blast annihilated fear, squashed and contained it to a size she imagined small enough to fit inside the bullet she wore around her neck.

The bullet was a touchstone that she reached for each morning. A totem, a solid thing to hold onto when so much else seemed vague. She held it in her hand whenever she heard the train pass through town, remembering the terrible noise from the wreck, knowing it had been a curse for her parents to die with that noise all around them. She drew strength from the bullet on her way to school, as she walked down Park Boulevard past the Feed & Seed, the small white church with its high steeple, and the motel where the drunks sat on the curb so close she could smell the whiskey on their breath. The bullet gave her the strength to jog until the air smelled clean again. She touched it when she walked through the lunch room trying to find an empty table where she could eat her bag lunch alone, when she left the school grounds in the afternoon, and at night when she crawled in bed. Her fingers were wrapped around the bullet when she closed her eyes and the last pill entered her bloodstream, traveled to her brain, and allowed her mind to go dark for a few hours.

She was dreaming of her granddad when she woke on Friday morning. She knew he'd been in the army years ago, that he would be proud of her aim and the skill she had in handling a pistol. After class she loaded Sloan's truck with the gun cases. He'd parked behind a stand of palmetto bushes, which made it easy to hide while she slipped the smallest revolver from its case and stuffed it in her backpack.

Alone behind the gun range, she loaded the bullets she'd stolen from Sloan's truck. She spun the cylinder a few times, feeling the metal's satisfying clicks, snapped it closed. The weight of cold steel resting in her hands, the power she felt stirring in her gut. It made no sense how much she loved having this thing all to herself. She touched the bullet hanging around her neck, remembering her father's wedding band and how she would play with it on Sundays while listening to her granddad preach. The church was hot on those mornings.

Air-conditioning wasn't in the budget and the windows were too high up for a decent cross breeze, but it wasn't considered Christianly to complain. Before the heat pulled her into a stupefying sleep she would sit on her father's lap and play with his ring. His hands were big, the ring too small to slip over his knuckles, but she would try until her eyelids grew heavy.

She thought about waking up in church with her father's arm draped over her shoulder as she walked to the retirement home. The old man had aged fast and seemed to be caving in on himself more each week. After his stroke they kept him strapped in a wheelchair, his head bobbing, drool spilling on the pajamas he wore all the time. He never talked but moaned often and loudly. He was on the front porch when she arrived, watching an egret over by the oleanders stalk its supper. It stabbed a lizard and ran to the edge of the grass.

The pill she was supposed to have taken at lunch was still in her pocket. She popped it in her mouth and chewed it to make the calm come faster.

She showed him the bullet on its chain. He nodded and it seemed he understood. She wiped the drool off his chin with the blanket draped across his lap. She told him she'd brought a gun to show him, that it was inside her backpack.

He grabbed her hand and she was surprised at his strength. He knocked her hand against his sternum, mouthed the word *Here.*

"Yes," she said, "I have it here."

She told him how anytime she touched the bullet she felt better.

His hand dropped to his knee and waved like a dying fish, perturbed, uneasy. A squirrel came onto the porch, sniffing around for the peanuts the staff set out every afternoon. Callie hated squirrels, thought of them as rodents with fluffy tails. She kicked at it and it jumped into the grass.

"Me," he said.

"What?"

He grabbed her hand and placed it over his heart. "Right here."

A red truck pulled into the parking lot and she thought briefly of how almost everyone in town had a relative in this place.

It was the first time her granddad had touched her in years, but now she understood. She'd taken the gun for one reason, loaded it for one reason.

She slung her backpack over her shoulder and wheeled him back inside, through the dining hall where the staff was putting out fresh bibs and juice boxes, down a corridor of rooms with noisy televisions, past the aide at the medicine cart and the janitor mopping the tiled floor.

She got her granddad inside his room and locked the door.

The gun was wrapped in a hand towel inside her backpack. When she unwrapped it and showed it to him, his eyes turned bright. He mumbled some words that might've been a prayer. She took it as a sign. He was rocking back and forth. He was excited and so was she.

Someone tried to open the door and her granddad hushed. The handle jerked a few more times then stopped.

He tapped his chest and mumbled more things she couldn't understand.

Red lights hit the windowpane. Another ambulance, another resident, another old-timer with a stopped heart. He stared out the window briefly then looked back at her. She brought the pistol close to him. He reached for it and knocked it out of her hand.

It was disgusting having to put her hands on the floor under his bed, guessing at the kind of germs that were sticking to her palms. The pistol had slid next to some half-eaten toast and a ball of used tissue. She grabbed the gun and crawled out from under the bed.

She understood this was scary for him, yet she knew what was right. She had aim. She had this one skill. She was a natural. Then she had a moment of doubt. Maybe he didn't understand. Maybe waving his hand like that meant something else entirely. Maybe she had it all wrong.

A voice shouted from the hallway. Someone banged on the door.

There was always doubt before she swung at the ball, before she lit the match, doubt before swallowing a pill. She knew not to give in to doubt. She had intuition. When it came down to it, she had follow-through.

She put the pistol to her granddad's chest, took a deep breath.

The blast knocked her against the wall. She slid to the floor wondering how there'd been so much kick. Maybe she hadn't planted her feet. Maybe the gun had misfired.

The window was blown out. Her granddad still sat upright in his wheelchair, the floor and his lap covered in shattered glass.

Sloan stood outside the window, so close he could have stepped into the room, his mouth set in a hard line. He kept her gaze, kept the rifle pointed at her as the janitor swung open the door. Sloan lowered the gun and said, "The rules were easy, Callie."

The bullet, lodged somewhere in her lungs, spread a dull ache down each arm, up into her head, through her torso. The cold dead weight of the pistol sat in her hand and she tried to close her fingers around it. It was impossible to move, to reach for the bullet hanging around her neck. She heard the train approach, saw a mound of shredded paper targets in its path, endured the searing pain. Then, as the air of her final breath escaped through the hole in her chest, Callie saw herself standing at home plate, the bat resting on her shoulder, hoping for the right pitch.

PABLO ESCOBAR

BY YULY RESTREPO GARCÉS

Largo

On the Tuesday of my second week of eleventh grade in America, Nicole found me eating on the stairs by the soda machine and introduced herself. Several weeks later, I'd be clinging to the back of her sweater as we said goodbye for the last time before she got on a plane to somewhere in Oklahoma, but that Tuesday I was just scared to talk to her. The school floor plan dictated that at lunch students had to gather in a big rectangular space in the middle of the building, and there were few places where I could eat without being out for everyone to see me. The previous week, my cousin and her friends, who were in the tenth grade, had made fun of my ratty, faded Chuck Taylors and middle part and the fact that I was wearing jeans instead of a skirt and my general FOB-ness. After that, I stopped sitting with them at lunch. I wanted to talk to no one, especially some girl who couldn't speak Spanish.

Nicole put a lot of coins in the soda machine and pushed some buttons and took out two plastic bottles with what looked like blue liquid in them. She walked over to the stairs, where I was failing to take delicate bites out of what the cafeteria sign said was a sloppy joe sandwich. Nicole handed me one of the bottles.

The liquid inside was, indeed, electric blue, and the label said *Fruitopia*.

"You're in my French class," she said. "I don't think you've seen me because I sit in the back. You're always in the front."

Nicole was short and chubby, with brown hair that she had styled in stiff curls, and small, incandescent blue eyes. Even as my heart raced with the responsibility of answering, I thought of my mom, who would have loved the color of Nicole's eyes as she had been loving the blue eyes of people we encountered in the overly air-conditioned grocery stores of Largo since we'd come to America a few weeks earlier. Nicole was wearing cargo pants, a tight navy T-shirt, and crisp white sneakers that she later told me were K-Swiss, as if that was supposed to mean something to me. She'd soon be my first real American friend, and I'd lose her just as quickly.

"Thank you," I said. "We're in French together?"

"Yeah, I sit in the back. Might as well because I never know the answers to the questions. You know all the answers, but I can never hear you when you say them."

"I know a little French," I said. Before leaving Colombia, I had been in college for a semester, studying foreign languages. My French was good, but English was what I liked to study the most. Now it made me feel dumb when Americans spoke to me and I couldn't keep up, or I pronounced a word I knew well in a way they couldn't understand, so silence became my refuge.

Nicole opened her soda and drank three big gulps, pointing with her eyes at my bottle, asking me to do the same. The soda tasted like cotton candy. I thanked her again.

"Where are you from?" she asked. When I told her, she said she didn't know where Colombia was, but that some cousins on her mom's side were from the Virgin Islands.

"South America," I said. She nodded.

Outside, a blindingly bright and hot late-August day

raged, but any natural light that entered the building did so through a row of small windows high on the walls above student lockers. The spotless white floor, the blue lockers, the cafeteria tables—all had the sheen of fluorescent lighting.

"Did you know there was a shooting at this school a long time ago?"

"Someone shot in here?"

"Yeah, my dad told me two kids brought guns to school and started shooting people at lunch. I think the principal died or something. But it was a long time ago. Anyway, they were fucking crazy."

I kept trying in vain to eat daintily while Nicole told me tales of the place where I had come to live. She told me about the rainbow stain in the shape of the Virgin Mary that had surfaced on an office-building window in Clearwater, about a town full of psychics and mediums, about alligators in people's swimming pools and ghosts in an old hotel that was now a university building in Tampa. She said her dad was a huge nerd and liked to collect all kinds of things, including these bizarre Florida happenings. She said we could eat together from now on, and that I could go over to her house whenever I wanted.

That night, my mom and I dragged a beige leatherette sofa we had found on the curb of our street into our duplex. It was the only piece of furniture we now had, aside from a TV-dinner table my mom's boss had given her. The previous night, the aunt we had come to stay with had yelled at my mom for not doing anything around the house, and we'd had to leave and move into the apartment we had found only a few days earlier. We had planned to move into it after we got some furniture. My aunt didn't work and spent all day watching tennis matches on TV and sipping vodka out of an iced tea can and crying while showing me clothes she had worn when she was younger and thinner. I didn't know what to do with all that, so I pretended I had something else I needed to do. I didn't even have the guts to tell her she was being unfair to my mom, who worked two jobs. Eventually, I understood this was what made being friends with Nicole so easy. She expected nothing of me but what I could give her. She didn't even expect me to talk.

The morning I met Nicole, before I'd left for school, my mom had given me a piece of paper with the address of the apartment we were moving into. It was one street over from my aunt's place, a street full of duplexes just like ours, whitewashed, with overgrown front yards and chain-link fences and old cars parked outside. Ours was a 1975 Chrysler Cordoba a coworker had sold to my dad for five hundred dollars. It had no air-conditioning.

I told my mom about the Virgin on the window, and she said we could go see her when my dad felt better. I also told her about Nicole. She said she felt happy I had made a friend, and that it was good that she spoke English, and not Spanish, because my English would improve.

We dragged the sofa into the living room. Then I laid a sheet over it and claimed it as my bed for the night. My mom had already put some thick blankets and bed covers on the carpet of the master bedroom for my father, and that's where she'd sleep too. The three of us drank iced tea and ate a pizza my mom had bought at the grocery store and heated up in the oven. The pizza was topped with tiny, spicy meatballs, which I hated, but the iced tea was sweet and cold.

After dinner, I finished what was left of my homework and lay on the couch, ready to sleep. The neighborhood felt wholly quiet in a way I wasn't used to. At night, my neighborhood in Medellín was full of the sounds of passing cars and neighbors' conversations and music and, even after people had gone to sleep, the steady whistle of the night watchman. Now all I heard was the hum of the air conditioner and the fridge, which made the apartment feel emptier.

In the middle of the night, I went back to the bedroom to ask my parents if I could spend the night on the floor with them instead. The couch, it turned out, was riddled with ants.

My dad's accident happened three days before my aunt kicked us out and four days before I met Nicole. Only a couple of days after arriving in the States, he got a job at a recycling plant. He hadn't even had time to visit the beautiful Clearwater Beach my aunt kept telling us about before he went to work. The day of the accident, one of the plant's conveyer belts stopped working, and my dad, who had been a mechanic back home, offered to take a look at it. He climbed onto the belt, which was about two stories high, and removed stuff that had gotten it stuck, at which point, one of his coworkers, who didn't realize my dad was up there, turned on the belt, and my dad fell into the machine at the end of it. His whole body went through the grinder before anyone could help him. He broke no bones, but he bruised some ribs, and when my aunt brought him home from the ER, he looked like someone in one of the many stories I'd heard back home of people being given scopolamine and taken to various ATMs around the city until their bank accounts were empty and they didn't know who or where they were. His dark hair was gray with debris and his eyes were bloodshot and his shredded work pants barely covered his scraped-up legs. Upon seeing him, a flood of heat and tears rose in me, and he said, "Don't worry. Things can only get better now."

I'd never seen him so frail. Even on the day his brother was murdered on a street corner for helping as a messenger for one of Medellín's branches of the liberal party, at a time when being open about any kind of politics made you someone's deathly enemy, my dad had been sturdy as he grieved.

Now the sight of him told me the opposite of what his mouth said, and that's what I should have listened to. If I had, I could have protected myself at least, but now it was me, in high school after having attended college; my mom, working two housekeeping jobs that kept her away from home from six in the morning until ten at night; and my dad, trying to heal his bruised bones even as he slept on the floor. We shared an empty duplex, and we had no one but each other.

Or at least I thought so. My parents wanted me to think otherwise.

"How do you think we got this car?" my mom said. "And who helped us get this apartment?"

We were sitting on the carpet, sharing another pizza. This one had only vegetables on it, and I liked it much more than the one before.

"Well, it wasn't our family," I said.

"Don't say that," my dad chimed in. "If it weren't for your aunt, we wouldn't be here."

"Yes, but that's money you still owe," I said. "And how are you going to pay her now?"

A few days after we moved into the new place, Nicole asked if I wanted to go to her house after school, and when I said I couldn't because I had to go take care of my dad, she asked what was wrong. As best I could, I told her about my dad's accident and our empty apartment, about how we didn't have pots and pans for our kitchen and how all our money had gone into paying a deposit and first month's rent on the duplex.

"I'll come visit. I promise I won't stay long. I'll get out of your way if your dad isn't feeling well."

That afternoon she showed up at the duplex with two men. One was overweight, dark-haired, and pink-skinned, the other tall, lean, and blond. They both wore baggy jean shorts and black shirts, though the big man's shirt had bright-yellow and orange flames all around the bottom. Nicole's hair was in a high ponytail, and she wore olive-green shorts, a red crop top with spaghetti straps, and huge gold-hoop earrings.

"This is my dad," she said, pointing at neither of them. "I told him about you guys, and he wanted to help. God knows we have enough fucking stuff."

"Hi, I'm Jake," the tall, thin one said, shaking my hand. "This is my friend Cory. We brought you a mattress and some other things. The mattress is good, I promise."

"Okay, thank you," I said.

We all walked to the driveway, where a small silver trailer was hitched to a giant black pickup truck. Nicole's dad opened the trailer to reveal a mattress on which my parents would surely be able to sleep, and an array of chairs, tables, kitchen things, and even a twenty-inch TV.

"All that is for us?" I asked.

"We have an air mattress in there too," Nicole's dad said. "Nicole's going to inflate it for you. Listen, you have to tell your dad about worker's comp. He should have some money coming. Do you understand?"

My cheeks, already warm from the summer heat, grew warmer with tears. I nodded and thanked him. I could hardly speak from sobbing.

"Now girl," Nicole's dad said, "let's not turn this into some sappy moment. I know that whenever Nicole needs you, you're going to be there for her. This is purely selfish, okay?"

"Like everything else he does," Nicole said, and gave him a taunting grimace.

He didn't react, instead stepping into the trailer to push the mattress out. I thought that was so strange. I could count on one hand the number of times my parents had hit me, but saying something like that to them would have surely added to the count. And here was such a nice man doing kind things for us at her behest, and this was how she treated him. I stopped crying, mostly from feeling like I should behave extra obediently to make up for Nicole's brattiness. I decided to please Jake, to be as invisible as I could while they brought stuff inside. I let myself feel his kindness and the warmth of hopefulness.

In less than an hour, Jake and Cory had taken everything inside and dumped the ant-riddled sofa back on the curb. I went to get some iced tea, only to find them sitting on it when I got back. The thick August air made my hair stick to the back of my neck and my clothes feel heavy, as if I'd been swimming in them. The men's faces dripped with sweat, and they drank in big gulps and talked about other people they knew. Even though they looked so different, they seemed like the same person. They modeled each other the way children do their schoolmates. They both seemed good humored. They wore the same clothes and moved in the same jumpy, birdlike way. Both had patchy beards and wore chains that linked their wallets to their belt loops, but neither wore a belt. After they drank the tea, Jake took out a pack of Newports, gave one to Cory, and put one in his mouth. I could tell it was the same for everything else—they liked the same music, the same food and drink, the same women.

Nicole stood by the chain-link fence that separated our duplex from the one next to us, kicking the grass with her pristine sneakers and sending the gray sand that had been resting among the brown blades up in the air. This was how all the yards on our block looked—spotty, brown, equal parts grass and sand from the soft Florida soil.

"Why are you here and not there?" I asked Nicole.

"They don't want me there. They keep whispering shit to each other, so I might as well not fucking interrupt them. They're probably talking about my mom anyway. God, he's such an asshole."

"Your mom?"

"All they do is fight, and then they do shit like this—throw parties, volunteer at school, give away stuff. She hasn't even slept in their bedroom for months. She calls him an idiot for all the nerdy, creepy shit he's always been into that she knew about from the beginning. So then he brings Cory over and they stay up all night listening to music and watching their weird-ass movies at top volume and smoking weed. He yells at her for not letting him enjoy his life. They're both assholes."

"Don't they care? When you call them that?"

She shrugged. "My mom's threatening to move back to Oklahoma where my grandma lives. Anyway, if you ever want some weed, I can steal some of his."

Nicole's dad got up and crushed his cigarette stub, while Cory threw the iced tea cans in the garbage and shook off the ants that had managed to crawl up his legs. They both laughed softly at something one of them had said. I couldn't imagine Jake yelling at anyone, much less his wife.

"Does your mom work on Saturday?" Nicole's dad asked.

"No sir," I said.

"If she's going to take care of your dad, I'll take you and Nicole to the beach."

"If you let me drive, you wouldn't have to take us any-where," Nicole said.

"You're not going to drive this huge-ass truck, honey," he said.

"Can you even reach the pedals?" Cody said, and laughed until he was out of breath. I didn't know whether his face was flushed from the heat or the laughing.

"God, you two are such fucking dicks," Nicole said, then climbed into the truck and slammed the door.

Indian Rocks Beach was one of the hottest places I'd ever been. There was nowhere to hide from the light here. Even in the late afternoon, the air smelled of sulfuric heat, just as it had on the day we landed in Miami after our flight from home. On that day, as we drove up that lonely four-hour stretch of highway to Largo, to the apartment we'd be kicked out of a month later, I could see waves of heat rising up from the pavement. Before Jake brought me and Nicole to this beach, I had only been to Clearwater Beach once, when my aunt had brought me and my mom to eat ice cream by the pier. Mine was promptly stolen away by a seagull. That had been when my mom didn't have any job at all, and we all still pretended my aunt didn't have a drinking problem. We played the game of getting along, while I slept until noon every day and told myself repeatedly I liked this quietude, hoping the day would come when I'd believe it.

Now, Nicole, her dad, and I sat on towels on top of sand coarsened by millions upon millions of shells, and I wondered why the only people in the water were parents with their young children. Otherwise, we were surrounded by a few older people, often sitting in pairs on beach chairs and reading mag-azines or thick paperback novels. Nicole's dad said all of them lived in the condos that lined the shore behind us, their pastel facades a rainbow.

"Most of them only come in the colder months, so a lot of those apartments are empty now," he said. "It gets pretty cold up north. But some of them move down here for good. I'd like to own one of these myself when I get older."

I wondered how anyone could afford these beachfront properties in the first place, let alone as second, winter homes. I couldn't understand how I was here now, surrounded by luxuries I'd seen in movies, when only a few months ago our neighbors had pooled money so we could pay our power bill, so my mother could cook dinner and I didn't have to do my homework by candlelight. It was hard to understand how these places were within reach now, but I still had to wonder whether we'd make rent next month.

"I don't think I'll ever live in one of them," I said, pointing behind me.

"Sure you will," Jake said. "Anyone that comes to this country gets the same chance."

The air smelled like the older people who moved here wanted to be burned alive. Nicole had slathered on an oily lotion that smelled of coconut. She lay on her back with a towel covering her face, not saying much. Jake asked me a few questions about my family, like where in Colombia we were from and why we'd come to the States and how we'd ended up in Largo. There was so much I could have told him about those candlelit nights that came after the men who'd killed my uncle started directing their threats my dad's way, so his usual clients wouldn't do business with him anymore for fear of ending up like my uncle. I could have talked about the block parties the neighbors threw at Christmastime, about getting up at four in the morning to take the bus to the metro so I could be on campus in time for my six o'clock English class, and how sometimes I didn't have money for the fare and couldn't go. There was so much I wanted to tell him, so much that got stuck somewhere between my brain and my tongue, so I just said the things I knew how to say.

"Oh, Medellín!" Jake said. "Pablo Escobar, right?"

I smiled and nodded, holding in a sigh. He took a sip of his light beer and readjusted his black baseball hat. His brown eyes glinted in the inescapable sunlight. His face was covered in wheat-colored scraggly hairs that didn't do much to protect him from the sun. I hadn't seen him put on any sunscreen.

"I've read all about that guy," he said.

"He was a bad guy," I said.

"Oh, no doubt, but I've read all these articles online about all the money he stashed in all these places that people still haven't found. I mean, it's been like six years since he died, and no one has found it. That's awesome! But that shoot-out where he died was crazy, right?" He slapped his thigh. "The photo of all the soldiers posing with his corpse on that rooftop—that's hard core. I'm pretty sure I have it somewhere at home if you want to take a look at it."

I'd seen the picture, of course, and I didn't feel I ever needed to again, but I nodded. I knew he meant well. He was just trying to connect with me in a way his daughter didn't feel the need to. I remembered my mom's tearful gratitude upon coming home and finding the apartment full of things that made it look like a place where real people lived, and the note she had me write for Nicole's dad in my best English. He'd been kind to me, and it felt easy to be nice to him.

That's how I found myself at Nicole's house that evening, standing in the room where her dad kept all his memorabilia. As Jake went through drawers and piles of paper, Nicole plopped down on a reclining chair in front of the TV. Her skin still glistened with the stuff she'd put on at the beach, and her cheeks and the bridge of her round nose had turned pink as cotton candy. She was still wearing sunglasses, even though no natural light entered the room through the black curtains over the window. The walls were covered in posters for what he explained were cult horror movies—movies with titles like *Blood and Lace* and *Brain Damage* and *Kill, Baby, Kill!* There were also posters for movies I did know, like *Fight Club* and *Pulp Fiction*, and framed newspaper clippings of bizarre stories of living dolls and people being swallowed by sinkholes. Enormous speakers accompanied the enormous TV, and in a corner stood a small desk strewn with papers and action figures and guitar picks and DVD cases. The word that came to me while standing in the middle of the room as Jake frantically looked for the Pablo photograph was *reblujo*, which is what my mom called the small room where we used to keep junk back in Medellín. Here, even the carpet served as a resting place for guitars and exercise weights and junk food packages and soda cans.

"Can you hurry the fuck up?" Nicole said. "I want to get this gunk off of me before dinner."

"I swear I have that photo in here somewhere. Your mom must have hid it."

"Why would she do that? She doesn't set foot in this pigsty. You see how clean the rest of the house is, don't you, Vicky? That's because Mom cleans it."

I said nothing, but it was true. The rest of the house was spotless. It was all beige walls and pictures of palm trees and ocean sunsets and shiny glass surfaces and spotless white tile. The living room had a beige sofa, but I could tell it was real leather, and not an ant in sight.

"You know what? Fuck it," Jake said, throwing papers on the carpet and pointing a slender finger at me. "You stay for dinner. Call your mom. Change into some of Nicole's clothes. I'll drive you home later. I'll look for the photo in the meantime."

We left him rummaging through the junk in his room, huffing and throwing things on the carpet.

Nicole's mom found me and her daughter on the beige sofa, going through the family album. It contained picture after picture of a small, chubby Nicole holding kittens and blowing out the candles of her birthday cakes and standing next to Mickey Mouse. My parents had only brought a handful of family photos with them, of my grandparents and uncles and aunts, as well as one picture of their wedding and one of my first communion.

Nicole's mom, who introduced herself as Carmen, appeared in a few pictures in their album, wearing shoulder pads and hairspray, her lips fuchsia, just like my mom looked when I was a child. Now, as she sat across from us, she wore green scrubs and black chunky shoes, and her dark hair was up in a high, curly bun. Nicole was her spitting image, down to the only dimple that formed on the right side of her face when she smiled. As Carmen examined me, her shoulders slackened and a wide grin filled her cheeks. Nicole had lent me a pair of denim shorts that didn't quite hug my hips, and a large white T-shirt with the word *NASCAR* in big block letters.

"You girls having a sleepover?" Carmen asked. Her voice sounded salty to me, like the roar of the waves on the sea.

"Oh no," I said. "No, just dinner."

"We ordered pizza," Nicole said. "Jake's on one of his rants about a stupid photo. He just really needs her to see it."

"Oh, it's okay," I said.

"I know," Nicole said.

"We know," Carmen said. "Don't worry, honey. We'll eat dinner, and I'll drive you straight home. Sorry he's holding you hostage. Did you call your parents?"

I nodded. I didn't understand the word *hostage*, but I memorized the sound of it so I could look it up in my dictionary at home.

Carmen got up slowly and sighed while undoing her hair tie. The curls flopped down in one clump. She dug around in her purse and left a bill on the coffee table.

"I'm going to get changed before dinner," she said. "You be on the lookout for the pizza."

What followed was an hour-long screaming match behind the closed door of Jake's memorabilia room, during which the sausage pizza Nicole had ordered got colder and colder. I couldn't hear most of what they said after Nicole turned on the TV to a music video channel that people called to request their favorite video. I could hear pointed accusations like, "What is wrong with you?" but most of it was muffled or drowned out by the volume of the television and Nicole calling the number that scrolled at the bottom of the screen to request "You Make Me Sick" by P!nk over and over, using what she proudly announced was her dad's credit card number. Even though I couldn't hear most of the row, it reminded me of the last few months at home, when my parents argued over money they didn't have for bills they couldn't pay.

When Nicole's parents came out, Carmen was still wearing the scrubs and her hair was still tangled, but now her cheeks were flushed and her blue eyes glinted with a giddiness I hadn't seen before. Jake looked as collected as ever and, during our cold-pizza-and-orange-soda dinner, didn't mention a single word about the Pablo photograph. When he apologized for making me come over, I stopped bracing myself for another fight. Both were now in full couple mode, asking questions about my dad's health and my mom's two jobs, and because I didn't know the word *housekeeping* yet, I mentioned the things my mom cleaned instead: floors, windows, toilets.

My mom didn't work her second job on Saturday and Sunday afternoons, so one late-October Saturday we went to see the Virgin on the window. My mom's boss had written directions on a piece of paper, and I read them to her from the passenger seat of the Cordoba, while my dad's long legs cramped in the back. My parents wanted to go pay a promise they'd made to the Virgin of Chiquinquirá on behalf of our safe passage and transition to a new country. They still hoped to make it back to Medellín to pay the promise for real, but now that my dad could move around more or less normally again, this would do.

I would never tell my parents this, because their response would have been that God manifests in many forms, but I found the shrine unimpressive. The building where the Virgin had appeared was by the side of a highway, unceremoniously next to a Toyota dealership. The image of the Virgin itself looked like an oil slick that had spread over a couple of large mirrored windowpanes of what we were told used to be an office building. It was an outline of what could be the Virgin but also almost anything else, or nothing at all. In front of the window, someone had installed a life-size wooden crucifixion, in front of which was a church kneeler. Before the statue were countless votive candles and rosaries. People stood around or sat in white plastic chairs and prayed in the choking heat of fall.

A man who introduced himself as Guadalupe told us the image had appeared four years earlier, just before Christmas, and that was why so many people believed it was a miracle. He was short and wore brown slacks and a navy button-up, and he said he came to pray every Saturday. On seeing the slickness of his forehead, which he wiped with a white handkerchief, I wondered if he dressed the same way every time he came to spend a scorching afternoon with the Virgin. He offered my dad a chair close to the Jesus statue after my dad told him the story of his work accident.

"I should be dead," my dad said. "When that machine was grinding me, I felt like my organs were just going to burst out of my body. All I could think was that I'd brought my family all the way here just to abandon them."

"But here you are, standing after all of that," Guadalupe said.

"Yes, and I can walk and move. It hurts, but I can do it."

"That's a miracle," my mom said.

They sat together and prayed a rosary while I stayed silent, wondering what would have happened to my mom and me if my dad had died. Would we have stayed, alone in a new country where we were afraid to answer the phone for fear the caller would speak only English? Would we have gone back home and begged one of our relatives to take us in while we figured out what the rest of our lives would become without him? And what would our lives become now?

When we opened the door of our apartment, it was evening and the phone was ringing, but we didn't answer it. It rang and rang, until I got a look from my mom that had started to become familiar in this new life, which begged me to speak on their behalf to whomever they couldn't understand and couldn't understand them.

I recognized Nicole's voice through the receiver, but not

what she said. She was yelling rapidly, and the words sounded like they were reaching me from the other side of an ocean.

"What happened?" I asked a couple of times, but it was useless.

She yelled and cried, and the only word I understood was "Help!"

We drove to her house. The car still smelled of the remnants of our McDonald's dinner, which we had shared with Guadalupe. My parents didn't like the food, but it was cheap, and the air-conditioning inside offered relief from the heat. I loved it and had gleefully eaten my oily apple pie on the ride home. Now the smell made my stomach turn when I thought of Nicole's ragged voice. I wasn't even sure I could point my mom to her house without getting lost.

When we arrived at her street, the car got flooded with waves of blue and red light. We parked by the corner, where police cruisers and vans didn't obstruct the way, but as I ran toward her house, my parents yelling after me, cops standing around chatting to each other and looking at their watches and lazily shooing away the small crowd that was starting to gather behind the yellow tape that cordoned off Nicole's house, I felt as if I were the only one with any sense of urgency. That was until I saw Nicole, and she saw me and started running to me, her face a mask made of garish red and blue light, yelling, "He killed her! He killed her! He killed her!" and in that moment I remembered that earlier at McDonald's we'd seen a very old man making his slow way to the counter with the aid of a walker, and that having picked up his food, he couldn't maneuver his way to a table, and that my dad had said to me to go give him a hand, and having felt shy, I'd said no, so he'd gotten up himself and helped the old man in his own slow way. I thought of this as Nicole extended her arms to me, and I understood she had no one else, and that was why she'd called me, and she didn't have to tell me the whole story for me to now understand what she had said on the phone, which was that her dad had killed her mom and now she was all alone. I understood that when Jake had said that I'd be there for Nicole someday, that his help to us had been purely selfish; he'd meant it not in the way of self-deprecation, but in the way of a payback he expected me to give someday. Well, that day had come, and as the steam of Nicole's breath gathered on the skin of my neck when I took her in my embrace, I knew it was time to pay back the things America had given us.

WINGS BEATING

BY ELIOT SCHREFER

Safety Harbor

I guess I should have figured a Florida vacation would have lots of cars in it. This trip has been red arrows, four-way stops, ogling the rare pedestrian, hailing a car on this app or that, or waiting for a crusty cab with a crustier driver. How much of a life around here is spent wallowing in seats, hands at ten and two or a pinkie at six, waiting for a light to tell you when it's time to act?

I'm driving around all the time in Maryland too, don't get me wrong. On Darren weeks I'm chauffeuring him plenty. Violin lessons or swim practice or trips to the mall food court with his girlfriends. Darren's a busy kid—the only thirteen-year-old I know who uses his calendar app—but driving with him back home means not having to talk. Now we're on vacation so we're pressed in the back of these hired cars, not me in front and him on his phone, but right next to each other, shoulder to shoulder, like we're sweethearts on a date. Like we're me and his mom, back before the split.

We're done with the sightseeing part of the vacation and onto the spa stay, the whole point of this trip. I'm no spa guy, but I was the third-place-out-of-three winner of an episode of *Guess It Now*, and this spa trip was my prize. I thought Darren and I could bond a little. Maybe we can laugh about it.

That's why we're in the back of a car whose upholstery smells like nightclub cologne, driving down the main street of this town called Safety Harbor, even though there's no ships here. Pretty safe though!

"Nearly there, kid," I say. "The glamorous resort and spa."

Darren puts his phone away—he's pretty good about that stuff, not an addict like most of them—and casts his liquid staring attention toward the spa. I guess it's the same place as the cutaway graphic on the game show: curved brick drive, blue rectangle of a pool behind the front windows, a restaurant that looks like the conservatory from Clue. There's something a little seedy about all of it too, which I definitely didn't expect. Hard to put my finger on. There's probably microscopic grime between all the tiles.

Valet boys in polo shirts lounge in front. One says, "Good afternoon, sir," when I pass. It's in this put-out way, though, like his mom just made him say it.

The other boys look at Darren, with his skinny jeans and gay or at least rainbow-spectrum-y designer eyeglasses, and I can feel the smirks they're all hiding, each and every one.

I don't know, maybe I thought the game show would have called ahead, said, *Hey, a prize winner's coming in to stay for a while, give him a congrats when he gets there*, and Darren could have had a moment of being proud of his dad, but I guess we're just like any other guests, because the lady behind the counter says, *Enjoy your two nights with us*, as she gestures me and Darren toward our room.

The hallway's covered in aggressively ugly carpet, a blue-green run through by ship's wheels and nautical rope. It saps the sound from our feet and our luggage wheels.

The room is perfectly clean. It's also perfectly stale, like a mock-up that was never meant to be lived in. While we slot our clothes into drawers the window air-conditioning unit rattles and chugs, goes quiet, rattles and chugs, goes quiet. I open the blinds, see the license plates of the cars parked right in front, the gas station on the far side, and close the blinds again.

It's a third-place-winner sort of joint, I guess.

Darren's messaging on his phone for a while. When the air conditioner's off, I can actually hear the sound of his thumbs on glass. I wonder, not for the first time, if he's cruising nearby guys. A little young, sure, but I'd have taken up any chance to have sex at his age, though willing girls are harder to find and I didn't have apps or anything.

It's not like he's come out to me, but I'm operating on the assumption that my son is gay until proven otherwise. I work with three gay dudes—maybe four, actually—and I find it hard to keep up with their fast and mocking conversations, but they're good guys. My son has their same armoring wit, the same tendency to check his hair, the same examined life.

Darren looks up from his phone and asks if I want to go for a walk. My son has made a request that involves spending time with me. I try to play it cool—but yes, I would like to go for a walk!

We haven't said much during our days working on our sunburns on Clearwater Beach. We don't ever talk much, to be honest, but I think that's what we both want. At least I know it's what *I* want, or at least it's the only way I know how to be. Darren, though—when he's with his mother he can't shut up. The number of TV shows they manage to watch and then discuss, it makes me wonder if he's ever sleeping when he's in his bedroom with the door closed.

There's an old pier right near the spa, and we walk along its curving and pitched wood. The constant sea air's made the surface waxy. Our sneakers tilt and squeak. At the end of the pier is a fisherman, a young guy with a University of Florida

T-shirt who I figure is plucking fish out of their water for kicks and not for food. He doesn't catch anything in front of us, thank God, Darren would not be into that, but I can feel my kid getting withdrawn as he smells the blood and scales.

Darren dutifully plucks up any scraps of loose fishing fila-ment we come across, balls them into his pockets. He doesn't want them flying into the sea and garroting mermaids or whatever he's worried about. He doesn't want to see things that aren't even human get hurt. He's an absurdly sweet kid, my son.

Amelia called me a week ago, saying Darren had been moody until he'd finally explained to her that I'd said it didn't matter if he was gay, or if he was green-skinned or ate babies or was a terrorist. Did that seem like the right way to talk to him about that? she wondered. I told her that I was sure I didn't put it that way, and if I did it was a joke because I was nervous because I love the kid so much. Of course I don't think being gay is the same thing as being a terrorist, but how am I supposed to find the words to tell Darren that? And now it's like we're never allowed to discuss the topic ever again.

I stop to talk to this nice woman in a tight top about where she's from and whether she knows good places to eat near here, and when I look up Darren's gotten away from me and he's almost back at the spa. He's a fast kid, his skinny legs made twitchy by all the swimming. I say goodbye to the lady, she was probably too young for me to be flirting with anyway, and catch up to my kid.

He's at the entrance, where there's this two-lane road clogged with glossy cars pumping out exhaust while they wait for the four-way stop to clear. Something's caught Darren's attention, but I can't tell what. On the other side of the road is nothing special, just a six-story apartment complex that's under construction. The earth around it is ripped and raw, and the apartments aren't finished or anything. It seems like a nice enough place to live, though. I'd take it.

Darren looks upset, and I get worried that all the dried fish guts we saw on the pier are going to make this spa stay go blammo. I'm sure he'd be telling his mom just what was the matter, but I don't know how to get him talking. I like everything he says to me, I just don't have a lot to say back, that's all. I scratch at the sweaty small of my back. "Something wrong?" I finally try.

"Nothing, Dad," he says. But I know there's something. It would be a bummer if your view got blocked by that new building, but I can't see why he'd get upset about that.

He's looking toward the spa, like he's ready to go back and chill in the room, but I focus on where he was looking before, and see there's an egret, a white spindly thing, pretty and harmless unless you're a fish. It's fluttering beside a stopped tractor, beating its wings uselessly against the side of the machine. It's only going to hurt itself. That tractor's not going anywhere until the crew returns on Monday.

What does a bird have against a tractor?

We have nothing to do with ourselves anyway—I'm at a getaway spa with my kid, and the awkwardness is hitting me more and more hard core—so we wander into the construction site. We poke around the boundary of the scalloped orange tape, check out the derelict backhoes and the homes without doors as we make our way to the bird. If you don't count the line of stopped cars or the egret or the ladies in white jeans going to the Starbucks on the corner, we're on our own. Eventually Darren and I make it to where we both know we're heading: as close as we can get to the tractor and the egret.

The bird goes all still when we get near, like it's trying to camouflage itself into the tractor. It seems to me that something spindly like an egret should fly away if a couple of humans approach. But it doesn't, and the wrongness of that leaves me fluttery. Darren, too, he gets this posture like, *Let's leave, Dad*, but he doesn't say any words, he just folds his arms over his slight chest and stares at the bird.

Look, I'm not a knucklehead, I had enough smarts to get onto that trivia show in the first place. I put it all together quick enough: new construction, maybe getting ready to show a model apartment to prospective clients, first-time landscaping around the building, someone knocked down the bird's tree or whatever, and its nest and its eggs or—God, little birds?—are gone now, but it's still fighting the tractor, like it can get the babies back. Maybe the dead birds are still under?

"All right, Darren, let's not bother the bird anymore."

"What do you think happened?"

"I don't know, but we've upset it, look."

"I don't think we upset it," Darren says quietly. "It was already upset when we were back across the street."

"Okay, but it's not going to calm down with us around. Come on, let's check out the pool."

I walk away, but Darren doesn't move. He's like a kid in a horror movie sometimes, his attention gets so focused that all other things fall away.

"Can we help it?"

"I don't think so," I say. "Whatever it's upset about is over now."

"Poor egret," he says in a whining way that makes me worry about how guys treat him at school. But he's always tight with the girls in his violin section, chatting away, and I bet they'd all be making friendship bracelets for this egret right now. I decide my kid's life is fine. In general, at least. For the next two days, I'm not as sure.

"You hungry?" I ask.

He shakes his head. I don't need to look to know that his eyes are wet. "Okay, we can just stand here and look at the bird, if that's what you want."

That's what we do. Cars are going by, sweat is dripping down my back, more ladies in white jeans are going into the Starbucks, and the egret is still freaked out, but not about us, and I wonder how long it's been there, fighting this metal thing, and it's making me sad too, even though my emotions are cinder blocks, so I go and try to investigate, like maybe if it can show me the broken eggshells the bird will feel better, but it flutters its wings at me, with its beak open, and that's when Darren says, "We can go check out the pool, Dad," so we head back to the spa.

While we walk I ruffle the hair at the back of his neck. It's limp and wet. I know he's gotten sad. He and his mother have always had plenty of melancholy in them, and I've never been able to do much about it for either one. They're just not sturdy, but my own dad made me be sturdy above all else and I've come to realize that sturdy isn't an especially healthy thing for a person to be.

"Maybe there's chicken fingers at the spa restaurant," I say.

No reaction to that one. He's always loved chicken fingers. But thirteen is different from twelve.

The valet kid welcomes us back in that same go-tell-Aunt-Bertha-thank-you tone. By the time we're at the indoor pool and steam room, my sweat has chilled.

The pool was probably something to behold back in 1980. It's hidden away from any natural light, occasional tiles darkened like age spots. An old lady in a bathing cap is doing slow laps, and two more are sitting on chaise longues around one of the little tables with pebbled-glass tops. The ceiling is dentist-office low.

"Nice, huh?" I say.

The kid's staring at a landscape with ceramic vases painted on it, which makes it look like we're in a low-res Greece or maybe Rome or something. He taps the fakey-jake sky and looks back at me smiling, like he's finally figured out the answer to some frustrating question.

We lie on our striped towels in the chill AC around the warm pool, and take turns diving in. He keeps his T-shirt on, like I'd have done at thirteen. I display my padded hairy belly to the world, then we go back to the room and put the TV on and drop into our phones. Someone can't figure out the software licenses in accounting, but otherwise everything at work seems to be going along fine without me. Amelia asks how Darren's getting along and I text her back a pic of him staring at his phone on his drooping hotel bed, and it all feels nice, like we're still married. I compose and delete a few texts to her, then finally put the phone down to stop myself from sending any of them.

I say it's time for dinner, and Darren doesn't change out of his T-shirt, so I tell him it's a special occasion. I'm grateful I don't have to explain that I want the game-show prize to be something special. He puts on a button-down shirt, pleated khakis, and a clip-on tie—it's a bit much but also pretty damn sweet.

We go tripping along the nautical hallway, my kid's loafers—loafers!—squeaking on the plush plastic-y fibers. When we get to the restaurant there's a printout taped to the window, seventy-two-point Calibri telling us it's closed for a private event.

Kid and I peer in anyway. He's on his tiptoes to see what's going on, bringing his white athletic-socked heels right out of the backs of his loafers. At first I think it might be a wedding, but then I see that it's probably a work event. There's an easel with some poster board I can't make out through the foggy glass.

I'm not the kind to go places I'm not wanted, so I bring Darren to the host desk and ask where the spa's other restaurants are. The lady explains that there's just the one, and sorry it's closed for a party, someone should have told me. I ask what else is within walking distance and she explains that there's nothing unless we want to get a sandwich from the Starbucks. That's when I start getting really mad, but Darren's there so I swallow it all down. He heard enough of my yelling back when I was married to his mom.

We stand in the hallway and I pull out my phone, but just looking at the car apps, imagining sitting in the back of a Camry in traffic, pits my stomach. I don't want to get back on the highway, don't want to wait at lights and pass three Applebee's on the way to what other chain restaurant we've chosen. I put the phone away. "Come on, we're going in," I say to Darren, and before he can protest I've pushed through the doors and gone into the private event.

"Whoa, Dad," he says under his breath as we step to one side, into the shadows. I crashed enough weddings back in my crazier days to know that you stay as still as possible until you've picked your strategy.

Looks like the event has been underway for a while already—maybe it's technically a lunch?—and the conversation is drunken, the buffet mostly picked over. There's plenty of waxy little cheese cubes, though, and some raw broccoli, and, no way, what looks like chicken fingers! The placard is in

French, but I know a chicken finger when I see one. Darren can eat around the creamy blue cheese center.

I tell him to wait at the quiet end of the buffet while I grab some plates, since that'll bring me close to the nearest clot of drunk office-party guys—this office does seem to be all guys, at least the ones who've stayed this late. I nod to four hair-wave polo-shirt bros with their napkin-wrapped beers, like to say, *Hey, office stuff, that work we all do, crazy, amiright?*

I get four nods back, then return to my kid with the two plates, their porcelain scuffed gray from innumerable meals. Feeling the office bros' eyes on the back of my head, I hand Darren one and ask him if he doesn't want to make up his own dinner and has he seen the chicken fingers yet? I'm hyper aware of these guys' focus, am sure they're passing around theories about us, because they're in that late-party zone where no one has anything to talk about but they're intimate and cheerful and a topic you've discovered together is proof of how amazingly everyone gets along, them against the world. Them against me and my kid. Potentially. I dunno where this is all going to go.

We get our food and then find an empty table where I can move enough smudgy wineglasses and napkins to one side so that we can eat together. Darren's laying into his chicken fingers and I'm eyeing the bucket with the open wine bottles and we're just being peaceful and companionable until I sense those guys nearby.

"Hey, are you two with—" Here they say the name of their company, which I honestly can't remember, but it was one of those full-name-of-a-hometown-guy kind of small-fry investment joints.

"Nope," I say, keeping my eyes on my plate.

Darren keeps his eyes furiously on his food too, but in

a maybe overdramatic way, like we're in a black-and-white movie avoiding Nazis.

"We were thinking this little guy could be a new junior analyst or something." It's the same bro speaking, and he's probably the one drunk or naturally aggressive enough to make this confrontation happen. Not that I think they're going to start an actual fight—they just want to make us feel shitty for a while so they can feel un-shitty together. I get it. I've done it before.

I look right into them. "Look, guys, we're just trying to have dinner here. We're not causing any trouble."

They make side-eye at one another, and that's how I know I've taken the wrong tack. Now I've turned from a foreign adventurer to a freeloader taking handouts. I could have explained that the spa rented out its restaurant without thinking about its guests, and that's why I'm here eating food they don't want anymore anyway, but I don't feel like I owe these bros any explanations.

"Guess you didn't see the sign," lead bro says. "This is a private party."

"We're not doing any harm," Darren mumbles.

I raise an eyebrow at him. He just said that? My kid?

"What did you say?" lead bro huffs.

"We're minding our own business," Darren says. "You should try it." He takes a preposterously large bite of chicken finger and starts chewing.

Maybe it's called cordon bleu, this chicken?

"*We're just thinding our own thisness,*" lead bro says, with an extravagant lisp. "Well, this is a private party, and you're not on the list, so you being here is our business, faggot."

My world clanks and drops. Blood buzzes through my ears.

"They're not causing any trouble, man, just let it go," says one of the other bros. They suddenly come into focus, a trio of pastels—pink, green, and blue—behind lead bro's orange. One of their hands is on lead bro's shoulder.

"They're not done ramming themselves down our throat on every TV show, now they're coming to our parties and eating our fucking food."

For the sake of Darren, I will myself motionless despite the rage pushing my limbs to move and fight. Do these douchebags think we're together? Me and my thirteen-year-old kid? Whatever version of the truth lead bro is thinking, it's not working for me. I push back hard from the table, enough to send my chair clattering to the floor. A couple of other guys in blazers look over, and go back to their conversation.

Pastel-blue bro picks up the chair. Maybe this is going to work out fine.

Lead bro puts down his beer and rubs his knuckles. Maybe this is not going to work out fine.

I've been in my share of fights before, and the whipsmack of this lifetime-achievement prize trip being so sucky has definitely given me the urge to connect my fist with something that'll scream back, but as I start to do my chest-forward-bumping-the-air toward lead bro, I catch a glimpse of Darren and he's got this look on his face—not scared, exactly, but more tired, like he'd give anything to be surprised by what's about to happen.

If I'm a good dad, my priority should be getting us out of here.

For the sake of my kid, I put my hands up and turn away from the bros. They start chuckling and victory-snarking, and it makes my shoulders square off and the hair on my forearms rise, but I still walk away. Darren stands up, looking all meek and lanky, but he takes one last chicken finger from his plate and waves it like a Potter wand. "Faggot out!" he says, before sauntering after me and out of the restaurant.

The fight fury fades. It's replaced by a queasy middle zone, where the pastel voices join together behind me and I'm waiting to feel a beer bottle or a hock of spit hit the back of my neck, things men have done to me and will do to my son for decades to come, but also my mind is skimming along the new reality that my meek sensitive kid stands up for himself, has developed a whole gay arsenal of zingers. Who taught him how to do that?

We're out of the room, and I've got my arm around him, rubbing his birdlike shoulder, and then I'm laughing. "*Faggot out*," I say. "Amazing."

"I dunno, that just came out of me," Darren says.

"I should use it," I chuckle. "*Faggot out*. Awesome line."

"You don't need to use it, Dad."

That can mean ten different things, and I try to ask him to tell me more, but the words stop before they get to my mouth.

Darren looks back where we came, to the closed doors. "I'm glad those guys aren't following us. They were total assholes."

"Yep," I say.

Without quite meaning to, we've wandered back into the pool area. I lean down and slap the warm, slightly cloudy water. "Want to take a swim again?"

Darren shakes his head. "I think I want to go back to the room."

I knew that would be his answer. We don't even have our trunks and towels with us or anything, and after nearly getting gay-bashed, neither of us is exactly inclined to any father-son skinny-dipping.

We walk past the steam room, and since it's still barely sunset and we have a whole night of sitting on our hotel beds on our phones ahead of us, I drag my feet by looking inside. Narrow tiled box, dingy without officially being dirty anywhere. It's like sitting under a giant hand dryer that blows wet. I've never gotten the appeal of those rooms.

Darren's waiting for me, worrying his fingers and tapping his knees, so I close the steam room up and walk with him down the corridor of nautical carpet. We get to our room, and he's immediately absorbed in his phone, unclipping it from the charger and hurling himself onto the bedspread. I take a piss, then waffle in the doorway. "Did you get enough to eat?"

He nods and pats his belly.

"I'm not sure I did," I say. The hair on my forearms has risen again. "I might go back out there and see what I can scrounge up."

He nods again.

"Sure you don't want anything?"

Headshakes.

"Okay, see you soon."

I step out, and press the door closed behind me. My palms are sweaty, my mouth full of a metallic taste. All I hear beyond my racing heartbeat is the feeble roar of air conditioners behind closed doors. Where are all the other hotel guests? In their cars somewhere, out to dinner, I guess. But not here.

My feet bring me to the restaurant. I could do with another beer, a cracker, a leaf of lettuce, anything, whatever I can steal from those assholes. I want them to see it, and I want to see the consequences. I listen to the door, then crack it open. There's just a server left there, cleaning the tables and putting chairs up. She gives me a *Hey, stranger* smile and I give one back. There's still some food left, so I could get some, but since the party bros aren't there it wouldn't count as stealing, and stealing is what I want to do. I do grab a beer, though, and start it going down quick. That gets a genuine smile from the server. She might like me.

She's way too young, though, so I leave the restaurant and lean against the door, drinking my beer and listening to the nothing happening all around me. Male murmurs in the distance, the sigh of the steam ticking on and ticking off, the constant hum of the pool pump. An old lady in a bathrobe shuffles down the hallway. I nod and smile at her, she nods and smiles at me. Think she's the same one who was doing laps in the pool.

I wish I had a cigarette. But I don't smoke anymore unless it's at a party. This is not a party.

The question that got me was geography. I wasn't stuck in the moment; I wouldn't have gotten it even from the comfort of my living room. I wasn't meant to be more than a third-place contestant on *Guess It Now*.

The Amazon River passes through Peru before entering Brazil.

How hard is life going to be for my son?

A roaring janitor passes me, his industrial vac advancing and retreating, advancing and retreating. He dips into the pool room, keys jangling. He comes out a few minutes later, closes the door, and flips a sign on a chain.

The vac roars back to life, then fades as the janitor passes around a corner and out of view.

My fingers flick over my phantom cigarette. Alone again.

Until I'm not. Voices approach from down the hall, voices I recognize.

I don't hide, but I do go still.

The bros, only two of them now, orange bro and pink bro, lurch along the hallway, coming from the same direction where the janitor disappeared. Pink has his arm around orange's shoulders, and the pressure of his heavy limb makes orange trip as much as he walks. They're staying upright, but only just.

My fingers drop the phantom cigarette and make a fist instead.

The bros go right up to the glass door to the pool area, peer in. They totally ignore the *Closed* sign and push through.

Their voices fall away beneath the hum of the pool pump. I'm alone in the hall. It's as if the bros were never here, as if they dropped into the water and were sucked away.

I stand there for a moment, resisting the urge to check my phone, just wondering about people being here, people being gone.

I step toward the pool entrance.

I'm totally silent, not from any special source of elegance, but because the carpet is so plush and so thick. I reach the door and peer in.

In soft focus through the blurring glass, the bros are doing midnight laps, laughing and splashing as they kick against either side. Their polo shirts stick to their torsos, and as they pull themselves out of the pool their shorts cling. Would my son enjoy the sight of this? The bros probably wouldn't want to be seen by my son, and tonight that matters.

The lights are out, but the streetlight silhouettes the bros as they jostle and push, as they scamper along the edge of the pool, frantic and agile, like little boys at a sleepover.

They head toward the door, toward me. I tense, ready for a confrontation. My fist on a jaw might just be the answer I need, the thing that will clear this murky unease.

The bros turn before they're at the exit, though, and head

into the steam room. I hear the crank of the knob, the clink of the heater, the whoosh of the steam.

I walk toward the entrance to the pool area and lay my hand on the doorknob. I push it, and head into the chill, chlorine-tanged air.

The bros are mere smudges of pink and orange behind the small fogged window of the steam room. If they looked toward the window, I think they might see me, but I'm also sure that they won't. I can hear the barks of their drunken laughter.

Darren's waiting for me back at the room. I can almost imagine him here next to me, the stew of desire and self-consciousness he would be feeling.

I place my hand on the looping handles of the steam room's double doors, consider opening them, enjoying the shock of the bros as I confront them, as I lay into them with my fists until they turn the tide on me.

How would I explain the blood and black eyes to Darren?

Instead I look to the pool, to its painted scenes of meadows and vases, and finally to the bug net lying along the tiled wall. I pick up the net, test its metal pole between my hands. Hollow, but strong.

The pole passes right through the handle loops, holds there at an angle, one end pitched into the wall.

Unaware that they're trapped, the pink and orange smudges continue their jostling and laughter. Drunk as they are, the bros will probably stay too long before they try to leave. Before they find that they can't leave.

I want to see it happen, want to see their shock at their sudden powerlessness. But I also want to get out of there, get back to Darren, watch whatever horrible show he's found on the room's greasy TV, lie there in quiet in our shared space.

I give the steam room door a kick.

The bros go silent, and the smudges near, resolve into shirts below red faces. Voices shout, but I can't make out the words. I back up, in a horrible kind of awe at what I've done, what I'm doing.

I head to the exit, give one last look at the steam room door, at the narrow rectangle of the window. Pale arms beat at it, like wings.

THE BITE

BY Colette Bancroft

Rattlesnake

These days it has some sunny upscale name focus-grouped by developers, but when I was a kid there the neighborhood was called Rattlesnake.

Back in the 1930s, some guy opened a rattlesnake canning plant in Tampa, off Westshore Boulevard near the Gandy Bridge. The suburbs hadn't sprouted there yet; the land stretching south toward Port Tampa was a couple of miles of pine and palmetto scrub with a hem of mangroves along Tampa Bay, perfect habitat for the plant's product. Locals caught the snakes by the bagful, pygmy rattlers and big diamondbacks, and sold them to the plant to be skinned and cooked. Around the South roadside gift shops sold the cans, labeled with an illustration of a coiled snake with its fangs bared over the slogan *Tastes like chicken!* It doesn't.

By the 1960s, when my family moved to Rattlesnake, the east side of Westshore was lined with streets of neat, new little two- and three-bedroom houses with carports. We were civilians, but lots of our neighbors were military families. MacDill Air Force Base was so close that the howl of fighter jets taking off for training runs was as ordinary as birdsong.

Our next-door neighbors were the Mendozas. He was a staff sergeant in the military police on base, and she was a nurse at the base hospital. They had two little girls, Julieta and Luisa, and sometimes in the afternoon when their shifts overlapped I'd babysit the kids.

Sergeant Mendoza would come home in the evening, unstrap his holster, and set it on the kitchen counter, gun and all. He'd point at his two little daughters and whatever other kids might be around and say, "Don't touch that," then make a little clicking noise.

The summer I was twelve, a new family moved into the house across the street. The tenants were a woman and three girls, the oldest about my age, the youngest a toddler. The woman seemed older than my stylish mother, who went off to her job at a downtown bank every day in a smart suit, every hair in her blond chignon in place. The new lady was so skinny and pale she looked like her own ghost, and she never wore anything but faded housedresses (a wardrobe item my mother disdained).

The carport across the street was usually empty, but once or twice a week I'd see a gorgeous 1955 Thunderbird parked there, with gleaming deep burgundy paint and a white convertible hardtop with porthole windows. My dad ran an auto paint and body business, so I knew cars, and I knew a ten-year-old car that looked that cherry was pampered like a princess.

I also knew it was a two-seater, which seemed odd for a family's only car.

I met the oldest girl when I walked out of the Mendozas' house one afternoon. She was standing across the street on the sidewalk in front of her house, hands on her narrow hips.

"The colonel would have a fit if he saw us near those greasers," she said to me.

I wondered what that meant, but she went right on: "I'm Brenda Howard. That's my sister Nancy." She tipped her head toward the carport, where the middle sister stood. Brenda had her mother's sandy hair and angular face, but her brash attitude was her own. Nancy was softer, rounder, blonder, and gazed off to the side of me like she couldn't quite look at me directly.

As soon as I introduced myself, Brenda invited me in to watch TV. My parents wouldn't be home for a bit, so I followed the sisters through their front door.

The neighborhood was made up of typical Florida suburban houses, concrete block with terrazzo floors and a picture window in the living room. Ours was cozy, with my mom's pride-and-joy Scandinavian modern furniture in the living room and, in my bedroom, a pink-and-white chenille bedspread with the figure of a ballerina (although I was the least balletic of girls).

The Howards' house looked like they were camping. In the living room were one big corduroy recliner, an old black-and-white TV, and three folding chairs that did double duty at the scuffed dining table. Mrs. Howard was sitting there in one of them, playing solitaire. Her eyes widened when she saw me, but she said hello warmly in a twangy voice, not quite Southern.

"That's our mama, Mrs. Howard," Brenda said, and led me off on a tour of the house, which didn't take but a minute. Mrs. Howard's room had a double bed; in the other bedroom, Brenda and Nancy and the third sister, Susie, slept on a mattress on the floor, where the toddler was currently immersed in a sweaty nap. Old sheets were tacked over the windows.

Mrs. Howard went out to hang laundry on the clothesline as we sprawled in front of the TV. Talking over the dialogue of some old Western, Brenda said she and her sister had been born near Tinker Air Force Base in Oklahoma City, where their father was posted. "Me and Nancy's dad died and Mama got a job keeping house for the colonel."

"Our daddy was in a car crash," Nancy said, her eyes filling with tears.

Brenda's eyes rolled. "He was a drunk," she said, closing that subject. "At Tinker the colonel had a nice big house and we all moved in. So him and Mama got married."

For just a second, I thought Nancy looked surprised. "Then Susie was born," Brenda continued, "and then a couple months ago the colonel got posted here. He's in temporary base housing until they have a big enough house for all of us."

"How come he doesn't just live here?"

"He has to be available for duty at all times," Brenda said. "Military officers have very demanding schedules."

That wasn't what I'd heard eavesdropping on enlisted men while they were drinking beer at block parties, but I let it go. "Where's your car?"

"The colonel drives the car. Mama doesn't drive. If she has to go somewhere, he drives her. But she never goes nowhere."

That night at dinner, I gave my parents a reconnaissance report. "She says the colonel—"

"He's a lieutenant colonel," my dad cut in. In our neighborhood everyone knew everyone's rank. I wasn't sure my dad had even laid eyes on him yet, but that didn't matter.

"Well, she calls him the colonel."

"Well, he's not. But what does she say about him?"

"She says he lives on base and they're just staying here until they get bigger base housing. He's their stepfather. Except the baby, he's her father."

"Mm-hm," my father said. "He's got a sweet car, but how does he get all those kids in there?"

"It's ridiculous," my mother said crisply. I couldn't imagine her giving up her new pearly white Mustang and waiting around for my dad to drive her places, although she did drive his Plymouth station wagon to the grocery store. "Now hush up and eat your pork chop."

A couple of days later, Brenda came over to invite me to dinner at her house the next night. "The colonel will be here," she said, kind of like he was the Beatles or something. She told me to come over at six sharp.

At about five, I heard the T-bird's engine. The colonel climbed out as all three girls swarmed him on the carport, then they carried a bunch of grocery bags into the kitchen. It was the first glimpse I'd had of him. He was tall and rangy, with a tight brush cut that could have been blond or gray, and a khaki uniform so well starched it could have stood up on its own.

I reported at six. Brenda introduced me with a stream of chatter, which he interrupted. "Good to meet you," he said. He smiled, a handsome smile, but his eyes made me feel like I was on inspection.

I could smell steak grilling deliciously in a cast-iron pan, but it turned out to be the colonel's dinner. Mrs. Howard served her daughters and me beanie weenies on paper plates.

Susie was perched in a high chair, while the colonel, Brenda, and I occupied the three chairs at the table. Nancy sat cross-legged on the floor by the TV, and Mrs. Howard, her hands empty, started to sit in the recliner.

"Aren't you going to have dinner, Mama?" the colonel said sharply. "Brenda can sit on the floor."

Mrs. Howard jumped up halfway through her sit. "Oh, no, sir. I'm not hungry."

He chewed vigorously for a moment, then smiled. "Well then, Mama, you can sing for us."

"Oh, no," she murmured.

"Sing for us," he said. It sounded like an order.

She clasped her hands behind her back and closed her eyes.

Pack up all my cares and woes,
Here I go, singing low,
Bye bye, blackbird.

She had a thrillingly beautiful voice, so lovely it seemed unlikely coming from someone so washed out.

Where somebody waits for me,
Sugar's sweet, so is he,
Bye bye, blackbird.

It's a sad song anyway, though she sang it sadder than anyone. The colonel was happily sawing off big bites of his steak, but I couldn't swallow, felt like I might never swallow again. Just as I began to fear I'd burst into tears, the baby did.

Mrs. Howard didn't finish the song. She scooped up Susie and carried her off to wash the tears and bean juice off her.

"May we be excused?" Brenda asked the colonel a few minutes later.

"Yes," he said, "for cleanup duty."

As we stepped into the kitchen, I started to flick my paper plate at the trash can. Brenda snatched my wrist. "We don't waste," she said sternly. "You can use them more than once." I watched as she carefully scrubbed the paper plates and Nancy gingerly dried them, and the colonel worked his way through the rest of that big steak.

When I left a little while later he smiled at me, warmly

this time, and put his hand on my shoulder. "Thank you for coming. I hope we see you again."

I reported the paper-plate business to my parents, of course. They just rolled their eyes in unison. "We can't even get this one to wash a *real* plate," my dad said.

The Thunderbird was gone by morning, and I didn't see it for a few days. One afternoon Brenda and Nancy and I walked to the nearby playground, but the sweltering Florida heat soon sent us back.

At the Howards' house, Brenda said, "Mama, can we take a nap in your bed? You have a fan." Almost no one had AC then, so a fan was heaven. We stretched out under its cool stream of air. I fell instantly asleep but sometime later was pulled partway from dreams by the sound of the Thunderbird's engine.

I had started to sink back into sleep when I felt a hand. I lay on my side, my back to the door of the room, and the hand slipped between my legs from behind.

The hand slid inside my shorts and underwear like it knew where it was going. It curved where I curved. A fingertip moved as if searching for something, a side-to-side tremor like a snake scenting prey.

I rolled and jerked up against the headboard to a sitting position. No one else was in the bed. The colonel kneeled next to it, looking at me calmly, his left hand resting where my hip had been.

"I'm sorry," he said. "I thought you were Brenda." He smiled, rose, and walked out.

I felt frozen. I don't know how long it took me to stand up and walk out of the room, but when I did there was no one in the house.

* * *

I didn't see the Howard girls for a few days. I could tell they were home, but they didn't come looking for me, and I didn't feel like knocking on their door, even though I had just about convinced myself I'd dreamed the whole episode.

The rattlesnake canning plant that gave the neighborhood its name was long gone, but the snakes were still around. They had adapted to suburban life, staying mostly invisible but occasionally slithering through a yard or being discovered under a pile of boxes on someone's carport.

My mother had a reputation as the neighborhood snake killer, having learned her technique from her father, who grew up on a farm in Slovakia where he sometimes dispatched adders. Armed with a shovel, my mother had coolly chopped the heads off more rattlers—and copperheads and water moccasins—than I could count.

One long summer afternoon, my mother had been home from work just long enough to change into her pedal pushers and Keds when we heard screaming from next door. Julieta came barreling into our carport shrieking, "Snake! Snake!" and Mom was out the kitchen door and into the utility room off the carport to grab her shovel.

Next door, Mrs. Mendoza was standing at the backyard gate. "Luis has a gun but he's not home yet. Please help her!"

Luisa was in the corner of the backyard, in a little slot between the fence and the shed. Blocking her path was a pygmy rattler, a coiled ball of fury, its tail vibrating with that unmistakable warning. I couldn't breathe.

"Stand real still, honey," my mother said to Luisa in her kindest voice. "Don't move."

The snake was focused on Luisa, but when my mother took a step forward and stomped one foot, it swung its head around. She struck, the shovel blade flashing through its extended neck. The coils convulsed, the jaws snapped, the tail fell silent.

She swept the beheaded snake aside with the shovel, then grabbed Luisa, who was still standing frozen as a little statue. "Did it bite you, baby?"

Luisa shook her head and began to cry as her mother swooped in, kissing her all over and inspecting her for bites at the same time.

Julieta craned toward the snake.

"Don't touch it," my mother said quickly. "They can bite even after you cut their heads off." By way of demonstration, she touched the severed head with the tip of the shovel blade, and the snake's jaws jerked wide, then snapped.

Mrs. Howard was standing wide-eyed on the sidewalk, hugging herself. I wouldn't have thought she could look any paler, but she did. I realized I'd never seen her cross the street. She motioned me over.

"Has your mama done that before?"

"Yes ma'am. She's the Rattlesnake snake killer. She's not afraid of anything," I boasted, reflecting a little of my mom's badass glory.

Mrs. Howard seemed as frozen as Luisa had been a few minutes ago. Then she took a shuddering breath and said, "Could you tell her I'd like to speak to her, please?"

I did. Mrs. Howard stood on her carport waiting until my mom had stashed the shovel and swaggered across the street. I went inside to watch TV, and when my dad got home I realized Mom was still at the Howards'.

They were on the carport, huddled in a corner. Mom was was talking intently, her voice low. Mrs. Howard was nodding but looking utterly miserable, tears standing in her eyes.

I got close enough to hear my mother say, "You have to. You have to go now. My God, the little one is his own child."

Mrs. Howard closed her eyes, and my mother took hold of her shoulders and shook her a little bit, so that the tears ran down her face.

Then they heard my feet crunch on the dry grass. Mom turned and said, "Go tell your father to get a pizza from Maria's. And you go with him."

When we got back she was home. My dad raised his eyebrows; she cut her eyes at me and shook her head. At least I got pizza. They talked long after I went to bed, though they shut my door so I couldn't hear what they said.

The next day I took a bus to swimming lessons at the Davis Islands pool, as I did a couple of days a week in the summer. The lessons consisted of a couple of teenage lifeguards throwing us all in the deep end and laughing, but the pool cooled us off.

The bus dropped me near home just in time for a classic Florida summer thunderstorm. I was drenched in a minute. I didn't mind that—I was still damp from swimming—but I was terrified of lightning, so I started sprinting the four blocks home.

A car pulled up beside me and slowed. It was the Thunderbird. The colonel cranked down the passenger window. "Jump in."

I felt frozen again. He swung the door open just as a thunderbolt crashed so close I could smell the ozone. I jumped.

He pulled into the empty driveway of my house, then turned to me and smiled. "This storm will pass in a minute. I can tell you don't like that thunder. Let's wait."

Rain hammered the roof. He reached over the back of the seat and fished out a towel. He rubbed my hair with it briskly, then slid it over my shoulders.

In the tiny car, his face was close to mine. "So pretty," he whispered. His hand moved over my wet shirt. I was as flat-chested as a boy, but his fingers found my nipple and pinched it, hard. His arm tightened around me and his mouth was at my ear.

"You remind me of the little girls I used to know in Saigon." He sighed deeply. "All those sweet little girls."

I swung the door open, twisted sideways from under his arm, and bolted into the dark house. The Thunderbird sat in the driveway for a minute or two, then slowly drove away. It didn't stop across the street.

This time I knew I hadn't dreamed anything, but I didn't know what to do. That night my parents seemed distracted, sending me to watch TV and murmuring in the kitchen. When my mother came into the living room, she said, "You look tired," and I realized I was exhausted. I went to bed without argument, figuring if I slept on it I'd know what to say tomorrow.

Voices woke me deep in the night. My parents talking in low tones, but someone else too. From the hall I could see Mrs. Howard and her girls in the kitchen. Susie was asleep on my father's shoulder. Nancy was backed up against the counter, weeping silently and sucking a lock of her hair. Out on the carport, I could see the back end of our station wagon, piled with loose clothes and my mother's tan suitcase.

Standing so close to her mother their noses almost touched, Brenda was shaking with anger. "I'm not going anywhere, you old bag," she said. "I'm staying here with him."

She turned toward the door, and fast as a cat my mother blocked her. She seized Brenda's arm and hissed in her face, "You get in that car now, or I'll hogtie you and throw you in the back."

Brenda wrenched her arm loose, and I thought she would strike my mother. Instead she whirled and slapped Nancy so hard she staggered. "Come on, you fucking moron," Brenda said.

I crept back to bed before anyone saw me. In the morning my father told me that my mom got a phone call in the middle of the night and had to go visit her aunt up the coast in Masaryktown because she was in the hospital; she'd be home soon, he added. I didn't ask him why I hadn't heard the phone ring.

A day later, walking home after swimming lessons, I spotted the T-bird on the carport across the street and saw the colonel standing at our front door. I cut off through the alley before he could see me and went into our house as quietly as I could through the back.

"Where are they?" the colonel was saying, not shouting but in that voice that sounded like he was giving an order. "I know you know. I know that damn wife of yours has something to do with this."

"My damn wife is *my* business," my father said, "and I'd appreciate you not talking about her that way."

The colonel snorted. "They're mine. You have no right. She has no right."

"All I can tell you is they're not here."

From where I stood in the kitchen, the colonel couldn't spot me, but I could see a gun in his hand. He held it loosely, pointed toward the ground, but he twitched it back and forth in a nervous way I didn't like.

My father must have heard me. Behind his back, he flicked his hand toward me in a get-back gesture, then pointed toward the Mendoza house. I went out the back door, holding it so it wouldn't slam, and jumped the fence into the backyard next door.

"The colonel is yelling at my dad," I said quietly through the Mendozas' kitchen screen door. "He has a gun."

"The colonel has a gun?" Sergeant Mendoza was already moving, his hand swinging the holster toward him. "Call the base," he said to Mrs. Mendoza. To me he said, "You stay here."

As soon as she was on the phone, I snuck out and slid behind the hedge along the side of our house so I could see the front yard.

Mendoza moved even more quietly than I did, stopping a few feet behind the colonel. "Drop the gun, sir."

The colonel grew still. He didn't drop the gun, but he stopped twitching it. "I'm your superior officer," he said without turning.

"Drop the gun, sir," Mendoza said again. "Then put your hands up."

For an instant my father's eyes met Mendoza's, and my father took one step back from the doorway, pivoted, and flattened himself against the wall. The colonel's hand twitched once. Mendoza moved one foot a little forward. Once again I felt as if I couldn't breathe.

Then we heard the siren.

The colonel never looked at Mendoza, but he put his gun down on the driveway, very slowly. Mendoza kept his weapon trained on the colonel until the MPs handcuffed him and drove him away.

After Mendoza holstered the gun, my father shook his hand. They looked at each other silently for a moment, and then my father said to me, "Come out of those damn bushes."

* * *

For about a week, Mendoza came over while Johnny Carson was on TV and slept on a lawn chaise on our carport, his holster on.

My mother pulled into the driveway two days after the colonel was taken away, just her and her suitcase, and she never said a word to me about where she'd been. I never saw the T-bird again. By the time school started, the Howards' house had new tenants.

A few weeks after she returned, my mom had to go to some kind of hearing on base. She came home looking tired and poured a double Scotch.

"Did you tell them where you took her and the kids?" Dad asked.

"They didn't even ask," she said. "But I told them what he did."

I was babysitting Julieta and Luisa late one afternoon not long after that. Mendoza and my dad got home at the same time, and I walked out to see them talking in our driveway.

"You know how the brass are," Mendoza said. "They cover each other's asses, sweep everything under the rug. All they did was transfer him. But they did send him someplace that might make him regret what he did. Things are getting real hot there."

My dad's eyebrows went up. "Where?"

Mendoza smiled. "They sent him back to Saigon."

ABOUT THE CONTRIBUTORS

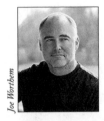

ACE ATKINS is the author of twenty-four books, including nine Quinn Colson novels, the first two of which, *The Ranger* and *The Lost Ones*, were nominated for the Edgar Award for Best Novel. He is also the author of eight *New York Times* best sellers in Robert B. Parker's Spenser series. Before turning to fiction, Atkins was a crime reporter for the *Tampa Tribune* and played defensive end for the Auburn University football team.

COLETTE BANCROFT has been the book editor at the *Tampa Bay Times* since 2007. In addition to writing reviews and interviewing authors, she directs the annual *Tampa Bay Times* Festival of Reading. She served two terms on the board of the National Book Critics Circle. Bancroft earned degrees in English from the University of South Florida and the University of Florida, and she wishes she had finished her dissertation on the novels of Raymond Chandler.

KAREN BROWN is the author of two novels, *The Clairvoyants* and *The Longings of Wayward Girls*, and two prize-winning short story collections, *Little Sinners and Other Stories* and *Pins and Needles: Stories*. Her work has appeared in *Best American Short Stories*, *The O. Henry Prize Stories*, and many literary journals, most recently *Kenyon Review* and *One Story*. She teaches creative writing at the University of South Florida.

LUIS CASTILLO grew up in Los Angeles and graduated from the University of Southern California. For three decades he has been a television sports producer, working for CNN Headline News, TBS Sports, and Fox Sports. He currently lives in Largo, Florida, with his wife, son, and daughter.

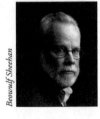

MICHAEL CONNELLY is the author of thirty-two novels, including the #1 *New York Times* best sellers *Dark Sacred Night*, *Two Kinds of Truth*, and *The Late Show*. His books, which include the Harry Bosch and Lincoln Lawyer series, have sold more than seventy million copies worldwide. A former newspaper reporter, he has won awards for his journalism and novels and is the executive producer of the Amazon show *Bosch*. He spends his time in Los Angeles and Tampa.

Janine Dorsey

TIM DORSEY grew up in a small town an hour north of Miami. He graduated from Auburn University, where he was editor of the student newspaper. He was a reporter for the *Alabama Journal* in Montgomery before joining the *Tampa Tribune* in 1987, becoming the night metro editor. He left the paper in 1999 and has since published twenty-two novels in several languages, most recently *No Sunscreen for the Dead*, and regularly hits the *New York Times* best-seller list.

Rick Ochoa

SARAH GERARD's most recent book is the novel *True Love*. Her essay collection *Sunshine State* was a *New York Times* Editors' Choice, and her novel *Binary Star* was a finalist for the *Los Angeles Times* Book Prizes' Art Seidenbaum Award for First Fiction. Her work has appeared in *T Magazine*, *Granta*, *Electric Literature*, and the *Baffler*. She was the 2018–2019 New College of Florida writer-in-residence.

Vilma Samulionyte

LADEE HUBBARD's debut novel, *The Talented Ribkins*, was published in 2017. Set in Florida, the book received the Ernest J. Gaines Award and the Hurston/Wright Legacy Award for Debut Fiction. She is also a recipient of a Rona Jaffe Foundation Writers' Award and has published short fiction in *Virginia Quarterly Review*, *Callaloo*, *Guernica*, and *Copper Nickel*, among other venues. Her latest novel is *The Rib King*.

Kevin Maloney

DANNY LÓPEZ (A.K.A. PHILLIPPE DIEDERICH) is the author of the novels *Playing for the Devil's Fire* and *Sofrito*, and the Dexter Vega mysteries *The Last Breath* and *The Last Girl*. The son of Haitian exiles, López was born in the Dominican Republic and raised in Mexico City and Miami.

Laurie Ross

GALE MASSEY's debut novel, *The Girl from Blind River*, received a 2018 Florida Book Award. Her award-winning stories and essays have appeared in the *Tampa Bay Times*, *Sabal*, *Seven Hills Press*, and other places. She has received fellowships from the Sewanee Writers' Conference and Eckerd College's Writers in Paradise, and has been nominated for the 2019 Clara Johnson Award for Women's Literature. Massey, a Florida native, lives in St. Petersburg.

YULY RESTREPO GARCÉS was born in Medellín, Colombia, and came to the United States nearly twenty years ago as an asylee. Her writing has previously appeared in *Catapult*, *PRISM International*, *Natural Bridge*, and *Zone 3*. She is an Iowa Writers' Workshop graduate, a MacDowell fellow, and an assistant professor of English at the University of Tampa.

LORI ROY is the two-time Edgar Award–winning author of five novels, the most recent of which is *Gone Too Long*. Her work has been named a *New York Times* Notable Crime Book twice, a *New York Times* Editors' Choice, and included on numerous "Best of" lists. Her debut novel, *Bent Road*, was chosen as a Notable Book by the state of Kansas. Roy lives with her family in Florida.

ELIOT SCHREFER is the *New York Times* best-selling author of *Endangered* and *Threatened*, both finalists for the National Book Award for Young People's Literature. His novels have also been named Editors' Choice in the *New York Times* and have won the Green Earth Book Award and the Sigurd F. Olson Nature Writing Award. He grew up in Clearwater and now lives in New York City, where he reviews fiction for *USA Today*.

LISA UNGER is the *New York Times* best-selling author of seventeen novels, including *The Stranger Inside*. Her novel *Under My Skin* was an Edgar Award and Hammett Prize nominee. Her short story "The Sleep Tight Motel" was nominated for an Edgar Award. Her books are published in twenty-six languages and have been named Best of the Year or top picks by *Today*, *Good Morning America*, *Entertainment Weekly*, Amazon, and IndieBound.

STERLING WATSON is the author of eight novels: *The Committee*, *Suitcase City*, *Fighting in the Shade*, *Sweet Dream Baby*, *Deadly Sweet*, *Blind Tongues*, *The Calling*, and *Weep No More My Brother*. His work has been widely praised, including by Dennis Lehane, who says, "The novels of Sterling Watson are to be treasured and passed on to the next generation."